SPY TRAP

A.P. MARTIN

© A. P. MARTIN 2021

The moral right of the author has been asserted.

Apart from any fair dealing for the purposes of research or private study, or criticism or review, as permitted under the Copyright, Designs and Patents Act 1988, this publication may only be reproduced, stored or transmitted, in any form or by any means, with the prior permission in writing of the publishers, or in the case of reprographic reproduction in accordance with the terms of licences issued by the Copyright Licensing Agency. Enquiries concerning reproduction outside those terms should be sent to the publishers.

This is a work of fiction. Names, characters, businesses, places, events and incidents are either the products of the author's imagination or used in a fictitious manner. Any resemblance to actual persons, living or dead, or actual events is purely coincidental.

Cover design by Michael Moden (mickey19830@gmail.com.) Cover images courtesy of Shutterstock.

This is an edited and revised edition of Spy Trap by A. P. Martin, published in 2017.

Books by A.P.Martin

Spymaster Pym Series

Codename Lazarus
Spy Trap
Sacrifice of Spies

Clavel and Snow Series

Sentence of Death
Death of an Asylum Seeker

Chapter One

Tuesday 25th June 1940, Headquarters, Army Group C, Frankfurt, Germany.

Five pages. That's all it was. But, if things went badly, those five, type-written pages could be responsible for having her shot. Or even worse, tortured and hanged like some animal carcass. *Don't think like that. Don't think like that*, the young secretary told herself repeatedly. *Just get on with typing it and act normally*.

Annaliese Fischer had been secretary to Captain Otto von Menges for several years, accompanying him as he moved, first to the Army General Staff and later to Army Group C. A practising Protestant, she had initially been enthused by the aims of the 'Confessing Church', created after the Nazi seizure of power in 1933 with the explicit aim of asserting Christian values in a rapidly changing German society. However, Annaliese had been disillusioned by the church's evident inertia and had struggled to understand its reluctance to engage in more forthright opposition to Fascism. In 1937, therefore, she had joined a clandestine group which sought actively to oppose Hitler. Since the outbreak of war, she had even passed information to colleagues who were able to transfer it to the Allies. Given the appalling trajectory of Nazi policy, this had seemed ethically purposeful, exciting even. And with von Menges's latest transfer, the chances of being able to pass on something of real importance had rocketed. However, as she had become much closer to material of great significance, so too had the degree of risk she was running.

On arriving at work that morning, Annaliese had gasped and immediately covered her mouth in shock. Von Menges had stroked the dark stubble on his normally immaculately shaven chin and smiled ruefully, 'I imagine I look a bit of a sight.' A handsome thirty-two-year-old, ex show-jumping champion, he was sitting, bleary-eyed and dishevelled at his desk. Annaliese followed his eyes as they homed in on the handbag she had dropped, scattering its contents at her feet. 'Here,' he said gently as he raised himself stiffly from his chair, 'you've had a bit of a fright. Please allow me to help you with that.' As he picked up first the bag and then the various items from the floor and passed them to her, he produced the smile which had captivated so many young women. 'You've got some really important work to do this morning.'

Von Menges had quickly explained to her how, late the previous evening, he had received an urgent order to prepare an initial action plan which was to be passed up to his commanding officer as soon as possible. He had worked through the night and had just finished it. 'You know Annaliese,' he'd gabbled excitedly, 'this is the first time that I've been ordered to prepare such a report myself. I was told that the instruction came from the Führer himself. Can you imagine that? So, make sure you're extra careful with it. Type it up straight away, while I clean myself up and get some breakfast. I'll be back in an hour.'

Annaliese had known what she must do as soon as she'd read the 'Streng Geheim' scrawled at the top of the first page. *So, it's Top Secret. I'll do an extra copy and smuggle it out.*

As soon as she was alone, she quickly inserted one more carbon sheet than necessary into her typewriter. She then tried to close her mind to the appalling risk she was running and focus on the mechanical business of typing. Tense, her heart racing, she soon began to feel hot and crossed the room to open the window which overlooked an immaculate garden of early summer flowers. Forcing herself to take in several deep, calming breaths of the scented air, she returned to her desk to complete the report without making a single mistake. Having lost the calming focus which typing had provided, her hands began to shake as she shredded the tell-tale carbon sheets and folded the additional copy into an envelope which she hid underneath the rug, on which her office chair stood.

Restored to his habitual, impeccably groomed appearance, von Menges returned after forty-five minutes and read the document with obvious satisfaction. He then carefully placed both copies in his briefcase and turned to his secretary, 'I doubt I'll be back today, Annaliese. You've done very well with this, so take it easy for the rest of the day. There's just the last part of the quarterly report to finish off.' Flashing another of his trademark smiles, he added meaningfully, 'Oh, and don't forget to wish me luck. If the Führer is impressed, we might both be on our way back to Berlin.' Annaliese's face twisted in a poor impression of a smile, but von Menges was far too preoccupied to notice the terror in her eyes as he strode out of the room.

Having too little work was the worst possible set of circumstances for Annaliese. She had to type unnaturally slowly, otherwise she would face an excruciating final couple of hours with nothing to occupy her mind. Before going to lunch she had decided that she would leave the envelope underneath the carpet in the locked office. *With Captain von Menges away for the day, no one should even come into the room*, she reassured herself.

Over lunch, her work friends commented on how quiet she seemed and, like young women the world over, tried hard to get to the root of their friend's unusual behaviour. In the end, Annaliese simply said that she had a headache and feared that maybe she was coming down with an early summer cold.

Despite her best efforts, her task was completed before 4PM and the office clock crawled its way through the rest of the afternoon, mocking her frequent glances in its direction. At last it was time for her to check that no one was about to enter the office before she retrieved the envelope and stuffed it into her handbag. Fighting the impulse to creep stealthily down the familiar corridor, which now seemed like enemy territory, she nodded and waved through the open door of the general office, where several young women were finishing off their work for the day. Self-consciously aware that she was sweating, Annaliese heaved a sigh of relief as she entered the deserted toilet, where she immediately threw open the door of an empty cubicle. The loud crack of the door hitting the tiled wall startled her. *For goodness sake, calm down,* she berated herself silently.

She quickly removed her jacket and blouse and struggled to trap the slim envelope between her bra strap and back. A fit of giggles erupted, as if Annaliese had only just realised the riskiness of what she was about to do. Her simple plan relied entirely on the probability that today, a random sample of people leaving would not be selected to undergo a thorough body search. *Come on, relax, they've done it three days running. They can't do a fourth. Can they?* Almost crippled with terror, Annaliese dressed, splashed her flushed face with water, checked her appearance and made her way towards the check-point at the entrance to the building.

Oh God! Her legs began to quake beneath her as she noticed a girl being selected for a full search, but she managed to keep her lowered eyes fixed firmly ahead as she moved towards the door. *If all the female guards are busy, he'll just look in my bag.* At the exit, she opened her bag for the bored soldier who gave it a negligible inspection before waving her through. Heart thumping with relief, she grabbed her bag and hurriedly tried to fasten it. Still fiddling with the clasp, she turned to the door and inadvertently barged into another burly guard. Irritated, he barked, 'Not so fast Fräulein! Get ready to be searched.' Annaliese's stomach lurched as she was directed towards a small cubicle, where she was instructed to wait for a female officer. She knew, both from past experience and gossip with her work colleagues, that such body searches would be very thorough. In panic, she wondered, *Dare I say I feel unwell? Maybe I could go back to the toilet and flush this stuff away?* Miserably, she realised that this would simply arouse suspicion and she stood, resigned to her fate and all too conscious of the envelope rubbing against her back.

Just as a particularly brutish female guard was approaching to conduct the search, a young army officer entered the building and, recognising Annaliese waiting by the cubicle, saluted crisply. 'As ever, it is a great pleasure to see you, Fräulein.' He smiled warmly, before turning to face the waiting guard. 'I can personally vouch for Fräulein Fischer. A search will not be necessary. Let her pass immediately.' Annaliese almost fainted with relief, before pulling herself together and walking calmly past the officer, to whom she offered a grateful smile. 'Perhaps we could have lunch tomorrow, Fräulein?' he asked hopefully. 'I'll pick you up from your office at twelve on the dot.'

'Oh, that would be wonderful, Captain,' stammered Annaliese, conscious of the furious look on the guard's face as she hurriedly left, before anyone could countermand the young officer's order.

Chapter Two

Thursday, June 27th, 1940, Heidelberg, Germany.

A less than perfectly fit forty-two-year-old, William Blake had that unremarkable appearance and demeanour which perfectly suits the professional spy. Standing a couple of inches under six feet tall, slim, with regular features and hair that used to be fair, but which age had darkened and flecked with grey, he was the ideal man never to be noticed. But he was tiring of the constant strain. He'd had his fill of the terrifyingly risky assignments, undertaken almost constantly during the nine months since the outbreak of war. In fact, he had been trying unsuccessfully for some weeks to persuade his controller to withdraw him from field duty.

'It's not that I'm in a funk, or anything,' he had lied. 'It's just that any cat has only nine lives. And I must've used all mine up by now. I'm just being realistic.' Deep within himself, he was certain that he would soon break down completely. He knew all about the tell-tale signs and had recognised them in himself. He'd almost lost the ability to sleep, he was increasingly and, worse still, conspicuously edgy and he was making more and more mistakes. If he could not get out of the front line, he hoped with genuine desperation that when his collapse did happen, the only life he might endanger would be his own.

A mere ten minutes after stubbing out his last cigarette, he quickly extracted another from the gaudy packet. His favourite was a strongly aromatic Turkish brand called

Murad, to which he had been introduced during his time in Switzerland. He greedily sucked the first of the heavy smoke deep into his lungs and sighed the contented sigh of the true addict. As he made his way towards the second-floor flat on Pfaffengasse, hidden away in the maze that was the old town of Heidelberg, he frequently turned off the direct route and made what he would have once blithely dismissed as nervous and unnecessary detours. His eyes constantly scanned the street for signs of danger. *Did that middle-aged man in the dark overcoat look at him just a little too long for comfort? Was the youngster in the Hitler Youth uniform making notes on passers-by as he lounged at the street corner with a pencil and a small notebook? Is that the same young woman with the long blond hair who followed him out of the train station?*

Of course, in enemy territory he had to be on constant guard, but he now feared that his neuroticism was beginning to inhibit his effectiveness. He had started to review his mission repeatedly for high-risk points, even when he had concluded a hundred times that there were none. He simply had to pick up the documents from his contact at the agreed location and courier them back to Switzerland. It should be child's play, using his regular, or, he now worried constantly, his too regular cover as a representative of one of the most significant Swiss trading partners of Nazi Germany.

The rain was teeming down from a slate grey sky as he approached the brooding residential block. A young couple, with eyes only for one another, were hesitating at the communal entrance as the uniformed man struggled to open his umbrella. Blake darted up the steps and, with a polite thank you and comment on the terrible weather, he prevented the door shutting and passed swiftly into the dimly lit hall. The smell of steaming cabbage was overpowering as he scanned the various Nazi propaganda posters which covered much of the available wall space. His eyes settled on a gap between two of the more rabidly anti-Semitic notices and he wondered if there might be some courageous soul who had defaced, or even removed one of the official posters. The threadbare stair carpet did little to muffle the creaks as he crept up the two flights of stairs to the top floor. The closed umbrella had been placed to the left of the door, confirming that everything was safe and, as soon as he rang the bell, he was admitted by an improbably young-looking woman.

'Die beste Bildung findet ein gescheiter Mensch auf Reisen,' she said slowly and softly, before looking expectantly at Blake. Without hesitation, he replied with the agreed Goethe quotation, *'Es ist nichts schrecklicher als eine tätige Unwissenheit.'*

'I'm glad you've made it, Ovid. Please, call me Homer,' the smiling woman said, before leading him into the flat. A good fifteen to twenty years older, Blake instinctively felt uneasy about her age. It wasn't that he doubted her bravery or commitment. In fact, that was a big part of his concern. In his experience, such people often had the overconfidence, even foolhardiness of youth. And all too frequently they took what he had come to regard as unjustified risks. *Take it easy,* he reassured himself, *just get the documents and get on your way as quickly as possible.*

Likewise, the woman unashamedly studied Blake's grey eyes and open face which still possessed a certain boyish quality, despite the deeper set lines and wrinkles which had been developing at an alarming speed over the last six months. Her attention was quickly drawn, however, to his trembling hands, as he first took out and then lit an unusual looking cigarette. For all her youth, she was sufficiently experienced to recognise someone who was decidedly edgy and silently echoed Blake's resolve to get the business conducted and get safely away from someone who may well prove to be a liability.

She quickly produced a thin envelope and laid it on the table between them. Reluctantly placing his cigarette in an empty ashtray, Blake extracted the sheaf of five papers, immediately recognising the identifiers of a Wehrmacht 'Top Secret' document. *I've seen far too many of these bloody things over the past few months,* he reflected ruefully.

As he delicately leafed through the carbon copied sheets of typing, the woman murmured, 'Doesn't look much, does it?' Shrugging her shoulders and smiling again, she added quickly, 'But, this is why we're both here. I'm told that it's the highest priority, so maybe we should….'

Her next words were drowned out by the roar of a heavy engine on the street below, immediately followed by the sound of boots hitting the pavement. Eyes swivelling away from the document, Blake moved rapidly across to stare through the front window, his breath coming in ragged bursts. 'The bloody Germans are here! What the hell's going on, Homer?' All his anxiety about his inevitable fate came rushing to the surface and the papers dropped from his shaking hands. He looked sharply at the woman, instant distrust covering his ashen face as he spat savagely, 'Oh Christ! You've bloody well betrayed me, you bitch!'

In truth, Blake's default relationship to almost all other people was defined by suspicion, perhaps even hostility. Moreover, while it might be self-comforting for him to believe that this was inevitable for a spy, if he was honest with himself, he would have to acknowledge that this attitude had far deeper roots. For it was simply a product of always having been an outsider and consequently a loner. Born in Britain just before the turn of the century, he was an only child, whose father in 1902 took up a technical post with Bayer, the large chemical group based in Leverkusen, a small town north of Cologne. He grew up in provincial Germany as a clear odd man out – 'Der Engländer' – a status which became more and more difficult for him as the Anglo-German Arms Race really speeded up in the years before the outbreak of the First World War. Unsurprisingly, he had few friends when, in early 1914, his father decided that it was no longer sensible to remain in Germany and promptly relocated the family back to Britain. The young Blake received little love from either parent and his time in a typical English boarding-school was entirely miserable. He found himself back in his native country, but once again treated very much as an alien. Indeed, he frequently cursed his mother for having given him the name William. This was not because his fellow schoolboys ragged him for sharing a name with one of Britain's greatest poets and visionaries. They were, of course, far too philistine for such wit. They did, however, combine his first name with his dubious history in Germany to create the mocking nickname of 'Kaiser Bill.'

Just too young to risk death for King and Country, things did not improve for him when he won a place at Cambridge to study German. He should have felt at home in a university largely populated by misfits, loners and damaged young men, but even these peculiar examples of humanity found Blake 'a queer fish'. Fully bilingual, he found his degree a relatively undemanding experience and, on graduation, he took up a tedious administrative post in the Foreign Office. There, he became known as an effective colleague, though one with an almost total absence of social graces. And there he might have stayed forever, had a pushy young secretary not taken a shine to him, during the office Christmas Party in 1932. Totally lacking in experience of the opposite sex, he was easy prey for such an ambitious woman who, thinking him a prize catch, set her cap relentlessly at him. Within a year, and much against his ageing parents' wishes, Blake had married and settled down to a life of somewhat less than domestic bliss in a dingy flat in Tottenham.

It took only a couple of years for his unsociable character to combine in a volatile way with the extremely fun-loving nature of his younger wife and by the Spring of 1936, she was leading an existence almost entirely independent of his. This might not have been so great a problem, had she not taken to taunting him mercilessly with the special abilities of her succession of lovers. Although not by nature a particularly violent man, Blake had had to learn how to defend himself effectively during those miserable school days in Germany and Britain. It was, perhaps, inevitable that one day, after a particularly graphic account, self-defence would metamorphose into pure aggression and he would take out his frustrations on the hapless lover. As a consequence, he found himself remanded for trial on a charge of 'Grievous Bodily Harm.'

It was while he was languishing at His Majesty's pleasure that he was first visited by the thoroughly unpleasant and self-important man who was to change his life. Claude Dansey had just established Section Z of MI6 and was on the lookout for people with competence in German. To Dansey, Blake seemed like manna from heaven – basically an isolate, not without intelligence, able to handle himself physically and very much in a pickle. In fairness, Dansey put his cards on the table during that first prison visit, when he breezed into the cell and casually offered Blake a wretched choice. 'Do your bit for Britain, or face a long stretch inside. It's your choice, sunshine.'

Undaunted that his initial approach did not have the desired motivational effect, the devious Dansey began to use his fortnightly visits to explore Blake's psychological flaws. For his part, Blake tolerated Dansey's visits, even though he quickly came to despise the man. He had soon accepted that they were his only contact with the outside world, save for the rare and pessimistic briefings with his solicitor, who consistently made clear that he could expect a not insignificant custodial sentence.

One day, towards the end of September, when the wind was howling and the rain was being driven almost horizontally from a leaden sky, Dansey finally found the right button to press. 'Of course, Bill,' he suggested amiably, 'you'd be working alone. You'd be your own boss. No need to be polite to colleagues every day and nobody would be looking over your shoulder. Your precise function would be to be anonymous, not noticed and left alone to get on with things. Now,' he concluded with a calculating smile, 'how does that sound, old chum? Bit better than slopping out in here and sharing your cell with several other unsavoury brutes, eh? By the standards of the regular inmates, I daresay you'd still be regarded as something of a 'pretty boy.'' Dansey sat back contentedly and blew a lungful of smoke out into the room to await Blake's response.

Suddenly, the grim reality of his dreadful situation struck Blake like a hammer blow and he rapidly made up his mind that he had no choice. A lengthy prison sentence was utterly unthinkable, especially given Dansey's disgusting suggestion. Blake shivered as he recalled how one of the more dubious types had already made obscene proposals as to how his cigarette ration could be enhanced. Moreover, his Foreign Office career and marriage were both well and truly over. *What have I got to lose?* Blake convinced himself, *I may as well accept the bastard's offer.*

A few weeks later, the demands of justice having been silenced on grounds of national security, Blake reported for duty at Bush House, the Headquarters of Station Z in London. It didn't take Dansey long to realise that Blake was even better than he had dared hope. He seemed totally anonymous, had a prodigious memory, was absolutely perfect in German and quite good in French, was unattached and even possessed a reasonable competence at picking up the advanced skills of unarmed combat.

Consequently, Blake found himself rapidly transferred out of London to Station Z in Bern, where he became the 'go to man' for any mission inside Germany.

Now, however, almost four years later, on a wet evening in Heidelberg, Blake had simply had enough and he raised his hand, as if to strike the woman. 'What are you doing, you fool?' she hissed at him as she moved quickly out of his reach and looked out of the window. 'It's probably nothing to do with us. Calm down and let's think rationally.'

'Think rationally!' Blake retorted with barely contained fury. 'Do you have a death wish, or something? We've got to get out of here and fast! You stay here and take your chances if you like, but I'm getting out now!'

Sensing that the Englishman was about to lose control completely and fearing that he may either go blundering out of the flat, straight into the arms of the Gestapo or make such a noise that he would provoke their interest, the woman seized the initiative. Against her instinct to stay put, she reasoned with the frantic Blake. 'Look, it's almost certain that this raid has nothing at all to do with us. But I can see that you're concerned. So, let's not take any chances. We can get out through the back window while everyone's focused on what's going on out front. It's not really overlooked at the back and with luck, we won't be spotted.'

Blake stared at the woman for a full half minute, before nodding and accepting the documents which she had retrieved from the floor. With quivering hands, he shoved them back in the envelope and secreted this beneath the false bottom of his small case. Without speaking further, the woman gestured urgently that he should follow her to the rear of the flat, where she pointed to a sash window.

It was heavily overcast and still raining hard as she climbed through the window and, with the agility of a cat, dropped onto a sloping roof several feet below. Somewhat less confident, Blake hesitated, half out of the window. Suddenly, loud banging on one of the adjacent flat doors, accompanied by harsh, guttural shouts of 'Gestapo! Open up immediately!' gave him all the encouragement he needed to perch on the ledge, close the window, pull his hat more tightly onto his head and drop heavily down onto the roof below. A sharp pain immediately shot up from his right ankle. Evidently, it had twisted awkwardly as he landed on the wet roof.

'Damn!' he hissed. 'I think I might have broken my bloody ankle.' An uncompromising expression met his pleading look and the woman simply said, 'Come on, we can't wait here in this exposed place all day. Let's get down to ground level.'

Reacting to the obvious pain etched onto Blake's face as he peered at her through the steady rain, the woman took his small suitcase and swung down a convenient drainpipe into a back alley. 'Quick! I'll help you down,' she whispered and grabbed hold of the Blake's legs as they tentatively edged down the drainpipe. His hands lost their grip on the slippery pipe and he fell the last three feet, further damage to his ankle being prevented only by the woman's surprising strength in cushioning his fall with her arms.

After he responded to her enquiring glance with a quick nod, they crept cautiously along the narrow passage which ran between the rear of the apartment block and the wall of a factory. This, Blake noted with relief, had only blocked up windows. Desperately hoping that the man's clumsy descent had not been observed by any sharp-eyed neighbour, Homer led him down the alley and away from the apartment building.

Blake recognised quickly that the woman knew her way around this part of the city and they soon reached Dreikönigsstraße, which ran parallel to the Pfaffengasse at ninety degrees to the river Neckar. Adrenalin had started to course through his bloodstream and he was surprised at the lack of pain as he tentatively made his way through the rain. Unquestioningly, he followed her as they walked towards the river and turned right onto Neckarsteden. Since making their escape, they had seen only a handful of people, wrapped up against the downpour and focused only on trying to keep dry. This emboldened the young woman to say encouragingly, 'So far so good. It looks like we haven't been seen. If we carry on along here, we'll be able to take a quick look back up Pfaffengasse. Maybe we'll be able to find out what happened at the flat.'

She turned and caught sight of Blake's look of panic, to which she smiled reassuringly. 'Don't worry. It's not curfew yet and, with your case, we'll just look like a couple walking back from the railway station. We won't attract any attention. But maybe you should take it now.' As Blake took the case, she linked his free arm in a natural lover's gesture. She quickly shot him a concerned glance as she felt a clear flinch when she first touched his arm. Blake had enjoyed no physical intimacy for many years and immediately understood the woman's dubious look. Attempting a smile of apology, he muttered, 'Sorry, I'm not used to such pretty women grabbing hold of me in public.' *Christ,* he reflected morosely as he contrasted his non-existent love life with the inviting curves of the woman's breasts and hips which even her ill-fitting and drab raincoat couldn't quite conceal. *I bloody well hope I'm still enough of a man to appreciate a pretty girl.*

As they reached the junction with Pfaffengasse, they saw a small crowd gathered on the pavement facing the house entrance. Intrigued, they cautiously moved to its outer edge. An icy shiver ran the length of Blake's spine as he saw a man being dragged out of the building. His legs were trailing limply, his head lolling grotesquely to one side and, even through the driving rain, he could clearly see the bright red of blood on the man's face. Blake's evident shock, followed by the intense look of relief flooding his face, contrasted sharply with the impassive and inscrutable expression of Homer as she stared at the scene with hard, dry eyes. Grotesquely, Blake almost felt like laughing with relief, as this unknown man was bundled roughly into the Gestapo van. *Of course!* he realised. *He's probably the foolish bastard who defaced or tore down the poster. Shit! What a bloody fool I am.* Alarmed by the strange emotions which seemed to be working his face, Homer grabbed him firmly by the arm and pulled him back towards the river.

As they made their somewhat unsteady progress through the damp and thickening mist, the chill was causing Blake pain in his ankle and he asked if he could rest for a couple of minutes. Ignoring his request, the woman abruptly turned away from the Neckar and pulled him across the sparsely populated Fischmarkt. The square was grey and wet, but the smell of coal and wood smoke tantalisingly suggested to Blake the warmth and safety of home. The treacherous conditions underfoot forced him to refocus on the glistening cobble stones as the woman made for a small, narrow door to the side of the huge red stone structure of the Heiliggeistkirche.

'Quickly!' she urged him through the door which, after risking a glance back to ensure that they had not been observed, she closed behind them. Inside the gloomy church, she whispered, 'It'll be quiet in here now. I know one of the young curates who tidies up ready for the morning service. He should be alone and I hope he'll help us, at least until we can get your ankle sorted out. How is it?'

Blake looked up sharply, instinctively suspicious of having to involve someone else. Someone who may be untrustworthy. *But I've got us both into this fucking mess,* he told himself. *And what choice do I have with my bloody ankle?* 'Look,' he began apologetically, 'I'm sorry I got into a flap back there. I should've listened to you. But, you know, I've seen too many rounded up by the Nazis, often quite by accident or through ill luck. I just didn't want to take that chance. Anyway, I don't think I can go much further with this ankle. I'm pretty sure that it'll need some medical attention soon.' As if to emphasise the point, he began to shiver violently as he leaned against the cold stone of the interior wall, clutching his hat in one hand and his case in the other.

Despite feeling genuine anger at Blake for placing them both in danger, the sight of his contrite face and the beads of sweat covering his forehead, caused her to feel sorry for him. Cursing herself for this uncharacteristically soft-hearted response, she began to calculate what to do. She knew, of course, that the church could only be a temporary refuge, a place to get them safely off the street until she could work out some kind of plan. Despite her phlegmatic reaction, it had been a terrible shock when the Gestapo had arrived at the Pfaffengasse flat. *Thank God they were after someone else. But now I'm stuck with this nervous wreck. And he's injured himself! If those damned documents weren't so vital, I'd just leave him on his own.*

Feeling out of her depth in what had become a much more volatile and complicated situation than the simple handover she had anticipated, she decided to go to her older sister. Head of Housekeeping at the nearby Hotel zum Ritter St Georg, she was also an active member of the anti-Nazi movement in Heidelberg. *Uschi will know what to do,* the woman convinced herself. *And she might even be able to get someone to help with his ankle.* Hoping desperately that in midweek the hotel would be quiet, she resolved to go to the staff entrance of the hotel as soon as Ovid was settled in the church.

The woman reached out in the gloom and gently touched Blake's hand which, she noted with interest, reacted less severely. 'Look, Ovid, don't worry about that now. It was just a bad call. We all make them. You wait here while I go to find my friend. We'll get you somewhere safe to wait while I make plans for someone to look at your ankle.' Correctly interpreting Blake's rummaging in his pocket, she added firmly, 'And absolutely no smoking in here. Understood?'

Blake grimaced, but nodded as she tiptoed out into the huge nave, where several banks of flickering candles offered a dull illumination. In her sodden coat, she shivered at the echoing space and grotesque shadows, writhing on the huge stone pillars in the dancing light. Thankfully, as she had expected, the pews were completely empty and she moved quietly across to a door in one of the side chapels on the far side of the nave. Opening it caused a loud creak and, as she peered into the small room, she smiled in recognition of the startled face of her old school friend. The young man's shock transformed quickly into a broad grin as he recognised her. 'Cornelia! Well, this is a most pleasant surprise,' he said with genuine pleasure, his brown eyes twinkling as he got up from a threadbare chair. 'But what on earth are you doing here, especially at this time? It's not long to curfew, y'know.'

One look at his friend's anxious face as she bit her lip, turned his smile into a concerned frown. 'Are you alone here, Dieter?' she asked quickly and heaved a great sigh of relief as he nodded. 'I didn't know where else to go.' Quickly, she told him what had happened, including her suspicion that the British agent was close to a breakdown of some kind.

The young curate received the news with grim determination and immediately offered to let the agent wait with him in the church, while she went to her sister. 'Don't worry,' he said with a grin, 'It's almost curfew. No one ever comes into the church at this time. He'll be safe and away from inquisitive eyes here.' Cornelia made to say something, but before she could open her mouth he added, 'And I'm not so unworldly. You can rest assured I won't let slip your real name.' Cornelia smiled, reminding herself that, ever since their schooldays together, Dieter had always been able to guess what she was going to say and do, a skill which had frequently helped him to talk her out of getting into scrapes.

Blake nodded in gratitude, as he sat down in the small office and listened carefully as Cornelia explained that she would leave him with the curate for a while. 'But don't worry. I won't be gone for long. I just have to make some arrangements.' As soon as she had left them alone, the clergyman smiled reassuringly, offered Blake a cup of sweet coffee and, to his great relief, indicated that he could have a cigarette.

Having slipped unseen out of the church and into the shadows, Cornelia walked rapidly towards the Floringasse and the rear of the hotel. Her sister hid any surprise she might have felt as Cornelia was shown into her office on the ground floor. 'I'm sorry to bother you, Uschi,' she apologised as soon as they were alone, 'but I'm afraid I've got a situation.'

'Is it something to do with Ovid?' Uschi asked quickly, 'because, you know, those papers...'

Cornelia cut her sister off in mid-sentence and explained what had happened, including Blake's loss of control in the flat. 'But he seems to have calmed down now,' she added, unaccountably feeling the need to defend him.

Understandably, Uschi was furious with the British agent's behaviour, but focused only on the need for speedy action. Given the impending curfew, the only option was to hide him in an empty room at the hotel and to treat him there. 'I think I can get someone to look at his ankle,' she said, 'but, after what you said about his state of mind, maybe it would be better if he's also sedated. He'd sleep for at least ten to twelve hours, by which time he'll hopefully be fit enough to leave Heidelberg.'

Cornelia had returned to the church within half an hour to advise Blake of the arrangements. His initial scepticism caused her to fear another panic attack and she tried to reassure him that, even if he were seen, he would attract very little interest. 'Look, these are rooms for seasonal staff,' she explained patiently, 'And if they're not needed, the hotel always turns a blind eye to staff using them for relatives on visits to Heidelberg. They're in a quiet part of the building, well away from prying eyes.' Blake nodded pensively as she added, 'You'll be glad to know that we've also sent for someone to look at your ankle. All being well, you'll get the treatment you need and will stay in the hotel until tomorrow morning, when you can take your train south.

Blake couldn't fault the young woman's planning and was further disarmed when the curate produced an old walking stick from a stand in the corner of the room. 'Here, take this,' he said with a shy smile, 'It was left in the church several weeks ago. I've no doubt that your need is greatest now.'

His embarrassment at his earlier panic weighing ever more heavily on him, Blake felt an urgent need somehow to explain. 'Look, about earlier in the flat,' he began tentatively, 'I think I owe you an explanation...'

'You don't owe me anything,' Cornelia interrupted. 'All I ask is that you get those papers out.'

Blake nodded and, having bade a thankful farewell to the curate, he and Cornelia slipped out of the church and back out into the misty drizzle. Within ten minutes, the agent was resting his ankle on one of the four beds in a simply appointed room.

Cornelia briefly left him alone, but soon returned with a bowl of hot soup, several thick pieces of rich, dark bread and a steaming pot of coffee. 'Here's something for you,' she said with a surprisingly girlish smile which afforded Blake his first glimpse of the real, young woman who was bravely helping him. 'Try to eat as much as you can. You'll need your strength tomorrow. We hope that the nurse will be here soon.' He made a start on the food with undisguised relish and immediately began to feel stronger as the soup worked its way into his system.

Blake had finished his meal and was lying uncomfortably on the hard mattress of the bed, when he heard a gentle knocking at the door. The door opened to reveal a tall, red headed nurse. Even the dark rings beneath her green eyes ︎nd her generally exhausted appearance could not disguise ︎natural attractiveness. Aware that he should try to help ︎h as possible, he tried to sit up and was immediately ︎hed. 'You just stay where you are while I check

28

your ankle,' she advised with an understanding smile. 'This may hurt, but I'm afraid there's no alternative.' She required only a couple of minutes to conclude that the ankle had been badly sprained, but was not broken. A relieved Blake relaxed as she strapped the ankle, before administering a quick injection. 'This will help with the pain,' she said, before offering him one small, white pill. 'I can only let you have this one painkiller. Don't use it until the morning, and, above all, try not to put too much pressure on the ankle. As soon as you are safe, rest it for at least a week.'

As he looked into the nurse's unfathomable eyes, Blake felt a deep sense of peace descend on him. Miraculously, as he listened to her soothing voice, he really began to feel that he could slough off his old life of isolation, lovelessness, cruelty and terror like an old, unwanted skin. He even began to contemplate a kind of rebirth. *Teaching's a worthwhile profession,* he thought dreamily, *and how wonderful would it be to settle down with someone like this in a family home, perhaps even have children.....*

The nurse nodded as she counted the time since the administration of the injection. As intended, the injured man was slipping into a deep sleep, where he would remain for at least twelve hours. After packing her things, she took one last look at his face, now calm and surprisingly young-looking in slumber. For some reason, she leaned over him to brush his damp forehead with a cloth and a tiny tear drop rolled from her left eye. With an almost palpable sense of loss, she began to think about another Englishman, who had all too briefly been part of her life.

'Is everything OK?' whispered Cornelia, from the opened door, concern lining her forehead.

'Yes, thanks,' replied the nurse, with a weary smile, 'he'll sleep until morning now. And I must get myself back to my beautiful little daughter.'

Chapter Three

Friday, June 28th, 1940, Heidelberg, Germany.

The door splintered open and the pounding of steel capped boots on floorboards, accompanied by fierce shouts of 'Hands up!' filled the room. His eyes were dazzled by the beams of several strong flashlights, careening crazily across the walls and ceiling, as he struggled to get out of bed. His mind began to whirl. *Fuck! This is it! Capture and torture.* His hands started to shake and perspiration to pour down his face, as he felt the first strong arms of the soldiers grab him and begin to pull him from his bed. How many times had he envisaged precisely this scene? How often had he punished himself, by playing out in lurid detail, just what it would feel like to fall into the hands of the dreaded Gestapo? Well, his worst fear had now come true and they'd finally caught up with him. Surrendering himself to the inevitability of the brutal treatment to come, Blake could feel the first sharp pain, as a succession of punches rained down on his body.

'Get off, you bastards!' he shouted, while raising his arms in a feeble effort at self-defence. Finally reduced to covering his face with his hands, Blake peered through his fingers with tear filled eyes to see the smiling face of the Gestapo officer, as he raised a Luger towards his face and pulled the trigger.

He sensed that he was falling down a deep, dark well and wondered, idly, whether this was what dying feels like. *But surely, I can feel a strong wind buffeting me? How is that possible in a well?* Even odder, he thought he was beginning to see a kind of light, impossible, of course, at the bottom of a well. *Could it be heaven?* He could hear voices now. *Are they angels singing?* Finally, his eyes opened to the light shining through a gap in the curtains and he felt the frantic attempts of Cornelia, as she shook him hard in an attempt to rouse him. 'Ovid! Ovid! Wake up! You've been having a nightmare. It's all right. You're fine.'

As his eyes began to focus, he realised where he was. His case was sitting quite safely on the bed next to his, exactly where he had left it the previous evening. His coat and hat remained, hanging on the hook behind the door and even the walking stick he had used the previous evening was leaning against the wall. Mortified, he realised that it had been another of his increasingly regular, 'special' dreams.

Cornelia looked on, aghast, as his whole body was convulsed by huge sobs. Unsure what to do, she reached for him and cradled his head against her breast and slowly stroked his damp hair. 'It's all right, Ovid. You're quite safe. Try to relax.' Blake's heaving chest eventually began to settle into a more normal rhythm of breathing and she released him from her embrace. As soon as he had disentangled himself, Blake looked away in embarrassment. 'I'm so sorry, Homer,' he began, only to stop with a harsh laugh. 'I mean, I don't even know your name, do I? Homer? What a bloody stupid thing to call you. Well, I've damned well had enough of it!' Ignoring Cornelia's startled look, he ploughed on, his eyes still full of tears, 'I want you to know that my name is..'

'No!' shouted Cornelia, 'You mustn't tell me. It's not safe! Please, remember why we are both here.'

Blake recoiled as if he had been slapped across the face. Rubbing his eyes with the heels of his hands, he muttered, 'Of course. I'm sorry. Forget I spoke, I'll be all right now.'

Despite her feelings of disgust at his weakness, her heart went out to him, as he gazed at her now with the eyes of a beaten, hunted animal. She gently took hold of his shaking hand and whispered, 'You were shouting in your sleep. I was worried that it might be heard by staff in the hotel.' Blake looked at her and nodded. 'Does this kind of thing happen often?'

Blake hastily withdrew his hand and reached for his cigarettes, 'More often than I'd care to say, really. But not usually as bad as that.'

'Then you must tell your commanding officer, Ovid,' Cornelia said decisively. 'You must tell him everything that has happened. He will understand. He must understand.'

An image of Dansey and his likely reaction crashed into Blake's mind. But rather than laughing at the idea of any sort of sympathetic response from that quarter, he calmly said, 'Yes, I will. Please don't worry. I'll be right as rain in a minute.'

'Then we must move as quickly as possible. How is your ankle? Do you think you can make it to the railway station? It's about fifteen minutes on foot.'

Blake shuffled to the edge of the bed and gingerly tested his weight on his damaged ankle. To his relief, he felt little pain. He tried to stand and, having finished his first cigarette, turned to face Cornelia. 'It feels good,' he said with a wan smile. 'That nurse definitely did a fine job.' Cornelia nodded and, after saying that she would return with his breakfast and some information to help him plan his return to Switzerland, she quietly left the room. Once he was alone, Blake carefully parted the curtains and peered through the window. He was in a single storey annexe to the main hotel building and he could see immediately that the drizzle and mist of the previous day had been replaced by a bright, sunny morning.

He had just finished another cigarette, when a brisk rap on the door was followed instantly by Cornelia entering the room and smiling broadly as she carried a sturdy breakfast tray. Seeing that Blake's hands had stopped shaking and that he had made an attempt to wash and smarten himself up, she said brightly, 'It's good that you're back with us properly again. I have promising news.' Blake arched his eyebrows in anticipation. 'One of my friends has been down to the main railway station and she says that there's no special police or Gestapo presence today. It looks as if we were totally unobserved yesterday. However, I suggest that, if your ankle can take it, you eat your breakfast as quickly as possible and leave Heidelberg while the going's good.' She handed him the tray, which carried a pot of coffee, some bread and cheese and a well-thumbed copy of the current railway timetable book. 'You've certainly thought of everything,' he said with a smile. 'And don't worry. The ankle's still fine. I'll soon be up and out of your hair.'

The door had barely closed behind her before Blake expertly plotted his route to the Swiss border at Konstanz. With luck in avoiding delays, he calculated that the journey would not take as long as he had feared. He would leave Heidelberg at just after 10AM and, with changes at Karlsruhe and Offenburg, he would arrive in the old, lakeside city just after 5PM. He should, therefore, be back at the Swiss safe house in Kreuzlingen by 6.30PM at the latest. *The biggest problem,* he reflected grimly, *is that I've only got one damn pain killer.*

When the time came for Blake to leave the hotel, Cornelia insisted on accompanying him to the station. She planned to walk twenty-five metres ahead of him and, should she see any significant risk, she would take her felt hat out of her bag and put it on. Blake would then abort his departure and meet her in the rear pews of the Heiliggeistkirche in the centre of the city. It was also agreed that the old walking stick didn't fit his cover as a prosperous Swiss businessman and, with some reluctance, Blake left it in the hotel.

The sun shone warmly as he made his way down the bustling Hauptstraße and on towards the railway station. He had taken his single painkiller with his breakfast and, while trying to avoid placing undue pressure on his swollen ankle, he felt reasonably confident in his ability to walk without a stick. He followed Homer onto Bergheimer Straße, where he passed the bus terminal and the grand façade of the Hotel Schriener. Almost at his destination, he carefully crossed the busy road, picking his way between the jumble of buses and trams. Finally, he entered the main station of Heidelberg, a long, low building with a distinctive row of arches, from each of which hung a huge swastika.

The ticket clerk showed only the most perfunctory interest in his papers, as he bought his single ticket to Konstanz. Against agreed protocol, Blake allowed himself a brief glance towards Homer, standing much further along the platform as if waiting to meet someone off a train. Having already bought the day's edition of the *Völkischer Beobachter* newspaper at the station kiosk, he joined the small number of people waiting for the next train. He could see no evidence of any unusual security presence, but nevertheless felt some relief as the train steamed punctually into the station. Given his cover, he had bought a first class ticket and easily found a spacious and far from crowded carriage. He had just enough time to stow his case in the rack above his head, before the train lurched into motion and he saw, for the last time, Homer's dark hair and pretty face sliding out of view. *And I don't even know her fucking name,* he reflected morosely.

***

The journey to Karlsruhe, and the subsequent hour's wait for his connection to Offenburg, passed uneventfully, exactly like ninety-nine percent of the time he had spent undercover in Germany. Sitting and enjoying his coffee and cake, among the cheerful buzz of the buffet in the pleasant and airy station, he did, however, keep his eyes open for likely Gestapo officers. Despite his acute desire to be out of Hitler's Reich for what he hoped would be the last time, Blake consciously tried to exude an air of utter normality as he awaited his connection. While climbing up into the train from the typically low German platform, he felt a sudden, sharp twinge in his ankle. He stared accusingly at the offending joint, before limping to the nearest free seat. *Shit,* he cursed inwardly, *the bloody painkiller's wearing off and I've fucking well run out of fags!* To his great relief, however, the motion of the train, combined with the warmth of the carriage soon dulled the ache in his ankle and the journey to Offenburg passed reasonably quickly.

There he faced a lengthy wait for his final connection to Konstanz and the walk to the safety of neutral Switzerland. Experience had taught him that such periods of waiting could be very dangerous. Security officers, for example, may have little to do, other than constantly check the papers of those travelling towards the Swiss border. Relieved that the pain in his ankle had not deteriorated too much, he tried to keep on the move, managing to buy some acceptable cigarettes and spending as long as he could risk, closeted in a toilet. Finally, he found a quiet table in the open buffet, where he sat drinking yet more coffee and noting with interest several large troop trains, steaming determinedly towards the Swiss border. Given that the Battle of France had been fought far to the north, it was something of a surprise to him that, the further south he travelled, the military presence and activity increased significantly. Uneasily, he pondered what this might signify.

His final train to Konstanz was scheduled to stop at several stations en route and, his newspaper having long since ceased to be a useful prop, he sat impatiently waiting for his long journey to end. Some two hours out of

Offenburg, the train stopped at the Black Forest town of Villingen and, through the window of his carriage, he could see several men climbing into the train. They all wore the classic Gestapo 'uniform' of long leather coat and wide brimmed hat. Blake, reflecting that he had expected a far more significant secret police presence on the journey, now prepared himself for their inspection. His carriage was about half full and he noticed, with a sense of relief that helped him to bring his nervous hands under a greater degree of control, that in this elite section of the train, the secret policemen were treating passengers with great courtesy.

A short, stocky officer, with a pock-marked face and round, milk bottle lensed spectacles, took Blake's passport and papers and peered myopically at them. In response to the German's raised eyebrow, the British agent explained in perfect Swiss-German, 'I'm travelling home after a successful business trip.'

'It is good that the Swiss recognise the importance of good relations and trade with the Reich,' the Gestapo officer responded with a crooked smile. 'After all, we ethnic Germans must stick together, mustn't we?'

'Of course. It's always a pleasure to visit Germany.'

'Then I wish you a pleasant journey home, sir,' saluted the German, before he moved purposefully further down the carriage.

It was still warm and sunny as the train trundled across the bridge over the river Rhine, which flowed in its timelessly sedate way out of Lake Constance and onwards into Germany. Vacantly, Blake gazed out over the water's flat surface, before stirring himself to collect his case and prepare to disembark. A moment of exhilaration swept over him as he realised that these may well be his last ever moments in Hitler's Germany. As soon as he stood up, however, a sharp pain darted up his leg and cut short his sense of euphoria. Struggling to avoid a noticeable limp, his body responded to the pain by beginning to perspire. To the suspicious eyes of the German border police, he feared that a limping, sweating man would definitely not match his cover as a reputable, middle aged, Swiss businessman returning home. *Come on, man,* he silently exhorted himself, while gingerly attempting to walk, *that gorgeous nurse did the trick with your ankle. Just pull yourself together one last time.*

To his relief, he found that, with great effort, he was able to move fairly normally. *But for how long?* As he disembarked the train and shuffled along the platform in Konstanz, he began to sense the onset of a headache, or perhaps even a fever. Determined not to give in at this last moment, he reminded himself that the walk to the border crossing at Kreuzlingen was blessedly short. *Keep going!* he urged himself, hoping that the warmth of the evening would account for his increasingly damp face and flushed appearance. Heart beating far faster than normal, Blake anxiously made his final approach to the border. He gulped as he saw the huge swastika and the 'Deutsches Reich' sign, newly painted in heavy Gothic script. Acutely aware that, without further medication, he couldn't hold out much longer, he took a couple of deep breaths to steady his nerves, tried not to grip the handle of his small case too tightly and trusted that his luck would continue to hold.

Just as he was arriving at the border control, the hazy air was cut by a loud shout of, 'Out! Get out!' from behind the opened rear door of a medium-sized, commercial vehicle, waiting at the wooden barrier. All eyes turned to see a pitiful huddle of Jewish adults and children as they were unceremoniously bundled out of the back of the van. The German guard, who had approached Blake to examine his documents, was evidently most reluctant to miss out on the arrest. Having given his passport the merest of glances and not having looked Blake directly in the face at all, he waved the agent through into Switzerland.

'Caught some more Jews trying to get out, did they?' asked the Swiss border guard sympathetically as Blake offered his passport and travel documents for perusal. 'Poor devils. Even if they'd got through, I'm not sure we would've been allowed to let them in.' He noticed the frown pass over Blake's face and, shamefacedly, added quickly, 'Things are tightening up, you see, sir. I don't like it any more than you. But there it is, I'm afraid. I just do as I'm told. But you don't look well, if don't mind me saying, sir. Do you need help?'

Blake shook his head quickly as he took the passport and papers back. 'No, thank you. I just feel a little light headed. It's the heat, I think. I don't have far to go. I'll be all right.'

'Very well, sir. Then I'll wish you good evening.'

Relieved beyond measure that the guard was giving all his attention to the tragic events unfolding on the German side of the border, Blake began to make his slow and painful way towards the centre of Kreuzlingen. Some ten minutes later, he had reached Neptunstraße and the safe flat, where he was to stay the night and undergo his initial debriefing. He would then travel to Bern the next day and demand a meeting with Dansey. The pain in his ankle was becoming more acute and his fever was rising as he all but collapsed into the flat as soon as its door was opened. 'Good God, man,' exclaimed the SIS agent who had clumsily arrested his fall. 'You look all but done in.'

'You look after him and let me take the case,' ordered the Duty Officer. 'London's very anxious to see what he's got here.'

The senior officer quickly took the case into his office and, once the door was closed, opened it and extracted the file from its hiding place in the false bottom. His eyes lit up at the sight of the OKW and 'Top Secret' on top of the first sheet, and he eagerly read the title of the document: 'Operation Tannenbaum: First Plan for the Invasion of Switzerland.'

Chapter Four

Friday, June 28th, 1940, The Bendlerblock, Berlin.

Berlin looked an amazing sight to Captain Ulrich Schulz as he strode purposefully down Tirpitzufer and on towards the headquarters of the Abwehr - German Military Intelligence. A career soldier since enlisting some twelve years earlier at age eighteen, Schulz was fully aware of the shameful crippling of the German armed forces by the terms of the hated Versailles Treaty. Now, walking among the happy masses thronging the capital, he also felt reason to celebrate the army's unbelievably quick defeat of the French and the British.

Despite the patriotic joy he undoubtedly felt, he had never been a committed Nazi. Like many army officers, he found many of Hitler's ideas and policies distasteful and most of the party's high command utterly absurd. In September 1939, as a junior member of a group of Abwehr officers led by Admiral Canaris himself, he had witnessed the manner in which the 'special groups' of the SS had conducted the invasion of Poland. To Schulz, this bore no relation to any defensible conception of an honourable and patriotic duty. Nevertheless, on this perfect afternoon in Berlin, he had to admit that the Führer had confounded everyone with his Blitzkrieg in Northern France.

A bevy of pretty young women, dressed in their best summer frocks, shot admiring glances at his tall, toned body and classic Aryan fair hair. In his neatly pressed officer's uniform, with its gleaming knee-high leather boots, Schulz could pass easily for a Nazi poster boy. Even the livid scar he wore with pride on his left cheek, the legacy of a duel he fought whilst in officer training, added to his attractiveness. Happily married to his childhood sweetheart Hildegard, however, he had no inclination to bask in such admiration. Moreover, he was a little late for the meeting with his commanding officer in the Bendlerblock.

'Come in, please, Ulrich,' beamed Colonel Erwin Kalz, as he rose quickly from behind his desk and offered his hand to the younger man. 'Come on, tell me, what do you think of our new home?' Kalz had recently been promoted and, though by no means a vainglorious man, he was clearly proud of his spacious and light, third floor office which overlooked the Landwehr Canal.

'Very impressive, sir,' replied Schulz diplomatically, for he had little interest in the trappings of seniority. He was happy to do his duty without any fuss and then to spend as much time as he could at home with his young wife and in his garden. 'But I'm not sure exactly what I'm doing here.'

'Quite so,' conceded Kalz. 'As you know, I've recently taken over the Foreign Branch of the Abwehr. But you certainly don't know that I have negotiated your immediate transfer to my command for a very particular purpose. I have had an urgent request from Lieutenant-Colonel von Ilsemann, our Military Attaché in Bern. He's a good man and a good patriot,' Kalz explained, using the conventional code to reassure Schulz that he was not some rabid Party man. 'He says that he needs a highly competent intelligence officer and I think you're the man for the job.'

Recognising Schulz's dubious expression, Kalz hastily continued. 'Von Ilsemann also acts as Head of Bureau F, the Abwehr's controlling unit for Switzerland. With the fall of France, Switzerland has become even more important to the Allies, both as a location for espionage activities and as a source of materiel. We are woefully under strength there, so your transfer is vital. You are to report to Bern on Monday July 1st.'

'But sir,' Schulz replied, acutely conscious that he was about to trade on the mutual respect between the two men, 'and with all due respect, Switzerland? Like most of my fellow officers, I was hoping and expecting that our efforts would be directed towards England. Surely, we must strike before they can recover? Dunkirk was a catastrophe for the British army, not least because they now have no equipment.'

Kalz sighed heavily, 'It's not quite so simple, Ulrich. After the campaigns in Denmark, Holland, Belgium and France, Army High Command thinks we need a little time to regroup and refresh ourselves. It's also extremely sceptical of our ability to control either the seas or the skies around Britain. Unless and until this can be guaranteed, the army is unenthusiastic about an invasion.'

'And the Führer?' asked Schulz. 'What's his view? Will the High Command have a voice in the matter?'

Kalz's lips twisted, as if he had tasted something unpleasant, 'Hitler believes the British will sue for peace. And he will be happy with that. So, for the time being, Switzerland, unlikely as it may seem, is our priority.'

***

At home in Karlsruhe, Hildegard was delighted when Schulz phoned to tell her that he was being posted to Switzerland, 'But that's marvellous news, Ulli!' she gushed. 'It surely won't be so dangerous and you may even be able to come home some weekends.'

Chapter Five

Saturday 29th June, 1940, Zürich, Switzerland.

'What on earth did Pilet-Golaz say, Karl?' asked Stephen Milton, as he handed his guest a second glass of Dôle wine. 'I missed his speech on the radio and I've been so busy since Tuesday that I've not quite caught up with things yet.

'You're better off not knowing, my friend. Believe me, it would dismay you,' replied the older man. 'Can you credit that he more or less said that it's great news for Switzerland that France has agreed an armistice with Germany and Italy? The idiot believes that we should all be relieved that our three most important neighbours have now found the road to peace. He's basically urging us to adapt ourselves to this new world.'

Milton shook his head in bewilderment, 'It must be a huge political risk for the Federal President to come out with a view like that. I'm an outsider, but even I am fully aware that most of your countrymen are very proud of your democracy. Even a vague hint that they should move in a Fascistic direction is sure to alienate them.'

'Damned right it is, Stephen,' shouted Karl angrily. 'Pilet-Golaz is a disgrace. Why the hell didn't he talk about our proud history of independence and, yes if necessary, about armed neutrality and even resistance? We need to show Hitler that, small as we are, we'd be no pushover. He's damned well hinting that we'd give up without a fight. The man even looks like Adolf with that stupid moustache.'

As a British citizen, Milton was not quite so personally offended as Karl Pfister by the Federal President's apparent acceptance of the domination of western Europe by Nazi Germany. Risky though it was, he could even see what the man had been trying to achieve with his speech. 'To be fair, Karl, the sudden and unexpected collapse of France and the comprehensive defeat of the British Expeditionary Force has left Switzerland having to deal with an altogether different, and far less comfortable, reality. You are, after all, now surrounded by hostile, Fascist regimes. I know you don't like it. God knows, neither do I. But, in some sense, it is understandable that Pilet-Golaz should try to reassure his people and not say anything that could be interpreted as a provocation by the Nazis.'

'Just roll over and let them walk all over us, you mean?'

'Not at all. But surely the experience of Czechoslovakia and Poland is ample proof of the unscrupulousness of Germany? We all know that Hitler wouldn't baulk at seeking specious justifications for an invasion. Perhaps Pilet-Golaz was just trying to defuse the situation, rather than inflame the rhetoric.'

'Yes, I see your point, Stephen,' admitted Pfister with a sigh. 'Let's not forget that about two thirds of those called up last year have just been released to undertake vital work on the farms and in the factories. We have to provide for ourselves, after all.'

Pfister was Milton's next door neighbour on the second floor of one of the recently renovated houses on the Münstergasse, in the pleasant Niederdorf part of Zürich's old town. Usually a measured man, happy to chat over a glass of wine, he seemed uncharacteristically agitated. He suddenly jumped up, drained his glass and said, 'I'm sorry, Stephen. I must go. There's an important meeting tonight and obviously we've a lot to discuss.'

Milton was aware that Pfister was active in Social Democratic politics and he would no doubt be meeting to discuss his party's response to this latest speech. 'That's fine, Karl,' he offered graciously. 'I've a lot to do myself. But don't be a stranger, especially now that I'm on my own.' Left alone with only half a bottle of red wine for company, Milton began to reflect on his current situation. A determined, though mild-mannered man, he was in his early thirties, tall, of medium build and with expressive blue eyes under neatly trimmed black hair. His regular features and open face still retained a weather-beaten quality, acquired during his days of active service in the Royal Navy.

Having proved himself to be an expert gunnery officer, his health had broken down and, much to his disappointment, he had been pensioned out of the service. While his appointment to the civilian staff of the Chief Inspector of Naval Ordnance didn't have quite the ring of an active service commission, he was persuaded of its value by no less than Louis Mountbatten. 'I know it's not what you want, Stephen,' Mountbatten had conceded. 'But I don't exaggerate when I say that your success could be crucial to Britain's chances of winning the coming war with Germany.' Since 1937, 'Dickie' Mountbatten had been waging a lone battle to persuade the Admiralty to consider refitting its ships with the Swiss made Oerlikon 20mm anti-aircraft gun. He argued persistently that its much higher discharge rate of more powerful bullets, combined with its lighter weight, meant that it was both more effective and much easier to fit than its major, Vickers produced rival. Mountbatten was also aware that, by the mid-1930s, German firms had been licensed to produce this weapon domestically.

'If we don't do something about this, sir,' he had urged Admiral Sir Roger Backhouse at a crucial dinner party in his Park Lane penthouse, 'the Royal Navy will be at a massive disadvantage in terms of its ability to withstand air attack. And if we lose control of the seas, sir…' Once a gunnery officer himself, the then First Lord of the Admiralty quickly recognised the clear advantages of the Swiss made weapon and, as a direct consequence, Admiralty interest in it increased. By early 1939, when many key decision makers in Britain had come to see war as inevitable, the Admiralty was keen to agree a contract with the Swiss manufacturers for the delivery of 1500 Oerlikon cannons.

Alerted to Milton's availability, Mountbatten had met him on several occasions and quickly decided that he was a perfect fit for the job he had in mind. To Mountbatten's eye, Milton had an unruffled presence, combined with a natural optimism and positive outlook. But, above all, he possessed the requisite knowledge of naval gunnery and a steely determination to carry out his duty. He was, therefore, the ideal man to go to Zürich to supervise the fulfilment of the contract.

'But I want you to do more than ensure delivery of the guns, Stephen, vital though that is,' Mountbatten had explained. 'I want you to negotiate the licensed production of the 20mm cannon here in Britain. The Germans and Italians are already producing it on home territory and we need to match them.'

'And what do you foresee as the major problems, sir?' Milton had asked, as he digested this significant addition to his mission.

Mountbatten had shuffled his papers distractedly around his desk in the Admiralty Building, before carefully framing his answer. 'Well, Stephen, for a start we've been pretty dismissive of Swiss engineering capability. When they first touted the 20mm cannon several years ago, the Admiralty rejected it in favour of the Vickers alternative. As you know, this was a highly questionable decision because the home-made weapon has a much more restricted range and its lighter bullets cause far less damage to an enemy.'

'So, I may have bridges to build there, sir?' Milton had asked, with the merest hint of a frown. 'But why do you think I'm the best chap for that kind of work? I'm no diplomat, after all.'

Mountbatten had laughed out loud and banged his desk in pleasure at this. 'But that's exactly it, Stephen! You aren't one of those mealy-mouthed types. You're a gunnery man to your bones and a damned fine one at that! You'll be able to get close to the engineers in Zürich, impress them with your knowledge and, who knows? Maybe you'll even make a couple of suggestions for modifications. First, they'll like you, Stephen. And then they'll do business with you.'

'But what about the major shareholder in the Oerlikon factory, sir. Isn't he German? Surely that's going to blackball me before we even start?'

'That could be a sensitive issue,' Mountbatten had conceded with a shrug. 'However, while it's true that Emil Bühler was born in Magdeburg, he was naturalised as Swiss in '37. I suspect that he won't be as much of a problem as the Nazi sympathisers among the Swiss staff. And, of course, there's bound to be one or two of those. Also, we shouldn't forget any German agents operating in the Zürich region.' Responding to Milton's concerned expression, he had swiftly added, 'though we shouldn't forget that, despite a great deal of effort, the Swiss Nazi movement has made very little inroads among the people. The Swiss are a fiercely independent lot and they value their democracy immensely.'

'But if you think there might be danger, then surely I can't take my wife with me?' Milton had protested quickly, only to be reassured by the older man.

'I'm certain that there's no danger to her, Stephen. I'd never allow you to take Helen with you, were that the case. The Germans would never risk any sort of strike against you on neutral soil and in peacetime. That's definite.'

As a Navy man, Milton knew little of, and had even less interest in, the landlocked Alpine Confederation. Nevertheless, he respected Mountbatten and had recognised the great strategic importance that he was placing on this mission. So, that was pretty much it. After an intensive course to bring up his passable German and French to a competent, if not fluent standard, Milton was dispatched to Zürich in April 1939, to be followed later by his wife. As soon as he had had the chance to examine the 20mm cannon, it was immediately obvious to him that Mountbatten was absolutely right. The Germans had taken a far greater interest in it than the Royal Navy for the very good reason that it was by far the best weapon available. Undeterred by having to make up ground, Milton spent a great deal of time with the Swiss designers and engineers, making himself thoroughly familiar with the gun, winning their confidence and, eventually, their friendship and trust.

   Despite his best efforts, however, production towards fulfilment of the order for 1500 guns had been painfully slow. This was not initially identified as a critical issue. Ongoing delivery through allied France was naturally considered a sufficiently straightforward business. However, after the outbreak of war, it had been recognised that disruption and delay, in both production and delivery, was far more likely. Milton had, therefore, been ordered to try to speed things up. Matters were a little more promising, as far as the franchising of production to Britain was concerned. He had impressed Franz Tröder, the Director of Production at the Oerlikon factory, with his astute suggestions for slight modifications to the gun, when it was to be fixed on board ship.

   'It's obvious to me that your heart is still at sea,' Tröder had observed in his good English as they walked past one of the older, low rise machine shops of the factory complex on a cold October afternoon, seven weeks after war had been declared between Great Britain and Germany. 'But you've made some very useful suggestions to us and I'm very grateful. So, I'll do you a favour.'

Milton had quickly turned his eyes away from the succession of steeply pitched roofs which suggested the appearance of a giant toast rack. He had squinted uncomfortably, as he paused and looked directly at Tröder, whose face was hidden by the glare of the sun directly behind him. 'Of course, the Germans are putting us under ever more pressure to cease sales of the 20mm cannon to the Allies and I have to tell you that there are one or two high up in the company who agree with them.'

'You mean Bühler?' asked Milton sharply. 'I'm not surprised. He is German after all.'

'No, Stephen,' replied Tröder firmly, 'It's not Emil. There are others with links to the *Fronten*,' our far right party. Seeing Milton's confused expression, he explained, 'You must remember that when he came to power in '33, Hitler made quite an impression here too. There were those who wanted an end to Swiss Democracy and for Switzerland to turn itself into an authoritarian state. Difficult to believe, after our centuries of devolved and direct democracy, I know. Anyway, thank God, they never got anywhere with their crazy plans, but there are some who still hold firm to those self-same ideas.'

'And your advice, Franz?' Milton had prompted.

'You need to forget the idea of your order being fulfilled. Has it not occurred to you that the frequent disruptions in production seem a little unlikely? Of course, I suspect sabotage. Admittedly on a small scale, but enough to make sure that you'll wait a long time to get your hands on your full complement of 1500 cannons. No, Stephen, you really need to push hard to get through the agreement to franchise their production in Britain. That's my advice and I'll help you all I can.'

'And what's the best way to achieve that, Franz? What's Bühler's position? Is he for or against?'

'That's difficult to say, Stephen. Emil is very inscrutable and, even though he has fully taken on what it is to be Swiss since his naturalisation, he is also keenly aware that he has a balancing act to perform. The company senior management's sympathies are, to a certain extent, split between those who prefer the pragmatic approach of a much closer working relationship with Germany and those who, perhaps more idealistically, favour the Allies and their democracies. It's up to you, but this ongoing 'Phoney War' has given you the breathing space to agree the franchise before hostilities begin in earnest. However, this situation won't last too long, so we've no time to lose.'

Mountbatten, while disappointed by the dismal news of delays in the fulfilment of the naval order for the Oerlikon, had nevertheless urged his agent to act on the advice offered by Tröder. As events transpired, Milton had found the factory owner sympathetic to the British request to franchise production of the 20mm cannon. Accordingly, an agreement in principle, had been reached before Christmas 1939. Moreover, Tröder had been as good as his word. His unconditional support for the British franchise had frequently irritated the minority of pro-Nazi senior managers, in what had proven to be very delicate negotiations over the terms of the licensing agreements.

However, the unexpectedly speedy loss of France and the retreat of the British Expeditionary Force across the English Channel had complicated matters greatly. As news of the catastrophe in France filtered through to neutral Switzerland, Milton had reflected bitterly on the wisdom of Tröder's words. For by that time, only 109 guns of the 1500 ordered had been delivered to Britain and, of course, further deliveries through France were out of the question. Moreover, as Switzerland was almost surrounded by nations hostile to its own democracy, concern about the wisdom of going ahead with the British franchise was more frequently expressed in Oerlikon Board Meetings.

The rapidly deteriorating situation had also forced Milton's wife to escape to the safety of British soil via a Royal Navy destroyer, which had called into the unoccupied port of Marseilles in Southern France. He, of course, had remained in order to bring the franchise negotiations to a successful conclusion.

As he peered through the sheer curtains of his flat, immediately recognising Karl's broad back disappearing down one of the quaint alleys of Zürich's old town, his mind returned to its most frequent concern. *How the hell can I complete the franchise agreement and get back to Britain before it's too damned late?'*

Chapter Six

Sunday June 30th, 1940, London.

Professor Bernard Pym had just settled down for his habitual Sunday morning review of the newspapers, accompanied by a Mozart Horn Concerto on the gramophone and a schooner of dry sherry. Both an Oxford academic and special consultant to the Security Services, with reference to the German speaking countries, he cursed softly at the telephone's insistent interruption. Nevertheless, he mentally sprang to attention as Mason, the concierge of his fine mansion block flat overlooking Lord's Cricket Ground in St John's Wood, informed him that a despatch rider from the Admiralty had arrived with an urgent message. An ex-Naval man himself, Pym was intrigued as he took the message from the attractive young Wren who advised nervously, 'With your permission, sir, I have to take back your immediate response.'

Pym nodded, tore open the flimsy envelope and read:

F.A.O Prof. B. Pym TOP SECRET.

Attendance at The Office of the Director of Naval Ordnance, Admiralty Buildings requested for 2PM inst., MOST URGENT. Confirm immediately.

'Please inform the Director that it will be my pleasure to present myself at the designated time,' said Pym with a smile.

'Thank you, sir,' replied the relieved Wren and, with a crisp salute, she left the flat.

***

Despite the psychological effects of the terrible disaster which had recently unfolded in France, Pym felt an unmistakable burst of excitement as he hurried through the main entrance to the grand building, commonly known as the Admiralty Extension. Even though it was a balmy Sunday afternoon, the place was a hive of activity. Having introduced himself at the reception desk, Pym was immediately led to a bright, third floor office, offering a magnificent view over Horse Guards' Parade. He was welcomed warmly and thanked for his prompt attendance by a middle aged, willowy man who introduced himself as Captain J C Leach, Director of Naval Ordnance.

'I don't suppose you've much idea why you're here, Professor,' suggested Leach with a warm smile, as he offered his guest a cup of tea and a biscuit. Pym barely had time to take his first sip, before the naval officer continued. 'I know you're a busy man, so I'll get straight to the point. We have a problem concerning the Oerlikon cannon.'

Pym was aware of Louis Mountbatten's long campaign to persuade the Admiralty of the benefits of equipping the Royal Navy with this particular weapon and nodded before interrupting. 'I understand what you are talking about, but what's it got to do with me? I'm currently engaged in a very important operation which is coming to a critical point here in London. It's led by a rather inexperienced chap and I'd be very reluctant to compromise my commitment to him by taking on a significant involvement in some other venture.'

'Of course, I don't know the details of that specific operation, Professor,' countered Leach smoothly. 'But what I can say, is that I have been told by Rear Admiral Bruce Frazer that the situation I am going to outline to you could be of the utmost significance both to Britain's chances of survival and of winning the war.' Leach smiled inwardly, as he saw Pym's eyebrows rise as he mentioned the Third Sea Lord of the Admiralty's name. Choosing his words carefully, he went on to explain that a member of the staff of the Chief Inspector of Naval Ordnance had been in Switzerland for more than a year, both supervising production and delivery of an order of the cannon, and negotiating an agreement to franchise their production to Britain itself.

'As you will appreciate, with the fall of France, the possibility of fulfilling that order is now negligible. Accordingly, the franchise has acquired even more importance. The problem is, you see, that Stephen Milton, our man out there, is a sound fellow, an excellent gunnery officer who has worked wonders in winning them over at Oerlikon. But he's not any sort of secret agent. He's a straightforward naval chap. Dare I say,' he added with a wholly disingenuous smile, 'rather like ourselves. And, what with the new situation across the Channel…'

'You mean the fact that Switzerland may be surrounded by Axis controlled territory before too long?' interjected Pym tersely.

'Precisely,' Leach replied glumly. 'I knew you'd see it straight away. While it should be a straightforward business to get out via southern France, we think it better if Milton has an experienced type alongside. Someone who knows the ropes.'

'But why don't you just involve SIS in Bern? Surely, they can help?' suggested Pym quickly. 'I really don't see what I could do better ...'

'Ah well. There we have it, you see,' murmured Leach, as he shifted uncomfortably on his chair. 'The problem is that this has been a Navy operation from the start. SIS and Station Z haven't been involved at all. Or, should I say more accurately, we chose not to involve them.'

Recognising Pym's look of surprise, the Director of Naval Ordnance explained. 'From its very beginning, we tried to present Milton's mission to the Swiss as a straightforward business matter. No espionage or underhand stuff at all. Remember, when he went out there, we weren't even at war with the Jerries. Now, of course, things are very different and it's not just a case of our fellow getting on a plane and flying home. So, er, you see...'

'You don't think SIS would take kindly to being asked to pluck the Navy's chestnuts out of the fire? Is that it?'

'Got it in one,' replied Leach, relieved that he had not, himself, had to put things so bluntly. 'My commanders would rather keep this a Navy operation, insofar as that's possible. But, as I say, they also feel our chap would benefit from a bit of support. So, as an ex Naval man and involved with SIS...'

'I'm the perfect choice to go out there, smooth things over and make the best arrangements I can for Milton to get home.'

Leach smiled in apology, 'I'm really very sorry, Pym. But if you set off tomorrow, you should have time to sort things out and be back in London within ten days, two weeks at the most.'

Thinking of the young agent, currently struggling to keep his head above water in his first, crucial mission, Pym immediately asked, 'Why doesn't this Milton fellow return with me? Presumably we could take the same route I use to get in?'

'Ah, well, there you have another problem you see,' said Leach sadly, his face taking on the appearance of a crestfallen spaniel. 'I'm afraid to say that he hasn't yet got the legal papers to permit us to produce the cannon ourselves. Nor the blueprints for the machinery and the guns themselves.' Anticipating Pym's next question, he quickly added, 'And we don't know how long this will take. We have to assume at least two weeks, maybe more.'

'I couldn't possibly be away from London for so long,' Pym responded firmly. 'That's absolutely out of the question. I have existing commitments and loyalties.'

'Of course, Professor, that's fully understood,' agreed Leach quickly. 'There's no question of you waiting for

Milton. All we want you to do is get yourself out there, liaise with Dansey of Station Z in Bern and make the most appropriate arrangements, as you see fit. I gather you know some of our people out there? Just select the best fellow for the job and then get yourself back home pronto. With luck, your other man won't even notice your absence.'

Pym immediately adopted a more rigid posture at the mention of Station Z. In response, Leach raised the palm of his right hand in a calming gesture. 'Don't worry, Pym. Menzies has squared this with Dansey. So, there'll be no problems from that quarter. He's the only one who knows the reason for your presence in Switzerland. As far as the rest of the station is concerned, you're on a fact-finding mission for the Cabinet.'

While Pym was relieved to hear that the proposal had the backing of the Chief of SIS, knowing Dansey as he did, he remained doubtful of his full support. Nevertheless, he accepted that he could not, in all conscience, decline the assignment and he reluctantly nodded his agreement.

***

Monday July 1st, 1940, German Legation, Bern, Switzerland.

Schulz could still sense the presence of his wife as he approached the solid, bourgeois villa which housed the German Legation in Bern. He had travelled to Switzerland by rail, rather than the speedier flight from Berlin. This had allowed him to enjoy a carefree afternoon and evening with his wife, followed by a night of passion and declarations of undying love, at his home in Karlsruhe. Glancing up towards the Nazi eagle, whose stone wings spanned the top of the entrance door, he regretfully banished from his conscious mind all thoughts of home.

His polished boots clicked in perfect time along the tiled, first floor corridor as he followed the clerk to the office of the Military Attaché. 'Good afternoon, Schulz,' smiled von Ilsemann in greeting. 'Come in and sit down.' A proverbial fly on the wall would undoubtedly have been able to amuse itself by watching each of the men try, as unobtrusively as possible, to run a ruler over the other. The senior officer nodded with approval at Schulz's immaculate uniform, his impressive physique and rugged, soldierly features set beneath his closely cropped fair hair. *He's even got a perfect facial scar to attract the ladies!* But above all, he liked the look of his bright, intelligent eyes. *This fellow looks like a thinking, flexible officer, rather than one of those blasted automatons, in which military training seems to specialise these days.*

For his part, Schulz estimated his new commanding officer to be in his late fifties. *But he still looks pretty trim and alert and there's no sign of the physical degeneration suffered by so many veterans of The Great War.* A smile flitted briefly across Schulz's face as he decided, *the man's grey hair and small military moustache give him the air of a minor aristocrat, looking forward to a day's hunting, fishing and shooting.*

After introducing himself, the older man began by observing, 'I suppose you're a little surprised to find yourself here in Switzerland, Schulz.' After politely listening to the younger man's agreement, he then continued, 'You come on the highest recommendation from Colonel Kalz. I believe you were assigned to his office for some time and moved with him when he became Head of the Abwehr's Foreign Section?'

'That's correct, sir,' replied Schulz confidently. 'After transferring to the Abwehr I saw action in the invasions of both Czechoslovakia and Poland.'

Despite receiving Kalz's unambiguous assurances concerning Schulz's traditional views on the role of the army, von Ilsemann was keen to explore further. 'And how, if I may ask, have you enjoyed your time with the Abwehr?'

Schulz was not overly surprised at the nature of this question. He was well aware that army officers, especially those like himself who were neither enthusiastic about, nor sympathetic to the Nazi Party, had to be very careful with the opinions they chose to express. Kalz had been quick to point out that his new commanding officer, 'shares our view of what it is to be an officer and a patriot.' Nevertheless, Schulz chose his words carefully, 'I must say, sir, and with all due respect, I was very disappointed at my transfer from Berlin. Even though it puts me nearer to my home in Karlsruhe and is indeed a promotion. I very much enjoyed working for Colonel Kalz. He is an inspirational leader and I was saddened to leave his office.'

'Oh, I'm well aware that all young officers think that the only place to be is at the front, or in Berlin,' suggested von Illsemann with a smile. 'But you must not, under any circumstances, allow yourself to believe that you have landed in some sort of quiet backwater here. For an intelligence officer, right now there is nowhere more exciting and important to operate than this small republic.' Von Ilsemann smiled paternally as he registered the disbelief on Schulz's face and asked, 'Tell me. What do you know of war related industries in Switzerland?'

'Not very much, sir.'

'I thought not. Well, it's not all cows, mountains and Heidi here, you know, Schulz. The Swiss have some of the most advanced engineering and technical industries in the whole world. And what happens to its output is of vital interest to the Reich.'

'You mean who they supply, sir?'

'Exactly!' agreed the older man banging his fist on his desk to emphasise his agreement. 'Would it surprise you to know that our latest intelligence suggests that 30% of Swiss war related industrial output is for Switzerland itself, some 50% for Britain, France and the USA and only 10% for Germany and Italy?'

'It would, sir, yes,' replied Schulz, before suggesting, 'But surely that will change now that the French have been defeated?'

'Indeed it will, Schulz,' agreed von Ilsemann with evident satisfaction, 'but that doesn't mean our work here is done. We know, for example, that the innocent sounding machine tool manufacturer in Oerlikon had agreed to supply 100 million Swiss Francs worth of 20mm anti-aircraft guns and ammunition to the British. These guns are widely regarded as the most effective of their type in the world and it could be a great problem for the Luftwaffe if the Royal Navy were to receive the full order.'

Von Ilsemann beamed as he noticed that Schulz was involuntarily leaning forward in his chair, fully focused on the conversation. 'How many have reached the British so far?'

'Not many, thanks to production interruptions caused by sympathisers in the factory in Zürich. And now that France has fallen, the supply route is cut permanently. But we know, from our informants, that the British Admiralty believe that their current weapon is unable to cope with dive bomber attacks. We think that it's most unlikely they'll give up so easily.'

'I see, sir,' Schulz said, even though he meant the opposite. 'But where do I come in?'

'It's vital that we know exactly what's going on at Oerlikon and take the necessary steps to prevent the British gaining the ability to deploy this weapon against our own forces. So, I want you to go to Zürich and to make yourself known at the Oerlikon plant. You'll pose as a regular army officer, with responsibility for trade negotiation in armaments. Try to find out how things lie there, especially if the British are cooking something up. And then report back to me.'

***

Thursday July 4th, 1940, Bern, Switzerland.

After hastily packing the essentials for what he expected would be a relatively short trip, Pym left London on the day after his meeting with the Director of Naval Ordnance. His roundabout journey to Switzerland, via neutral Lisbon, Spain and as yet unoccupied southern France, was tiresome and, given the rising threat of a German invasion of Britain, he was determined to complete his task and return to London as soon as possible.

On arrival in Bern, Pym met with Claude Dansey, a man with whom he had a polite, but scarcely cordial relationship. In truth, Pym had no taste for many of Dansey's attitudes and opinions, especially about foreigners. Given this personal history between the two men, and the nagging suspicion that Leach had sold him a pup about Dansey being 'onside' with the mission, Pym wasn't surprised by the coolness of his reception.

'Nothing personal, Pym,' said the Head of Station Z aggressively, 'but God knows why you've been brought in. We could easily have handled this thing ourselves, if only His high and mighty Lordships of the bloody Admiralty had had the humility to ask.'

Keen to avoid provoking Dansey, Pym stifled his irritation with the pompous little man and, exaggeratedly shrugging his shoulders, said, 'Well, there it is, Claude. Ours is not to reason why, eh?' Noting Dansey's half-hearted smile, he got straight to the point, 'I hope I can count on your support.'

Dansey responded with a thoroughly theatrical performance. Drawing in his breath between clenched teeth and shaking his head sadly, he promised, 'Of course, I'll do what I can, Bernard. But, as you know, we're very stretched. We've lost a couple of good men in the last three weeks and haven't received replacements yet.'

'Surely you have somebody,' urged Pym with a rising sense of concern. 'Otherwise, I suppose I'll just have to get in touch with my principals in London.'

'Oh, I'm sure there'll be no need for that,' suggested Dansey with an unctuous smile. 'In fact, now I come to think of it, I wonder if I can see a way in which we can help each other out.'

'Really?' asked Pym, uncertain what he meant. 'How so, Claude?'

'Well, it just so happens that we have a chap who's deuced keen to return to Britain. I haven't really felt that this could be justified, given the manpower problems I've just mentioned. But this situation might just give us the perfect rationale.' Recognising Pym's dubious expression, Dansey attempted some reassurance. 'Don't look like that, old chap. Actually, I think you know the fellow I have in mind. Bill Blake. He's just back from a mission in Germany and he's not quite one hundred per cent. A damaged ankle, but, given the timescale, that shouldn't be a big problem.'

In fact, Pym knew Blake fairly well and had a decent opinion of him. Their paths had crossed several times before the outbreak of war, when the Professor had been a frequent visitor to Germany, Austria and Switzerland. Since September '39, however, they'd lost touch with one another. *But surely Blake is one of Dansey's star agents, especially for the most dangerous work inside Nazi Germany,* mused Pym. *Why the hell is he offering him up so willingly for this mission? Can't Dansey see that he'd lose him for a significant time, maybe even for good? Or is he not telling me everything?*

Pym decided there was no mileage in pressing Dansey about such concerns. Rather, the best course of action would be to meet Blake as soon as possible and determine whether he's up to the job. Having been told that Blake still rented the tiny roof flat that he had visited previously, Pym immediately set off for Postgasse, deep in the heart of Bern's old town.

As he walked along the sheltered pavement, set into the ground floor of the solidly bourgeois buildings in an arcade style which was entirely characteristic of the Swiss capital, he reflected on how the everyday life and appearance of Bern and London had diverged since the previous September. To him, the small city seemed to be meandering sedately forward, as it always had. In contrast, London now showed many unmistakable signs of the change that war was inevitably bringing. Lost in his thoughts, Pym only became aware that he had passed his intended destination when saw the untypically pretty St Peter and Paul Church. Realising with irritation that he had crossed into the Rathausgasse, Pym quickly retraced his steps to the familiar heavy wooden door to number 44 Postgasse. Just as he was about to ring the bell, an elderly man came out of the house and Pym exchanged the customary Bernese *'Grüssech'* greeting.

As he plodded up several staircases, Pym recalled that Blake's top floor flat was what the Swiss, bizarrely, call a two and a half room apartment. Still smiling at the apparent absurdity of 'half a room', the Professor finally reached his goal and rang the doorbell. He had taken a chance on Blake being at home and was, therefore, not unduly surprised when no one immediately answered the door. A second, more insistent ring, however, resulted in an audible rattling of keys and a final opening of the door. Pym frowned in dismay at the state in which Blake presented himself. The rather unkempt, unshaven and decidedly grubby person standing in front of him certainly did not match his memories of the agent. Worst of all, his hands seemed to have a restless twitch, which could be indicative of acute stress.

Pym did his best not to let his concern show and smiled warmly, 'Hullo, Bill. It's good to see you again after all this time. How're you keeping?'

Blake studied his visitor in silence for a few seconds, before muttering, 'Oh, it's you Pym. What the hell are you doing here? I suppose you want to come in.'

The Professor followed his limping host into a living room cum kitchen, in which most of the flat surfaces were littered with unwashed crockery, old newspapers and empty beer bottles. The unpleasant aroma of stale tobacco mingling with the unmistakable reek of sweat filled the small, dingy space. Pym immediately marched over to the large window, drew back the curtains and opened it wide, saying cheerfully, 'Good heavens, man! Could do with a bit of fresh air in here!'

The Professor's initial concern at Blake's condition was partially relieved as the agent, obviously mortified at the state of his flat, clumsily began to tidy things up. 'It's the injury to my ankle, sir,' he gabbled in mitigation. 'It's been so bloody painful that I've had to be doped up pretty much all the time. To be honest, these last few days, half the time I've not been aware of very much at all. It's not normally like this, I promise. In fact, today the ankle feels a bit better, so I'll get this lot tidied up in a jiffy.'

'Don't worry about that, Bill,' said Pym gently. 'Just come and sit down, while I make us a nice cup of coffee and you can tell me what's been going on with you.' Over the next half hour, Pym's careful application of more indirect interrogation techniques allowed him to develop a reasonable picture of Blake's current state of mind. He quickly recognised that the agent believed that, during his last, highly successful mission into Germany, he had reached a turning point. He was adamant that he would not return to field duty.

'Just look at me, sir!' Blake cried desperately. 'I'm a bloody mess! Oh, I know the signs all right. And I've got 'em in spades.' Holding out his hands, he demanded, 'Just look at them shake!'

Pym attempted to reason with him, arguing that all field agents go through tough times; that they all feel they are one small mistake, or a piece of rotten luck away from falling into the enemy's clutches. 'But we carry on, don't we Bill,' concluded Pym firmly. 'It is our duty, after all.'

'That's easy for you to say!' retorted Blake angrily, 'sitting there in your bloody office in Whitehall, or wherever. You just push us pawns around on the board. When sacrifices must be made and losses taken, it's some other poor sod who picks up the tab.'

Pym instinctively felt that he should get Blake out of the flat. In its dishevelled state, there was a danger that it would reinforce the agent's sense of his own poor condition. 'Look, Bill, what say you get yourself smartened up and I'll treat you to dinner? Do you know anywhere discreet? Somewhere we can talk privately?'

Thirty minutes later, the two men were facing one another in the Alter Bock, a traditional Bernese restaurant, just around the corner from the flat. 'It's nothing grand, but they serve good, simple food and beer, have a decent cellar and it's blessedly free of the likes of us,' had been Blake's recommendation as he had quickly shaved off his five-day old stubble.

As soon as they had ordered and were enjoying their first taste of a rustic Walliser red, Pym began. 'I know you think that what I do is easier than being an active field agent.'

'Damned right I do,' interrupted Blake, to be cut off in turn by the older man raising his hand.

'All right. I'm prepared to accept your point of view. But just listen to me for a minute, please.' Blake was struck by the passion with which the Professor had spoken and, for the moment, he remained silent.

'I understand everything you say about the pressures under which you have to operate. It's true that I've never experienced espionage work behind enemy lines. But I do have sufficient imagination and empathy, not to mention having heard graphic, first-hand accounts from those who have, to get a sense of what it must be like.' Pausing only to take another taste of the wine, he went on, 'But, can I ask you to consider this for a moment? How would you feel, having to send young, inexperienced men and, yes women too, out on missions, which you know there's a near certainty they'll not survive? How would you feel, having to attend, like I did eighteen months or so ago, a memorial service for an agent who I knew was still alive? To commiserate with his parents and family? I certainly didn't feel proud of my role that day. Frankly, Bill, I'd have rather taken my chances with the damned Germans.'

Bloody clever old sod, thought Blake savagely. *How the hell did he guess that my biggest worry is that I'll be responsible for the deaths of others?*

Pym, however, had not yet finished. 'What do you think it's like, being trapped on a merchant ship in mid Atlantic? A sitting duck for the wolf packs of U Boats, searching out our inadequately protected convoys? Do you think it's easy being a nineteen-year-old pilot, still wet behind the ears, having to climb into a Spitfire and do battle with a numerically superior enemy in the skies over Kent and Sussex? Each time you climb into your kite, you know that, if your luck runs out, the best you can hope for is instant death. The worst is to go down in indescribable agony, like a human torch.'

'Enough, Professor, for pity's sake,' interrupted Blake, his palms bared in surrender. 'Don't embarrass me any more than necessary. I get your point. I really do. But, for now, I'm certain that the best contribution I can make to the war effort would be to return to Britain and undertake a back office or training role. My experience behind enemy lines would be more valuable there.' *Where I'll do less harm*, he added silently. 'All right, I don't rule out going back into active service after a few months away. But just now, I don't think I can hack it.'

'Look, Bill,' Pym responded sincerely, 'both you and I know that you're a damned fine officer and field agent.' Brushing off Blake's immediate shake of the head and hand raised in protest, Pym quickly continued. 'Yes, I accept that you've been pushed to the limit. And that can't go on. But that doesn't mean you've suddenly become totally incapable. I'm certain you can still do an important job.'

'That may be true, I suppose,' admitted Blake unwillingly. 'But, honestly Prof, I can't go back into Germany. Not just yet. That's for sure. So, whatever it is that you've come to say, you'd better get it said. I'm not fool enough to think you just dropped in on a social call.'

Pym smiled at Blake's characteristic sarcasm and replied as honestly as he could. 'Of course, you're right, Bill. But what I've got to say could work for both of us. And for Britain.'

An intrigued Blake looked up from his wine glass and asked quickly, 'You mean a Blighty ticket?'

'Yes,' replied Pym cautiously. 'But there's a price to pay. No such thing as a free lunch, after all old chap.' Recognising the conflicting signs of interest and disappointment in Blake's eyes, Pym explained. 'There's a fellow who will soon have some rather important documents that we need to get back to Britain safely. How would you fancy the job of making sure he gets there with them?'

Blake immediately began to shake his head slowly. 'Did you not hear what I just said?' he asked incredulously. 'I've told you. I'm finished with all that for now. I couldn't go back. It's impossible.'

'But this wouldn't involve going back into Germany, Bill. He's here, in Switzerland. You'd just have to get him out through southern France and into Spain. A piece of cake to someone like you.'

Pym prided himself on being a good judge of character. Sometimes, he even thought that he could see qualities in people that they didn't always recognise in themselves. In this case, despite both his reservations over Dansey's motives and his own concerns over the state in which he had found Blake, his responses during the conversation had been exactly as Pym had hoped. He was convinced that, despite the undoubted issues, Blake still had sufficient skill, determination and sense of duty that, once persuaded to undertake the mission, he'd make a good job of it.

Blake, however, remained doubtful. 'No. Sorry. I don't want to do it. I've earned my ticket home already. It's not right that you're asking this of me.'

Pym shook his head sadly, 'I'm afraid there simply is no one else, Bill. You know how thinly stretched we are over here. Especially after our recent losses.' Blake involuntary grimaced at this reminder of the grisly ends recently suffered by three of his colleagues and Pym disingenuously added, 'Besides, Bill. Even if I could choose anyone for this mission, I'd want you. No question. You're the right man for the job.'

'How long do I have, before you need an answer?' asked a defeated Blake and Pym knew that he had got his man.

Chapter Seven

Monday July 8th, 1940, Uetliberg, Zürich, Switzerland.

The second week of July dawned, bright and sunny, over the steeply pitched roofs and glittering lake of Zürich. After enjoying a small breakfast of Birchermuesli and a cup of dark, aromatic coffee, Milton left his flat to walk to the lower terminus of the Sihltalbahn. This funicular railway effortlessly carried passengers the 9.1 kilometres and 400 metre height difference from close to the city centre up to the top of Zürich's 'local mountain', the Uetliberg.

From his apartment, Milton made his way along Münstergasse. He craned his neck to smile at the blue sky, looking forward to feeling the warm sun which had yet to banish the shadows from this busy thoroughfare in the city's Bohemian Niederdorf. Crossing the river Limmat by the Münsterbrücke, he turned to gaze towards the lake of Zürich and the Alps in the distance. Shrouded today in the beginnings of a fine heat haze, they lazed sleepily in the distance and it occurred to Milton that first impressions can be dangerously deceptive. The Swiss mountains may look benign on a day such as this. But he was certain that no invader would relish having to root out determined opposition from such a redoubt.

He passed the twin towers of the Romanesque Grossmünster, which legend claimed was founded by Charlemagne, and was soon crossing the famous Bahnhofstraße. Despite the favourable weather, shoppers were not out in quite the force of an average weekday morning. Moreover, those who were evident seemed much more subdued in their general demeanour. In contrast, the pale blue and white trams clanged normally through the bright sunshine of Paradeplatz, where the two financial giants – Union Bank of Switzerland and Swiss Credit Institution – glowered uneasily at one another across a corner of the square, for all the world like two boxers before a fight. Several more minutes of easy walking found Milton at the lower terminus of the Sihltalbahn, where he bought a return ticket and waited for the next train.

Whilst waiting on the platform, he reflected on the rather sparse instructions which been issued to him by telegram on the previous Saturday afternoon. He had never met his contact, a Professor Pym. Neither was he quite sure what the meeting would be about. He was merely aware that Pym had been sent by the Director of Naval Ordnance and that he had been told to obey any orders issued by him. Despite his equable disposition and his undoubted concern about his situation, the habitually even tempered Milton was disturbed by this development. *Damn it all, I've been running my own show here for over year and I can't say that I'm overly enthusiastic about someone just breezing in and telling me what to do. At least*, he consoled himself, *it doesn't look as if that odious Claude Dansey, or one of his closest lieutenants, will be involved.* Milton was aware, from whispered gossip among the British he had met on his frequent visits to Bern, that the Head of Section Z was not at all popular among his colleagues. Moreover, from his admittedly limited experience of the man, he could readily see why. The term

'Blimpish' could have been invented for Dansey, who wore his huge list of prejudices like a badge of honour.

The meeting with Pym was scheduled to take place in the Restaurant Uto Kulm, situated atop the Uetliberg and, on previous visits, Milton had enjoyed its excellent coffee and cakes and marvellous views of the city, the lake below and the Alps in the distance. At last the electric train glided, almost noiselessly, into the station and, as is the logical preference of a man who faces life head on, Milton claimed a forward facing, window seat. The sparsely occupied carriage reminded him immediately of how sensible the decision to meet early in the morning had been. As he left the train at its mountain terminus and began the short, steep path up to the restaurant, he glanced at his watch and realised that he had arrived too early. Grateful for the shade offered by the overhanging tree branches, on what was fast becoming a glorious summer day, Milton smiled as the fine old building came into view. Its covered balconies, huge windows and generous dimensions gave it the air of a grand hunting lodge or an imperial summer retreat. He immediately recalled, with a pang of real sadness, the last time that he had dined there. It had been on his wife's birthday and the weather had been totally different on that December day. Moreover, the deep snow drifts had served to encourage Christmas spirit aplenty among the various diners.

Milton briefly wondered if he had time to climb the viewing tower, positioned adjacent to the restaurant building. Having decided against, he went directly to the restaurant, where he sat at a window table and ordered a café crème. He barely had time to savour his first taste, when a man fitting perfectly his written description of Pym sauntered into the room. To Milton's surprise, he was chatting amiably with a tall, rangy man of around forty, who was dressed very smartly in a fine woollen business suit. Milton's surprise that Pym was not alone must have been evident as he looked questioningly towards the tweed clad academic. Pym simply smiled broadly, swept over to the table and, for all the world like they were three business associates at a morning meeting, discreetly introduced himself and then Peter Graf of the Swiss Military Intelligence Service.

'I'm aware that you were expecting me to be alone, Milton. However, I'm sure you'll see the point of inviting Herr Graf here this morning,' explained Pym, after ordering more coffee.

'It seems to me that our young friend looks somewhat unconvinced, Bernard,' said Graf in accented English. 'Perhaps I should explain a little about our relationship?'

'Thank you, Peter, but I don't think that will be necessary,' replied Pym firmly. 'Suffice to say that, as we came in, we were just discussing a current case in which Herr Graf has been of great service to Britain. And I'm sure you will be interested in what he has to say. I'm not sure that you understand fully what happened at Dunkirk,' the Professor added with a heavy sigh. 'Whatever the Prime Minister may say for public consumption, I can tell you that it was a total disaster.'

'But I thought most of our chaps got away? That's what it said in the newspapers here,' protested Milton.

'That may be so,' replied Pym evenly. 'But the flotilla only had room for human cargo and they had to leave all their heavy equipment and vehicles behind. So, at this moment, Britain has never been more vulnerable to invasion. The Royal Navy is going to be even more crucial to our survival over the coming years and we think that the Oerlikon cannon is crucial to its chances of success.'

'And, of course, now that the import of ready-made weapons is impossible,' Milton added helpfully, 'getting the franchise agreement signed and the machinery blueprints and product specifications back to Britain is even more vital.'

'Exactly,' agreed Pym, 'and that's not all. An agent of ours has recently returned from a mission in Germany, during which he came into possession of outline plans for a Nazi invasion and occupation of Switzerland. They are only outline plans at this stage, but they indicate a clear intention.'

'This is something that, frankly, Swiss Military Intelligence had come to expect,' Peter Graf admitted, as he took out a cigarette from a slim, silver case. 'Shortly after the outbreak of war last year, General Guisan, the Commander-in-Chief of the Swiss Armed Forces, reached an agreement with the French.' He paused to offer a cigarette to his colleagues, Milton declining and Pym preferring to produce a pipe from his jacket pocket. 'This stated that, in the event of a German invasion of Switzerland, French troops would be permitted to enter my country in order to offer armed assistance.'

'But doesn't that contradict Switzerland's historic neutrality?' asked Milton sharply.

Graf smiled at the astuteness of the observation, 'Yes, it could be seen that way. But at the time, a German invasion of central and southern France, through Switzerland, was thought to be the more likely scenario. It was a sensible precaution, really, rather than an overtly anti German step.' The two British men nodded and Graf explained further, 'Of course, no one expected that Hitler's Blitzkrieg would be so incredibly successful. And its speed has had a potentially damaging consequence for my country. As a result of their advance, we believe that the Germans have discovered papers which detail this agreement. In these circumstances, there is increasing pressure on all Swiss people and organisations to do nothing to irritate or annoy Germany. Moreover, we have just demobilised about two thirds of the conscripted army, to permit badly needed manpower to deploy to our farms and factories. As you can see, gentlemen, the position of my country is perhaps even more vulnerable than that of yours. After all, we don't have your English Channel. Though,' he added with a rueful smile, 'we do, of course, have the Alps.'

A silence descended while the three men digested what had been said. Milton gazed through the huge window, towards the Uetliberg viewing platform, while Pym fiddled with his pipe and Graf lit another of his fragrant cigarettes. After a couple of minutes Graf resumed, 'My commander, Lt Colonel Roger Masson has stressed that I should advise you most strongly to conclude your franchise negotiations as quickly as possible. The climate, as you can see, will not become more favourable for some time. Now, Bernard,' he asked as he gathered his lighter and cigarettes, 'Is there any other way I can help you? If not, I would just ask you to remember me to Herr King. I hope his mission in Britain is going well.'

'I think you've been a great help, Peter,' replied Pym warmly. 'And thank you, he is well and his mission is exceeding all expectations. But, as you can imagine, we all feel that, given the heightened threat of invasion, it may now be entering it most crucial phase.'

'I wonder, sir,' asked Milton quickly, as he saw Graf begin to rise from his seat. 'Before you leave, could you perhaps let me have a method of contacting you? Only in case of absolute emergency, of course.' Pym shot a sharp glance at Milton, before looking apologetically at the Swiss. After barely a second's hesitation, Graf scribbled a telephone number on a piece of paper, saying evenly, 'This is my home number and it is secure. Please memorise it and destroy the paper. If I am not present when you ring, say that you are my tailor and that my suit is ready for a further fitting. I will then contact you. But, please, use this only in a dire emergency.'

After Graf's departure, Pym and Milton left the restaurant and decided to climb the viewing tower. The younger man was surprised at the Professor's fitness as he reached the deserted viewing platform without having to pause. As they gazed out over the city and lake sprawling below them in the sunshine, Pym gently chided Milton. 'I'm not sure asking for his contact details was quite cricket, Stephen. I may call you that, now we are alone? Nevertheless, Graf's a sound fellow and I must admit that I feel happier that you can call on him, if absolutely necessary. Now, let's work out what you must do.'

Pym explained to Milton that he had recently arrived from London via Spain and unoccupied France and that he would return by the same route the following day. 'The Germans themselves have been caught out by the speed of their advance,' he explained. 'They simply don't have the manpower to occupy the whole of France. So this is your best route out of Switzerland. But you'll have to make it quick. We don't know how long it will be before the noose is tightened.'

It was agreed that Milton would push to obtain the necessary documentation from the Oerlikon factory as soon as possible. At any event, he should be leaving for Britain before the end of the month at the latest. 'That should give you enough time and, with luck, the Germans won't be organised properly in France. Hitler clearly placed too much reliance on the Italians and, not surprisingly, they failed him. The Jerries are also trying to work out whether they should risk an immediate invasion of Britain. I must say, as things stand, the odds don't look good for us. But at least that makes southern France a lesser priority for them.'

Finally, Pym came to what he correctly suspected would be the most awkward part of the meeting. He had thought long and hard over his decision to involve Blake. *The man's evident state of stress is an obvious risk*, he had debated, *and Milton has been doing a good job on his own. I doubt he'll take well to having a 'babysitter' imposed on him. On the other hand*, he had reasoned, *show me a field agent who doesn't show some signs of stress and I'll show you one who isn't fully on his mettle. No,* he had concluded, *Milton could quickly find himself out of his depth if the journey home goes wrong and I have sufficient confidence that the prize of getting back to Britain will ensure Blake does a competent job. It's definitely a risk worth taking.*

Pym instructed Milton firmly that he would be accompanied back to Britain by an experienced agent, 'This is non-negotiable, I'm afraid, Stephen. This man must return to Britain and he will be a useful guide and protector for you. I won't say that you should take orders from him, but you should definitely follow his advice. He'll be in touch in the next week or so using the codename Ovid.'

Milton had liked Pym and been relieved that his instructions about getting out of Switzerland quickly were entirely consistent with his own views. *But this is altogether something else. I didn't see that coming!* 'Now, with all due respect, sir,' he protested, 'you've just said that the trip should be straightforward. And in any case, I'm used to working alone and would rather carry on that way.'

Pym shook his head and replied tersely, 'It's not an option, Milton. I carry the full authority of the Director of Naval Ordnance in this matter. Your orders are to meet and liaise with this officer who will arrange for both of you to return to Britain. I trust I have made myself clear.'

Chapter Eight

July 1940, Zürich, Switzerland.

As July began, the population of Switzerland became increasingly concerned about the existential threat which their country faced. They couldn't quite understand how, surrounded as it was by nations hostile to the very idea of democracy, the commanders of the army could have approved a policy of demobilisation. While the increased labour in factories and on farms was welcome, there was a widespread sense that by implementing such a policy, Switzerland was endangering its very independence. Indeed, after his poorly received speech of June 25th, Bundespresident Marcel Pilet-Golaz compounded his error by warmly receiving a delegation of Fascist supporting *Jung Fronten* members. This hardened public opinion against him and enhanced the worry that Switzerland was drifting towards a catastrophe.

The population did not know, however, that the military, under the astute leadership of General Guisan, had developed a new defence strategy based on the idea of a so called Réduit. Guisan and his senior staff were initially sceptical of this approach. In particular, they were very reluctant, effectively to abandon the flat, industrial heartlands of north and west Switzerland to an invader. However, they eventually accepted the military arguments that these areas could not be defended against numerically far superior German forces. By planning to fall back onto a defence of Switzerland in its core homeland of the mountains, the embattled democracy enabled itself to pursue a policy that made perfect economic and diplomatic sense. More labour could be devoted to producing that which Switzerland would need to survive in war time. But crucially, this would be a policy that Germany could not present as confrontational and, therefore, a possible justification for invasion. At the same time, however, should the Nazis attack, it would allow the smaller Swiss army to employ guerrilla tactics in favourably mountainous terrain.

Milton's sense of his security in a neutral country had been eroded greatly by the meeting with Pym and Graf and he was shaken even more when, exactly a week later, he kept an appointment with Franz Tröder at Oerlikon. As he made his way down the curved approach road towards the administration building, he gazed at the bulk of the main workshop which ran for over two hundred metres to his left side. Every time he arrived at the factory, Milton marvelled at the neat and tidy appearance of the whole site. To his eye, it had more in common with a university campus than with the equivalent industrial provision in Britain. This, he remembered as chaotic, uncared for and strewn with discarded material, in marked contrast to the straight roads, the clear signposting and, wherever possible, the patches of green and plant life of the Swiss factory precincts. *It's funny*, he mused, *but when I visit this factory my spirits are lifted, whereas works in Britain always used to shrivel them*. It was the same inside the production workshops. These were light, airy and meticulously organised, a far cry from the dismal, overcrowded and haphazard appearance of the equivalent at Vickers in Britain.

As he entered the administration building, he almost collided with a tall man with a prominent facial scar and a swastika lapel badge. The man raised his hat in a friendly gesture and smiled by way of apology. Milton responded politely, 'I'm so sorry, I'm afraid I didn't see you.' Caught unawares, he had instinctively spoken the first three words in his native language, before hastily switching to German. The other man's expression took on a more quizzical appearance, as he turned and moved away towards the reception area.

Milton swiftly made for the paternoster lifts and, as he waited for one to come around, he was able to hear quite clearly as the man used all his considerable charm to flatter the young receptionist. *Blast!* he cursed inwardly, *that damned German's gone to ask who I am and what business I have here*. As soon as Milton arrived in Tröder's bright and tidy office, the expression on the Swiss's face told him that this had been a far from easy day. 'Good afternoon, Franz,' the Englishman began cheerily, 'though I have seen you looking better. You look terrible, if you don't mind me saying.'

'Whatever gave you the idea that it's a good afternoon, Stephen?' replied a glum Tröder with uncharacteristic sarcasm. 'If you call having an unwelcome visit from our German neighbours good, then, yes, maybe it is a good day after all.'

'Ah, I see,' commiserated Milton. 'Actually, I ran into one of them in reception. Seemed quite a pleasant type though. All smiles and politeness itself. It was just his rather pronounced facial scar and his swastika badge that suggested he might not be quite as innocent as he seemed. That, and the fact that he was clearly asking your receptionist about me.'

'A scar, you say?' asked an obviously concerned Tröder. 'You shouldn't joke about the likes of him, Stephen. He may say that he's a regular army officer based with the German Trade Mission in Bern, but I'm far from convinced. He might indeed seem politeness itself, but he was certainly very interested in our international trade links. Of course, he wasn't so blunt as to ask outright about our links to the Allies, but I could tell that was what really concerned him.'

'Who do you think he was? SS or something?' frowned Milton.

'My gut feeling is no,' replied Tröder thoughtfully. 'He was a little too polished and polite for that lot. But I do believe he may well be some sort of intelligence officer. It's not a good sign that people like him are snooping about. And, of course, there will be those in management here who would be ever so keen to tell him all about you. I think the sooner you are out of Switzerland the better.'

'But how can I do that without the blueprints and the product specifications?' asked Milton flatly.

'Oh, don't worry,' responded Tröder, his spirits returning with a conspiratorial wink. 'I've had an idea on that score. After we've finished here, just let me put my plan into action and stay away from the factory until I contact you.'

***

Tröder's idea worked like a dream. The first part of his plan was to get the sympathetic Bühler to attend the next Management Board meeting, on the pretext of discussing a proposal for investment that he, as Production Director had made. Tröder knew that his proposal would never be accepted, but Emil Bühler almost never attended Management Board meetings, unless they were to discuss a proposed investment spend. His proposal was simply a pretext to ensure his presence, without arousing any suspicion among the less sympathetic directors. Tröder's plan was complete when, at the last minute, he requested that the British Franchise be placed on the agenda. The classic ambush had been set.

The July 17th meeting could scarcely have gone better; the bogus investment idea was speedily despatched and Bühler, in no uncertain terms, instructed the Finance and Legal Directors to finalise the already agreed British franchise within the week.

***

On the same day as Tröder's meeting, Bill Blake took the train from Bern to meet the civilian who he was to escort back to Britain. Unusually, this had departed ten minutes late and it amused Blake greatly that the ticket inspector seemed to think that his frown, as he stared morosely at the passing countryside, was caused by the delay. Indeed, the Swiss official went out of his way to apologise and cheerily to reassure the Englishman that the train would definitely arrive in Zürich on time. Hardened by years of dire experience with London's public transport, such a paltry variation from the timetable had not crossed Blake's mind. Rather, he was still irritated by Pym's insistence that his only chance to return to Britain was by acting as Milton's escort. *Well,* he resolved, *if I do have to take you to Britain, my lad, you'll come on my terms.*

The two men met at the main entrance of Zürich Opera House on the Sechseläutenplatz, where Blake tersely established his identity, grunting his agreed Ovid password like a sullen child. Milton further irritated him by smiling and responding correctly and politely, even offering the older man his hand. Milton's initial opinion of Blake was established when the agent sighed heavily to make clear that he regarded this as a wholly unnecessary courtesy and strode across the road towards the shore of the lake, leaving the navy man no alternative but to rush after him.

'Have you ever been to Zürich at the beginning of April?' Milton asked as he finally came into step with the silent Blake. 'This square is used for the traditional Spring celebration. They burn a huge effigy of Winter. It's quite something.'

As they reached the lakeside, Blake turned away from the city and ambled off in the direction of the Alps which stood, majestic and brooding in the distance. Disconcerted by the other man's continued silence, Milton took the opportunity to study him more fully. *He's definitely older than I expected. And the way he's coughing his way through that foul smelling cigarette and even beginning to limp, I'd say he hardly looks in the best of health. On top of that, his singularly uncommunicative, positively boorish attitude is damned poor, but, to cap it all, he seems as nervous as a kitten. Just look at his fidgeting hands and darting, nervous eyes. What the hell is Pym playing at? Lumbering me with this anti-social wreck.*

Milton was brought sharply back into focus, however, when at last Blake spoke. 'Look. Let's get something understood right at the outset,' he insisted, 'I didn't, and still don't, want this job. But I've been told I've got to do it, whether I like it or not. So, I hope that you've finally got hold of those blasted documents because I want to get out of here as soon as possible. If you bugger about, the damned Jerries will have us bottled up here for the duration.'

The pent-up frustration fuelling Blake's hostility reflected almost exactly Milton's own feelings and he could not prevent himself from laughing out loud. Blake's gaping response amused him even more and eventually he managed to splutter, 'Snap! You may be interested to learn that your appointment didn't please me at all. Far from it, in fact. I am perfectly capable of making my way back to Britain under my own steam and I resent strongly any implication that such a task is beyond me. Having said that, like you, I've got my orders. However, unlike you, I usually try to carry them out with rather more good grace.'

Blake stopped and turned to face Milton and for one bizarre moment he thought that the agent was about to raise his fists. The threat rapidly disappeared, however, and Milton was surprised to see the hostility replaced by the hint of a smile. 'Touché. Now, what about these bloody papers? Do you have them?'

'I'm afraid I've nothing firm to report there,' replied Milton defensively, causing Blake to take solace in lighting up another cigarette. Recognising his obvious disappointment, Milton quickly added, 'But I entertain every hope that we'll see some progress in the next few days.' Ignoring Blake's dismissive groan, Milton tried to steer the conversation to a consideration of their likely route home. *At least this should be less contentious,* he reasoned, *and with luck, it might even help me to begin to establish some sort of relationship with him.*

To his dismay, however, the British agent simply scoffed, 'You leave that to the grown-ups to sort out. You just damned well get a move on and get those papers, otherwise we'll be trapped like rats in a barrel.' Giving off all the signals that he saw no purpose in prolonging the meeting, Blake then handed over a contact telephone number, with the explicit instruction that this was to be used only to leave a message for Ovid that 'your appointment is confirmed.' Milton would then be contacted with the details of their departure from Switzerland.

'But surely I should have a say in the timing and planning of this?' Milton protested.

'Afraid not, old man,' Blake smirked. 'Pym made that very clear. I'm the professional here. You do as you're told.'

It was abundantly clear to Milton that the initial meeting could hardly have gone worse, and, with scarcely an acknowledgement, the two men parted. Blake limped back towards the city and a frustrated Milton sat down on an unoccupied bench, from which he gazed across the glistening surface of Lake Zürich.

Well, that went pretty much as expected, reflected Blake as he walked slowly back towards the main station. He had approached the meeting determined to give the man a hard time, in order that the pecking order be established at the outset. *I've certainly achieved that, but there are several things I'm not happy about. For a start,* he began his mental list, *he may well be a decent enough chap, but he's inexperienced, an amateur and, possibly, an interfering and unreliable civilian. He obviously has no idea about espionage.* Blake cursed Pym again as he recalled being advised that Milton had been pensioned out of the Royal Navy as 'unfit for active service.' *The bloody Prof, was deucedly cagey about the precise reasons,* he mulled. *Could the blighter have psychological weaknesses that would endanger the whole mission?* Blake then turned to the delay in getting the documents, *if he doesn't make it snappy with those, the bloody Nazis might encircle Switzerland and how the hell could we get out via southern France then? And what the fuck other options would there be?*

Having already thoroughly depressed himself, Blake made matters worse by reflecting that the more Milton's failure to get the documents dragged on, the longer they would be trapped in Zürich and the greater would be the chance that some nosy Abwehr agent would uncover their plans to escape. As he made his way along the Limmatquai, Blake reminded himself that *Zürich and Bern are so full of agents, émigrés and freelancers who would sell information to the highest bidder, that keeping this operation under wraps will require a minor miracle. All in all,* he concluded as he ripped the last cigarette from the packet and greedily lit up, *the whole thing's a fucking nightmare*,

***

Bureau F, German Legation, Bern, Switzerland.

Schulz was looking forward to his meeting with von Ilsemann. He had visited the Oerlikon machine tool factory a few times and felt that he could now offer a reasonably detailed report of the situation there. Punctually at 3PM, he made his way down the sunlit corridor to his superior's office, where he was greeted by the older man's smiling face. 'Ulrich, please come in. I'm very eager to hear how you got on in Zürich. Was it a worthwhile trip?'

'Indeed, it was, sir,' replied Schulz, flicking open the file on his lap. 'I would respectfully suggest that we need to discuss the situation at Oerlikon fully and decide what should be done about it.' Schulz began by summarising the information he had compiled. 'We know that the Royal Navy is now placing greatly increased emphasis on purchasing sufficient 20mm anti-aircraft guns. Their aim is to equip as many of their ships as possible with this weapon. It appears that they have finally listened to those officers who have been arguing for years that their current weapons offer little protection against dive bombers. We know for a fact that they have already placed a very significant order with the Oerlikon factory.' Schulz paused to savour the aroma of his unsweetened coffee, before continuing. 'Of course, for the British the situation has been significantly complicated by the defeat of the French and their own Expeditionary Force. They recognise that future deliveries of the cannon from Switzerland are now most unlikely.'

'Surely you mean impossible!' interrupted von Ilsemann with evident satisfaction. 'The routing of the Allies has fully solved that particular problem for us.'

'With respect, sir,' Schulz replied, 'while that is almost true, it is the case that Switzerland is not yet fully encircled. The defeat of the French was so rapid that the army has not been able to occupy the whole of southern France and the Italians are proving typically useless. There are even limited rail links from Switzerland that are still open.'

'Yes, but these will soon be closed,' protested von Ilsemann. 'You're surely not suggesting that the Swiss will be able to supply tens of thousands of these cannon from under our very noses?' Having made this conclusive point, he sat back in his padded leather chair and flexed his fingers. 'No, Schulz. I'm certain that we can forget any more deliveries to the British.'

'That may be true, sir. However, while I was at Oerlikon, I managed to discover that the British, having recognised that delivery of the 20mm cannon is now most unlikely, are planning to take production specifications and a franchise agreement back to London. In fact, I literally bumped into a British agent called Milton, who was entering the administration building as I was leaving. As soon as I got his name from the receptionist, I quizzed a sympathetic source at the factory about him. Apparently, he's an ex-Royal Navy gunnery officer, who has been hanging around Zürich since last year. He was trying to speed up the delivery of the Navy's order, but he's now concentrating on finalising this franchise agreement. Thankfully, our people on the production line managed to slow things down considerably and very few were actually delivered before we defeated the French and British.'

The news of the franchise seemed to trouble von Ilsemann. His face drained of colour and he balled his right fist into his eye, as if he had an oncoming migraine. 'Colonel Kalz and I suspected that something like this would be going on. That's part of the reason that I requested your transfer here and he agreed to lose such a capable man from his office in Berlin.'

Ignoring the compliment, Schulz immediately asked, 'Is there any pressure to remove this agent and stop their plan in its tracks?'

Von Ilsemann exhaled deeply and replied, 'No, thank God. We still act like military officers, not gangsters. There's no question of that, especially given the delicate political and military situation here. As you have said, the army is spread very thin in France, the Italians are of no help and so we want to do nothing to irritate the Swiss.' Seeing Schulz's look of confusion, the older man went on with his explanation. 'The Swiss have just demobilised the greater part of their conscripts for other work. While some may well argue that we would be fully justified in eliminating an obvious spy, the Abwehr doesn't want to risk this being presented as the assassination of a British civilian on neutral territory. Such a thing might just give the Swiss, the majority of whom, let's not forget, are hostile to

Germany, the perfect excuse to demand the recall to arms of these people.' Von Ilsemann then paused for effect, before delivering the decisive point, 'Especially not with plans being made for the invasion and occupation of Switzerland.'

The older man smiled at the effect of this information on Schulz, whose jaw fell in astonishment. 'That's right Ulrich, and, of course, this information is top secret. So, you see how sensitive the situation is at present. For the time being, keep Milton under observation, but do not touch him. At least, as long as he's in Switzerland. If he makes a bolt for it, that's when we'll get him!'

Chapter Nine

July 18-23rd 1940, Zürich, Switzerland.

During the days after his initial meeting with Milton, Blake's misgivings and irritation about the mission did not change. He still felt strongly that Milton had been foist on him and began to dwell increasingly on the likelihood that his habitual, isolated work pattern would be disturbed. The idea of having to work closely with someone he neither knew, nor trusted filled him with anxiety. Moreover, as if to heap more pressure onto his buckling shoulders, he was about to discover that Milton had acquired an unwanted shadow.

Characteristically suspicious, Blake had stayed in Zürich since their meeting and, while shadowing Milton, regularly saw a tall, athletic man with a facial scar following the Englishman. Blake grudgingly acknowledged the man's skill and was grateful that his sole attention was, perhaps understandably, directed at not being seen by Milton. He was, therefore, totally unaware that he, himself, had been spotted by a third person and Blake found it easy to put the watcher himself under surveillance. He even made time for a day return to Bern, to check out SIS's photographic file of recent arrivals at the German Legation. He found the man quite easily and snorted with derision when he read that he - Captain Ulrich Schulz - was part of the German Trade Legation. *Trade man, my foot,* he thought to himself as he carefully read the thin file. *I'll bet my bottom dollar he's Abwehr. Doesn't look brutish enough for SS, so he's military intelligence for me.'*

While this development was most unwelcome, Blake's first devious thought was to try to turn it to his own advantage by despatching a coded signal from Section Z to Pym in London.

M under hostile surveillance. Suggest I obtain merchandise and repatriate alone. M useful decoy.

To his intense frustration, Pym turned the idea down flat, arguing that Milton's expert knowledge of the blueprints, machinery and the cannon itself, was irreplaceable. Blake's mood was darkened even further by the tone of the Professor's final sentence:

Return of M most vital. Everyone else expendable.

***

Wholly unaware of the four eyes shadowing him, Milton was anxiously awaiting news from Tröder. Finally, late on Friday 19th July, during an ecstatic phone call from the Production Director, his patience was rewarded. 'The franchise contracts are all ready for your signature, Stephen, and the blueprints and technical papers you need are all collated. Please come along to the factory at 10AM next Wednesday morning and we can finally complete our business. It might be better if you come in a car, as I have a couple of surprises for you.' Before Milton could reply, the Swiss advised, 'Let's keep things as private as possible. Drive straight to the rear fire escape and I'll be waiting for you there. The fewer people who know you finally have the papers, the better.'

Milton spent much of the weekend debating whether he should alert Blake to this development. It was clearly his duty to do so, but the man's attitude at their meeting had been so poor and he'd issued strict instructions that contact should be made only when all the documents were in his possession. *To hell with him,* decided Milton finally. *I'll take him at his word and only tell him after the exchange of contracts on Wednesday.*

Milton's neighbour was perfectly happy to offer his car for the journey to the factory. 'Please be gentle with her,' Karl said as he handed over the keys with a broad smile. 'She's a grand old lady, but does things in her own time. And any traffic fines, you pay! You know how strict the Swiss police are.'

It was a genuine treat for Milton to be behind the wheel of a car again and a pleasant reminder of happier pre-war times. Given the efficiency of the public transport system in and around Switzerland, he had not felt the need to run a car during his stay. However, Karl's gleaming black Citroen, despite its undoubted age, was a delight and, as he pulled out of the underground garage, he was so involved in the thrill of handling the car that he didn't notice the tall man, studiously watching the front door of his apartment building. Neither, for that matter, did Schulz or Blake recognise the driver of the Citroen as he began his journey to Oerlikon.

On arrival at the factory complex, Milton drove the car straight to the rear of the administration building and parked adjacent to the rear fire-exit. As planned, Tröder was waiting for him. 'Good, now quickly, let's get you to my office before we attract curious eyes.' Once safely inside the office, the signing of the contracts, already completed on the Swiss side by Emil Bühler, went without a hitch. Less than half an hour after his arrival, Milton was sitting nursing a small glass of celebratory white wine. Despite the generally happy mood, the Swiss wore an expression of deep concern. 'You know, Stephen,' he said, while looking out over the factory buildings, 'my work is done in this matter. But for you, the really hard part is just about to begin.'

Milton nodded before replying with a tight smile, 'You're right, Franz, but I'm sure you'll understand that I can't say anything about how and when I will leave Switzerland.'

'Of course,' said Tröder, holding up his right hand in acknowledgement. 'But I do hope that you will be leaving in the next few days, because the Germans will soon have us totally surrounded. Also,' he added with a smile, 'I hope that you'll be able to make use of some small gifts which should help you when you get back home.' Tröder stood and moved to open a door which Milton knew led into a large walk-in cupboard, containing the factory production records.

As the Swiss stood back, he could see two large sacks, obviously full of small boxes and labelled with Swiss Post stickers. 'I'm sorry, Franz, I don't understand,' Milton said in genuine confusion.

Clapping him affectionately on the back, Tröder explained, 'Let's call it my personal gift to my good friend

Stephen Milton. They're full of jewel centres, vital for aircraft navigation. I'm sure the RAF will find a use for them, as they confront the Luftwaffe in the months to come. There's also a few more items which should help you to start production of the cannon.'

Genuinely overcome, Milton struggled to respond, 'I.. I don't know what to say...'

'Then say nothing, my friend,' interrupted the Swiss, 'let's just get you out of here unnoticed. And when you get home safely to Britain, get building these weapons and win the damned war!'

Tröder helped Milton carry the sacks to the car and, thankful that no one had seen what they were doing, waved Milton away from the factory for the last time. As soon as he had parked in the underground garage of his apartment building, Milton used his neighbour's small trolley to wheel the sacks into his own cellar. Relieved to have them safely stored, he went upstairs, returned the car key to Karl and rang the number provided by Blake, where he left the message for Ovid that his 'appointment is confirmed.'

It didn't take long for Blake to receive the news. He had been ringing the SIS office every couple of hours for any message from Milton and, as soon as the intelligence was passed on, he swung into action. Faced with the necessity of making good his escape with a man who was under surveillance, he had already decided that he would not give Milton any advanced notice of their flight from Switzerland. He was concerned that, as an amateur and, by all accounts, a well-liked man, he would probably want to say his fond farewells to neighbours, or even friends at the factory. This could easily alert the Germans to the timing of their escape. Now that he had received news that Milton had all the necessary papers, he planned to deposit a brief note in the Englishman's post box early the next morning. This would advise him that the documentation should be produced that afternoon, when its verification could be facilitated. Only then could their departure be finally planned. Of course, this was purely a pretext. After all, Blake himself could study the documents for ever and a day and he would still not know whether they were complete, or even genuine. Once in Blake's control, however, Milton would leave Zürich immediately. *There'll be no packing or preparations of any kind for him,* Blake told himself. *And if he doesn't like it, well, tough, I'm in charge of this mission.*

    A brown paper envelope, provided at Pym's request by Station Z, had already provided Blake with a plentiful supply of Swiss currency and Swiss and French passports for himself and Milton. Over the past couple of days, he had also bought and packed a few essential items for each of them. As he carefully put his own things into the small case he had used on many of his forays into Germany, he reflected anxiously on the greatest weakness of his plan. *I'm depending on Milton being able to shake off that damned Jerry shadow. And he is an amateur as well as being a pain in the backside.* Whichever way he looked at it, however, Blake couldn't think of a better strategy. Feeling far from certain that things would go perfectly, he sat down to write the note which he would deliver to Milton by hand very early the next morning.

Chapter Ten

Thursday July 25th, 1940, Zürich.

Milton left his apartment building early to take the short, pleasant walk down to the River Limmat. Since childhood, he had always enjoyed a good breakfast and a morning stroll to buy pastries from his favourite bakery had become something of a ritual. On his return, he checked the post box and found one hand-written, unstamped envelope. *Surely this must be from Blake*, he pondered as he sat down and, over his first cup of coffee, read the message. It was a disappointingly brief, even terse note which echoed the tone of their meeting. Blake had used his codename to verify his identity and had simply stated that the franchise and other documentation must be checked thoroughly, before detailed preparations for their departure could be made. It went on to make clear to Milton that he should follow the enclosed instructions to the letter, with no deviation or modification. These stated that Milton should casually enter Zürich main railway station from the Bahnhofstraße during that afternoon's rush hour. As soon as he was among the crowds, he should run, as fast as possible, to the exit on Bahnhofquai, from which he should emerge at exactly 5.30PM by the station clock. There, a black Mercedes sedan would be waiting to pick him up and take him to the meeting place. *Wouldn't have thought he was the melodramatic type,* Milton thought sarcastically. *I wonder if the bastard's trying to test me. See if I cock it up. Well, I'll damn well show Mr secret bloody agent Blake that I know how to carry out instructions, however ridiculous they are.*

***

Main Railway Station, Zürich.

Ulrich Schulz was becoming more and more concerned. An informant at the factory had told him that the franchise documents for the British had been finalised. *So why has Milton not been to Oerlikon to pick them up?* he wondered uneasily. He began to wonder whether he was being overconfident. *Surely, he can't be aware that he's being followed? He's definitely shown no sign of that when he's been out in the city.* Schulz's worries increased when, late in his afternoon surveillance watch, he saw Milton, carrying only a thin attaché case, leave his flat and make his way towards the Bahnhofstraße. *What's he up to?* the German asked himself doubtfully. *It must be too late to be going to Oerlikon and he doesn't look equipped for a long journey. I'd better stick with him and see where he goes.*

To his relief, Schulz saw no hint that his quarry was in any way aware of his shadow as he sauntered slowly towards the main station. The pavements were crowded with office workers eager to get home, or to enjoy a post-work drink in one of the pleasant pavement cafés and bars. Schulz experienced a momentary pang, as he remembered many such evenings with his wife in Karlsruhe. He became so caught up in his thoughts that he briefly lost sight of the Englishman as he passed under the beautifully decorated entrance to the station. *Nothing to worry about,* he reassured himself, *it's just a little crowded here. And he's walking so slowly, that I'll pick him up easily enough inside.*

***

Despite his doubtful opinion of the man who had issued his instructions, Milton freely admitted to himself that he got quite a thrill out of his sudden change of pace and direction. In some strange way that he could not fully explain, it made him feel almost as if he were on active service in the interests of Britain. As soon as he entered the station, all the pent-up frustration of his removal from the Royal Navy's active service list and redeployment into this, basically technical/clerical role, burst out in his sprint to the exit on the Bahnhofquai.

Blake was just approaching the station exit in the gleaming black Mercedes, when he saw Milton dash out of the wide door. *My God, he's bang on bloody time. Maybe there's more to this chap than I've given him credit for.* Blake glided to a halt in front of Milton, who, having initially registered uncertainty, soon recognised the driver and jumped into the front seat.

***

Damn the man! cursed Schulz, *where the hell can he have got to?* Having anticipated being able to pick Milton up again with ease once he had entered the station, the German was shocked to see no trace of him on the large concourse. *Shit!* he cursed. *It's not so busy here. I should be able to spot the damned Englishman … Unless….*The thought dripped into his brain like iced water down his spine. *Unless he moved much, much quicker once he was out of sight. But why on earth would he do that?* he asked himself angrily, as he desperately scoured the anonymous faces passing by. Infuriated with himself for making such an elementary misjudgement, Schulz immediately made for the nearest exit to the station, which led out onto Bahnhofquai. To no avail, he rapidly scanned the pavement and road, but was rewarded only by the sight of a stream of traffic cruising towards the Bahnhofbrücke. The Englishman had simply disappeared.

***

Milton barely had the time to close the passenger door, before Blake, to the sound of several loud hoots of protest, had pushed his way out into the thickening city traffic. Glancing in the rear-view mirror, he smiled contentedly as Schulz rushed out of the station and stared frantically about. 'You have the papers?' Blake demanded. 'All of them?'

'Of course,' Milton confirmed, while meaningfully patting the briefcase he was holding in his lap.

Sitting in the sun-drenched car after his dash through the station, Milton soon began to feel uncomfortably hot and he began to wind down the window. 'Stop that immediately!' hissed Blake, as he expertly manoeuvred the large car into a narrow road, bordered on both sides by functional looking, concrete apartment blocks. 'Leave that bloody window alone! We can't risk you being spotted.'

Blake's violent reaction so shocked Milton that he sat in silence as they began to move through the outskirts of the city. As he stared across the car at the concentrated expression of the driver, he glimpsed the glittering waters of Lake Zürich, framing Blake's head. With a start, he realised that they were leaving the city behind. 'Now look here, Blake,' he began amiably, only to be once more stunned into silence by the savagery of the response.

'For God's sake, man,' Blake shouted, 'just sit there like a good little fellow and I'll explain everything shortly.' Like a miserable child, Milton was reduced to asking, with increasing frustration, where they were going and how long the checking of the documentation would take. In reply, he received only pregnant silence and hostile looks as Blake worked his way frantically through his packet of cigarettes.

After about an hour and with the Lake of Zürich left way behind them, the British agent abruptly stopped the car on a deserted part of the road, near the village of Sattel. Climbing out of the driver's seat, Blake walked deliberately round the back of the car, opened the passenger door and asked Milton to step outside. As soon as he had inhaled sufficient nicotine from another of his endless cigarettes, Blake said with weary resignation, 'Look. I didn't ask for this job and, whatever Pym might say, nor do I particularly care what happens to you. But I am determined to get these bloody documents back to Britain, if it's the last thing I do.'

Milton felt the explicit rejection like a slap in the face and was preparing to reply in kind, when a warning hand stopped him dead. 'Did you know that, for the past few days you've acquired an interesting new friend? He calls himself Economic Liaison, or some such tosh. But, of course, he's German military intelligence and he's been shadowing you very closely.' Grinning manically and nodding at the evident disbelief on his passenger's face, Blake continued. 'Oh yes, with a gorgeously scarred face to boot! Why do you think I insisted on you taking that diversionary manoeuvre back there at the station? You may have thought that it was a joke. Or that I was playing cops and robbers. But I can assure you that it's no laughing matter to fall into the not so gentle hands of types such as him.'

Milton's face drained of colour and he looked around nervously, visibly shaken by this news. *Of course*, he remembered, *that German I bumped into at the factory! And Tröder's warning that he'd been asking a lot of questions about me.* Milton had never really considered that he was in any sort of genuine danger in Switzerland. But now, for the first time, he realised that the stakes he was playing for were very high. And not just for Britain. He instantly regretted taking no precautions to avoid being followed, nor trying to observe a possible tail.

Recognising the other man's evident discomfort brought his own recent embarrassment in Heidelberg back to Blake and he offered an olive branch. 'Look, don't worry about that now. Your man was there at the station. I saw him through the rear-view mirror as we drove off. You'll be pleased to know that he was punching the air. Frustration at losing you, I imagine. He's no idea where you are now.' Exultant that they'd got clean away, Blake awkwardly clapped Milton on the back and added, 'By the way, you played a blinder back there. Couldn't have done better myself.'

Milton was totally wrong-footed. He was still digesting the disturbing information, when he was hit by Blake's sudden change of demeanour. As the full situation began to dawn on him, he asked quietly, 'But if we've got to make a run for it, why the hell didn't you tell me beforehand? There are important things I've left behind.'

'Oh, don't worry about your pyjamas!' scoffed Blake. 'There's a small case in the boot, with enough clothes and other stuff for the journey. Or do you mean your passport? Come on,' he asked sarcastically, 'Do you really think it would be wise to travel under your own name? We're going into France, you know. A defeated country, in case you hadn't noticed.' Milton simply gaped at Blake in opened mouthed dismay as he tried to recapture his more sympathetic tone. 'Look, Milton,' he reasoned, 'I'm sorry. Genuinely I am. But you must see. I could only be certain that you'd behave naturally and not give the game away about us clearing out, if I left you completely in the dark. As I said, you played your part beautifully and you were tailed to the station, so that was a very necessary deception. Our first goal was to shake off that swine and we've done it. Now, we're going to take the scenic route to France, rather than heading straight for Geneva. But look, I accept that it's all been a bit of a shock to you and, don't forget, the Jerries will be trying to pick up our trail soon enough. So why don't you just sit back and relax? We'll be at our hotel soon and there I can explain the full plan over a good meal and a bottle of wine. What d'you say?'

In turn, Milton's response stunned Blake. Picking his words very deliberately, the official pointed out, 'The problem is this, my friend. I'd say you've just made one hell of a blunder.' Gratified by the look of utter confusion on Blake's face, he continued, in a parody of the agent's earlier sarcastic tone. 'You see, I have two large sacks of goodies for the Admiralty and the RAF. Given to me by my friends at the factory. I dread to think what the brass will say, if we do reach London and they find out that we left that stuff in my cellar. A spell in the Bloody Tower is about as likely for you as a medal, I'd say.' Blake immediately threw down his half-smoked cigarette and grabbed Milton by the collar. Grimacing at the sour, smoke-impregnated breath which was panting over his face, Milton once again smiled. 'That's right, Blake! Use fists before engaging brain. Why not break the habit of a lifetime and just listen for once?' To Milton's surprise, the other man released him, stood back and smiled, 'OK. You tell me. What's the problem?'

'The problem,' Milton explained slowly 'is that those bags contain sufficient vital jewel centres for aircraft instruments to keep the RAF going for months. And the way things went in France, they're damned well going to need them. There's also lots of parts and small components of the cannon itself, as well as tools to make them. All that would speed up no end the start of production in Britain. And they're all safely tucked away in the cellar of my flat in Zürich. As instructed, all I've brought with me are the papers agreeing the franchise and the technical drawings and specifications.'

'Why the hell didn't you tell me about any of this stuff before?' growled Blake, running his hand violently through his hair and kicking the car's rear tyre in frustration. 'Pym said nothing about stuff like that. He was only interested in the agreement and the tech drawings and,' he added with a sarcastic sneer, 'of course, you.' As the enormity of the missed opportunity flooded over him, Blake looked to the sky and shouted, 'Christ Almighty! What a fucking cock up! And to think, I thought we'd got away scot free!'

The two men stared at the deserted road, shivering in the distant heat haze, before Blake reached a decision. Squinting into the early evening sun, he concluded emphatically, 'Well, it's too late to cry over spilt milk now, my lad! We can't possibly go back to Zürich. The Jerries would be on the lookout for sure. So, His Majesty's Lords of the Admiralty and the R A bloody F are just going to have to damn well manage with what we've got. Now, get back in the car and let's get on our way.'

A tense truce settled in the car and the rest of the journey to Flüelen took place in a deafening silence, punctuated only by an obviously nervous tattoo, beaten onto the steering wheel by Blake, as he drove the Mercedes to its very limits.

***

As they approached the charming little village, situated on the shore of Vierwaldstättersee, Blake cursed at the extent of the military presence there. 'Bloody hell! We're trying to slip away discreetly. But we somehow seem to have landed in the middle of some massive Swiss army manoeuvres.'

'I wonder what's going on?' asked Milton, as he anxiously looked outside at the various army vehicles and personnel, positioned all along the promenade. 'They can't be after us, or the papers, can they?'

Blake replied with a non-committal shrug, 'I can't see it. But we'd better play it carefully. Let's just get to the inn and take it from there. Oh, and by the way, say as little as possible. We're supposed to be Swiss, and, while they tell me your German's good, I'm guessing your Swiss-German is none too hot. So, be a good chap, look charming and let me do the talking.'

It was just after 8PM on a pleasantly warm, high summer evening as Blake drove past the white tower of the local church and parked in front of the inn. By this time, many of the military vehicles were moving off, leaving just a handful of officers to enjoy the fine weather. As he locked the car, Blake nodded in approval as Milton automatically took the briefcase which he had been holding since they left Zürich. 'You'd better not let that thing out of your sight 'til we get to London. And I hope it locks.' Milton merely grunted in reply as Blake opened the heavy wooden door to the inn.

The mystery of the Swiss army's presence in such numbers was explained by the excited innkeeper, as they checked into the Gasthof zur Rose. 'You've caught us on quite an auspicious day, gentlemen,' the ruddy-faced man explained. 'General Guisan has just addressed the army General Staff up on the Rütli meadow. Apparently, he said that the army stands ready to resist any attempt at invasion by the Germans. And a bloody good thing too!' he added, whilst downing the last of a heavy cut-glass tumbler of some improbably strong mountain schnapps. 'What do you say?' he winked at his visitors, whose concerned expressions had quickly turned to relief. 'How about we toast the good General and all the valiant boys in the army. To hell with Adolf and his lot. If he tries to swallow Switzerland, he'll find out he's bitten off a bit more than he can chew.'

'Hear! Hear!' replied Blake in perfect Swiss German, as all three clinked their glasses, before downing the large measure of the fiery liquid.

'Now, gentlemen,' the innkeeper said apologetically, 'what with all the excitement today, we're still in a bit of a mess. Can you give us half an hour to get the kitchen ready to prepare your meal?' Seeing the swift look that passed between the two men, he suggested brightly, 'It's a lovely evening for a stroll down by the lake.' Blake immediately reassured him that a good half hour walk along the lake promenade was exactly what he and his friend needed and that he should think no more about it.

As they walked slowly along the water's edge, the first signs of clouds gathering over the surrounding mountains began to appear. In contrast to his earlier volatility, Blake seemed in more reflective mood and stopped to light a cigarette, before observing, 'What an incredible coincidence. To be here, today of all days!'

Milton supposed that the schnapps had served both to calm Blake and to make him modestly sociable. He was also grateful to see that his hands were no longer fidgeting and his eyes had stopped swivelling wildly from side to side.

'You know, of course, that this area is pretty much where Switzerland was created,' Blake continued authoritatively, while waving his arm expansively. 'Altdorf, the place where William Tell stood up to the Austrian Gessler, is just a few kilometres away. And the Rütli meadow, the one that chap just told us about, is just across the lake from here. I imagine Guisan chose it deliberately as the best place to rally his troops, because it's where the famous Oath of the Old Swiss Confederacy was taken in the thirteenth century. It's a very important piece of land to this little country.'

Milton freely admitted that the warm, inner glow of the schnapps, combined with the golden rays of sunshine, now breaking through the thickening cloud and reflecting on the still waters of the lake, gave the whole setting a magical, timeless quality. However, he was still smarting from the way he had been kept in the dark by Blake and the earlier argument that this had caused. 'You're quite a mine of information,' he said pointedly to Blake's back, as he gazed across the lake. 'Unfortunately, it seems about every damned thing, but what's important. So, where do we go from here?'

'OK, fair enough,' replied Blake wearily. 'I suppose it's only right that you know what's in store. Let's get back to the inn and I'll fill you in over dinner. Just remember to speak softly in German and about our plans only when we're alone.' The agent was as good as his word, for as soon as the food order had been taken and each man had an ample glass of red wine before him on the plain wooden table, Blake shrugged and said, 'Righto, now I'll outline the plan.'

If Milton had been expecting a fully thought-through strategy, with route, stopping off points, clear destination and arrangements for the onward journey to Britain, he was to be bitterly disappointed. Firstly, Blake's explanation of 'the plan' was extremely sketchy. 'We have a couple of identities each, one Swiss and one French, and we'll get into France between Martigny and Chamonix,' he began promisingly. 'It's relatively quiet, compared to the border near Geneva. So, with a bit of luck and our Swiss passports, there should be no problem. From there, we'll head towards Grenoble and try to get across the Rhône, well south of Lyon. Probably somewhere near Valence. The last part of the drive through southern France should be pretty straightforward; down the coast road though Montpelier, Narbonne and Perpignan and across into Spain. Our diplomatic people should meet us in Figueres and, from there, we're as good as back in London.'

As he listened to what he interpreted as the introductory overview of the route, Milton thoughtfully swirled his Walliser wine around his glass. When it was clear that Blake had concluded his account of the plan, he looked up incredulously and asked, 'Is that it?'

Blake looked him directly in the eye and, with an exasperated shrug, demanded, 'Well, what more do you want? A 'Thomas Cook' style itinerary, with hotel reservations en-route and places of special interest noted for your diversion?'

Milton grimaced at the barb, but quickly retaliated, 'Well, for a start, how long will it take us to reach Spain? What will we do for money? And have you the faintest idea how far the Germans have already reached in this part of France? We might blunder straight into them!' Having posed his questions, a smiling Milton sat back and awaited Blake's response.

'In sequence,' Blake replied dismissively, 'It depends. It's covered. And I haven't got a clue.' He then lit another cigarette and demanded savagely, 'Now, any more damn fool questions?'

As he stared at Blake's smirking face, Milton realised that things couldn't go on like this. 'Look,' he began in an effort to establish some sort of understanding between them. 'It's blatantly obvious that you don't like me at all and you resent having to act as my chaperone. I fully understand that, because, as you know, I feel much the same about you. I don't particularly care for you, or for the fact that you're involved in this operation at all. I'd have been perfectly happy on my own. But, like it or not, we're stuck with one another. We simply have to work together to get the job done. We've already made one monumental cock up in leaving that vital stuff in my cellar.' Recognising Blake's instant bristling and preparedness to retaliate, he hurried on, both hands held up, palms facing outwards. 'OK. I'm not saying that was all your fault. But I'm sure we can agree that it was a crass blunder. The point is, if we carry on like this, bickering and sniping at one another, we're likely to blow the mission altogether. And what bloody use would that be? What would that say about us, as men? That we were more interested in picking fights with each other, than in succeeding with something which is vital to the defeat of the damned Nazis – that's what! And I, for one, don't want something like that on my headstone.' Desperately trying to seem more emollient, Milton conceded, 'And, from what little I know of you, I'm certain that you don't either. So, I suggest that we try to bury our differences for now and do our damnedest to get this stuff home. And,' Milton concluded with a wry grin, 'I promise that as soon as we're safe and are about to depart for London, I'll give you first shot at punching me on the chin. If you still have the inclination, that is. How's that?' Just as he was finishing, the innkeeper arrived with their food, fixing them with a curious glance.

Blake used the time spent eating his meal to reflect on what had just been said. He still deeply resented being lumbered with this mission, but he had to admit that, the more he got to know him, the more he felt that Milton wasn't such a bad type. He knew, of course, that he himself was still potentially the greatest problem. Despite the warmth of the evening, he shivered as he recalled that it was his lack of trust that had caused the cock up with the materiel from Oerlikon. He just hoped that he would be able to keep things together until they reached Spain. Above all, he was terrified of letting anyone down.

Once the dinner plates had been cleared, Blake tried to deal with Milton's initial questions more seriously. 'Look,' he began cautiously, 'not even Hitler knows where his armies have got to. But we're crossing France much further south than Lyon, so there's a good chance we'll avoid them.' Emboldened by Milton's ready acceptance of this argument, Blake made the ultimate concession by proposing, 'You know, we'd be much quicker if you'd share the driving. What do you say?'

Milton was delighted to accept this vote of confidence from Blake and an awkward handshake, outside their respective room doors, sealed what he hoped was the first sign of an emerging peace between them.

Chapter Eleven

Friday July 26th, 1940, Switzerland and France.

In an area which is widely known for its extremely changeable weather, the fine, sunny day was followed by a grey, damp morning in Flüelen. Low clouds hung over the adjacent mountains like an unpleasant, wet blanket. 'It's normal here,' confirmed the innkeeper cheerfully, as he served steaming pots of strong coffee at breakfast. 'But you should be careful. Especially if you are planning to drive over the Furka Pass today. Visibility will not be good and the road is narrow and dangerous at many points.' Given the route they had discussed the previous evening, Milton was surprised when Blake swiftly replied to the obviously inquisitive innkeeper. 'Thanks anyway, but we're not going in that direction. We're heading towards Luzern as we've an important business meeting there.' The innkeeper nodded slowly, but the look in his eyes suggested that he didn't altogether believe what he had just been told. 'It's better not to trust anyone at all,' was Blake's answer to Milton's questioning look, as soon as they were alone.

Before they set off towards Andermatt and the Furka Pass, Blake was pleased to have the opportunity to fill up the Mercedes at a small petrol station on the outskirts of Flüelen. Both men had been excessively polite over breakfast and the silence which fell between them on the journey, while not exactly companionable, was at least better than the previous day's bickering. The early morning mist in Flüelen had developed into a thick fog, as they climbed ever higher into the dense clouds. Blake had to take things slowly and steadily as he skilfully negotiated the many hairpin bends of the Furka Pass. 'It's a pity the weather's so appalling,' he murmured in a tone of authentic regret. 'The views here are magnificent. But at least it'll keep the traffic down to a minimum.'

Eventually, as they descended into the Canton of Wallis and skirted the awe inspiring Aletsch Glacier on their right-hand side, the fog began to thin out. Sharing the driving in the early afternoon sunshine and meeting very little traffic, for a while they followed the River Rhône as it flowed surprisingly swiftly towards Lake Geneva. When they stopped for a bite of late lunch in Brig, Blake confirmed that they were more than half way to their destination at Martigny. 'I did consider trying to get into France in one day,' he confided. 'But, while that might have speeded things up, I didn't really want to be crossing the border late in the evening.'

Genuinely perplexed, Milton asked, 'Why? Do you suspect that checks might be more thorough at that time?'

'Well, there is that. But it's more that I'd rather get well away from the border and into France before we have to stop for the night. Safer to stay an extra night in Switzerland, I think, even though it will take us an extra day to reach Spain. Let's hope it doesn't cost us.'

The driving conditions were perfect and both men had the opportunity to enjoy the magnificent scenery as they progressed towards Martigny. They both remained content to avoid any further disagreement by restricting their exchanges to banal comments on the condition of the roads, the traffic and the views. Having arrived at a small inn just outside Martigny in the late afternoon, the two men decided to take an early dinner and make a prompt start the following day.

Over dinner in the otherwise deserted dining room, Milton asked the question he'd been itching to ask since the two men had met. 'How on earth did you get into secret service work?'

'If I told you, you wouldn't believe me. And you'd probably think me a prize ass. Let's just say that I was made an offer I couldn't refuse.'

'You know, Blake, I don't think that I could regard you as an ass at all. It's one thing to face the enemy square on and shoot at one another, like I did in the navy. It's quite another to venture, often unarmed and alone, into the belly of the beast, as you must have done. That takes real guts.'

'I appreciate the sentiments, Milton. But don't be taken in by all that 'King and Country' claptrap. It's not heroic. It's not noble. It's terrifying and brutal and quickly makes you abandon exactly those values that you're supposed to be fighting for.' Milton judged it better not to pursue the issue further and, over post-dinner coffee and cognac, he listened as Blake briefly outlined his plan to enter France the next morning. Their aim was to cross into France as soon after 9AM as possible and reach their Rhône crossing at Valence before nightfall.

'I imagine,' Milton suggested hopefully as he enjoyed a mild cigarillo, ' that once we get across the river, we should find it pretty much plain sailing down to the Spanish border.'

After savouring a long draw of his cigarette, Blake cautioned, 'Well, we're certainly not out of the woods yet. But I agree. I'd say that, if we're to encounter the Hun anywhere, it's likely to be at the river. So, keep your fingers crossed for us, eh?' With that, he announced that he was going to take a stroll outside to check that the car was secure and that Milton should turn in.

***

The control post between France and Switzerland at Le Châtelard, was little more than a wooden pole across the road, guarded by two small cabins on either side of the border. Blake, who had once again insisted on taking the first turn behind the wheel, cursed under his breath as he saw the Swiss official raise his hand, instructing them to stop. 'I bet until France bloody well fell, there was no bugger here at all,' he muttered. 'Anyway, it's to be expected, I suppose. Look, just let me do the talking again, all right?'

As it turned out, the Swiss border guard was eagerly anticipating the morning coffee break that is almost obligatory in his country at around nine o'clock. He cheerily waved them through, with barely a glance at their false, Swiss passports. On the French side, their experience was helped by Blake's use of an exaggeratedly thick, Swiss-German dialect as he tried to communicate with someone who only spoke French. This ploy ensured that he had to divulge only the vaguest of details of their fictitious, business appointment in Lyon and, with a surly nod, they were permitted to enter France.

'Phew!' exclaimed Milton, as they pulled sharply away from the border, 'well done! Initially, I thought that things might get a bit awkward back there. Still, it seems that he's happy.'

'I wouldn't be so sure,' groaned Blake, as he squinted into his rear-view mirror. 'The nosy shit has already made a note of the car's number plate and now he's darted into his office. Probably getting on the blower to his collaborationist bosses further up the line.'

It was immediately apparent to Milton, that Blake was reacting badly to this development. His hands once again took up their rapid, nervous tattoo on the steering wheel, accompanied by frequent expletives. Moreover, he had roared away from the border as if the hounds of hell were on his tail. 'For goodness' sake, Blake. Calm down,' Milton urged, while looking pointedly at the steep fall to the left-hand side of the road. 'Otherwise we won't have to worry about the Jerries catching us. We'll be at the bottom of one of these ravines.'

Blake seemed to relax a little and he drove in a more measured way until, on a deserted stretch of the road between Chamonix and Passy, he unexpectedly turned onto a curved track which disappeared into a dense wood. 'This'll do,' he said enigmatically and, having jumped out of the car, began rummaging in the spacious boot. Ten minutes later, with authentic, French number plates attached and French passports in pockets, the two were back on the road towards Grenoble. 'That should throw any nosey gendarmes off the scent,' Blake said more optimistically. 'They'll be looking for two Swiss heading towards Lyon. Whereas we are two Frogs, going in a different direction altogether.'

By evening, after a journey blessedly free of sightings of German troops or security personnel, they were approaching their intended crossing point over the Rhône at Valence. 'If we can just get across this damned river,' Blake said quietly, 'we're as good as in Spain. Given that we've seen no Germans so far, it's very unlikely that we'd run into them even further south.'

'Seems like it was a good idea of yours to avoid Geneva and Lyon then.'

'Let's wait and see. The bridge is just the other side of town and we approach it on a wide curve. We'll stop half a mile from it. You stay in the car and have a kip if you like. I'll go and recce up ahead.'

As soon as they had passed through Valence, Blake searched for a place to park the car off the road. Having found a suitable spot, he climbed out of the car and whispered, 'Just wait here. I'm not sure exactly how far away the bridge is, so I may be some time. Sit tight and get some rest.' Without waiting for a reply, he disappeared into the surrounding trees.

Blake cursed the heat as he forced his way through dense woodland at a ninety-degree angle to the road which ran on towards the Rhône bridge. Finally, he reached a vantage point high above the river, from which he could clearly see the elegant span of the bridge across which they hoped to travel. It was a good half mile distant and he decided to risk the climb down through the shrubbery to the water's edge. He reasoned that he could get much closer to his target from there. He paused about a hundred metres away from the bridge and, having satisfied himself that it was deserted, he was just about to return to the car when he thought he heard a low, rumbling noise. *What the hell's that?* he wondered, before deciding that he may have simply confused the river's gurgling with some other sound. *But hang on! Surely there it is again. But now it's a high pitched mechanical whine.* Blake peered anxiously through the settling dusk and saw flashes of light on the far side of the bridge. To his horror, he then observed a platoon of German motorcyclists, with machine gun sidecars, pull onto the bridge. His heart sank as he realised that, should they continue over the bridge towards Valence, they would ride straight past the Mercedes with Milton inside. He was acutely aware that, while he had parked a little way off the road, the vehicle was by no means so well hidden that none of the Germans would spot it. *Jesus Christ,* he mumbled to himself, as a feeling of panic began to grow, *what bloody rotten luck. All this damned way and if we'd been an hour earlier, or even half an hour, we'd have been home free.*

Filled with a wretched mixture of despair and anxiety, he realised with a jolt, just how important the successful completion of this mission had become to him. He still wasn't deliriously happy about the whole thing, but somewhere on the road today, he had decided that he fundamentally agreed with what Milton had said. They were damned well going to succeed, whatever the odds. Only now, it was beginning to look as if they'd already failed. He was still crouching, so frozen with hopelessness that he didn't initially notice the first motor cyclist stop at the near end of the bridge. *What the fuck's going on now?* he wondered, as he saw the others line up their machines to make a mechanised barrier, with a gap just wide enough for vehicles to pass in single file across the bridge. *They're making a road block*, he realised, *and it looks pretty damned permanent.*

Despondent, he recognised that there was nothing to do, but get back to Milton as quickly as possible. He could smell the smoke from his cigarillo long before he reached the parked vehicle. Without speaking, he snatched it from the surprised Englishman's mouth and waved it in his face. 'What the hell do you think you're doing,' gabbled Milton angrily, 'There's no need for that, especially given those foul things you smoke all the bloody time!'

'Maybe you'd like to just go out on the road and introduce yourself to a squad of nice, German motorcyclists? They're busy making themselves at home on the bridge,' answered Blake contemptuously. 'They've got some lovely looking machine guns which I'm sure they'd love to try out.'

'Germans?' asked a horror-struck Milton, forgetting all about his discarded cigarillo. 'But I thought you said they couldn't be as far south as this.'

Blake brushed off the implied criticism and remarked glumly, 'Well, they flaming well are. It's just damned bad luck. Half an hour earlier and we might well have been over the river and away, before they'd even turned up. But now, let's face it. It's over as far as this route's concerned. There's nothing we can do.'

Milton stared at Blake, with a mixture of pity and disappointment. In some vital way, the agent even seemed to shrink before his eyes. 'Come on, man,' he said soothingly, 'it can't be so bad. Let's think about our options.'

'Options!' retorted Blake in a suppressed roar, 'we don't bloody well have any! I lost my options when I was saddled with this idiotic mission.'

In an effort to calm the situation, Milton began slowly and methodically to analyse their situation. 'OK. You say the Jerries have just arrived. Well, we could take a chance on them being not quite set up properly. Our fake French passports are pretty good and the papers are well hidden in a secret compartment in the boot of the Mercedes. So, why not have a go at getting through the checkpoint?'

Of course, Milton was no fool; he realised that this was a very risky suggestion and had not meant it to be taken seriously. He simply wanted to draw Blake back from his despair and get him to think strategically about how they should get out of their current predicament. To his relief, the tactic seemed to work as Blake responded, 'Too dangerous! The Germans may well be bored and, with little other traffic to concern them, they may well take their time over an interrogation and search. And neither of us has perfectly fluent French. It'd be touch and go whether they'd even buy that we're Frogs. So, no. Going on isn't an option. As I said, we don't have any.'

'What about trying further south? We could try our luck at the next bridge,' suggested Milton hopefully.

'That would cost us at least another day and it's hard to think that Jerry wouldn't be even quicker than us in reaching the crossing points,' replied Blake flatly.

'Of course, we do have one clear option, Bill.' The amicable use of his first name caused Blake to look up sharply, a strange, almost grateful look in his eyes. 'We can go back to Zürich and simply find another way out.'

'How?' demanded Blake abruptly. 'The Jerries are after you and I don't see how SIS can help us out. All its men and almost all its places are known to the Huns. So, if we made contact with my outfit, they'd be on our tail as quick as a flash. No,' he concluded miserably, 'this route was the best that I could come up with. And look where it's got us. Bloody nowhere.'

'Ah,' replied Milton quickly, a slow smile coming to his face, 'I've just remembered that I have the promise of help from an officer in the Swiss Military Intelligence. He seemed a very resourceful chap. If you can think of a place where we could lay low while I contact him, I'm sure that, if anyone can sort us a passage out to safety, it'd be him. What d'you say? Shall we give it a go?' In truth, Blake could see no better alternative and grudgingly agreed to this threadbare plan. 'Good show!' responded Milton enthusiastically. 'And, of course, I can ask our Swiss guardian angel to get those sacks of vital equipment that I had to leave behind. There you are, you see,' he concluded with an optimism that he scarcely felt, 'it's working out much better this way.'

Chapter Twelve

Sunday July 28th, 1940, Winterthur, Switzerland.

The return journey to Switzerland, via an overnight stay midway between the Rhône and the border, proved to be surprisingly uneventful. An early morning start on the Sunday, the restored Swiss number plates and passports and the astute use of a different border crossing out of France, ensured that only the most cursory of interest was shown by officials. Moreover, no further evidence of German troop deployments in France was encountered.

As they were driving through Bern, on the last leg of their long journey back to Zürich, Blake suddenly turned to Milton. He gestured with his thumb at the sleepy city and said in a strangled voice, 'Don't be deceived by this place's appearance, my friend. It's full of people who'd buy and sell you for less than the price of those bloody documents you're carrying, let alone the information you've got in your head.'

Milton twisted in his seat to look at Blake, his face working to keep up with his train of thought. 'Oh yes, Milton. I know all about Bern and the way they'll stab you in the back. And not just the Jerries and the Eyeties – there are loads of Swiss on the make and even some of our own chaps. Not to mention all the Central Europeans who've supposedly fled the Nazis. Dansey, the obnoxious little shit in charge of our espionage efforts here 'in der Schweiz', can be seduced by anyone with a story that fits his blimpish worldview. I tell you, I'm ruddy well glad to be out of it.'

Milton had mixed feelings about Blake's sudden outburst. On the one hand, it indicated that he was opening up a little more to the possibility of a friendlier, even trusting relationship between them. On the other, perhaps it demonstrated Blake's paranoia. He decided to respond gently, 'Surely things aren't that bad. Aren't you exaggerating just a little bit.'

Blake immediately swerved the car alarmingly, as he turned round to face his passenger. 'Exaggerating? You really think so? Why d'you think Dansey agreed that I should do this escort duty? Because he thinks I'm his best man and that's what the mission needs?'

'Well, er... I don't really know Dansey at all...' stammered Milton, only to be interrupted by a harsh laugh from the driver.

'I think you deserve to hear the truth, old chap. Dansey gave Pym permission to use me, because he thinks I'm damaged goods.' Squinting sideways to note Milton's confused expression, he went on savagely. 'He believes that my nerve has gone. That I'm all washed up, a liability and that I'll probably make a mess of anything I'm asked to do.'

While Milton had his doubts about Blake, he certainly didn't see him in quite such a negative light and replied dubiously, 'Surely not. Professor Pym spoke very highly of you.'

'Pym had no option but to give me the job,' explained Blake. 'He's hoping against hope that I don't blow up. Whereas that bastard Dansey positively wants me to fail.'

'Now come on, Bill,' interrupted Milton, 'Dansey must be aware of how important this mission is. I'm certain he'd never do anything to endanger it. We're all on the same side, after all.'

'Are you really so naïve, Milton?' asked Blake sarcastically. 'Do you actually believe that we're all jolly good chaps and all playing for the same team? All for one and one for all and all that crap?'

'I don't know what you mean. If you mean that we're all fighting for our country and what we believe in, then, yes, I do believe that,' protested Milton.

'Then let me put you right. Dansey wants the mission to fail because, from the day of your arrival here in Switzerland, he resented it being a Royal Navy operation and Station Z being excluded. When it all goes belly up, he'll be able to say a great big 'I told you so' to the powers that be.'

'And what about Pym?' asked Milton, 'do you think he's just as bad?'

Blake paused before replying and when he did, it was in a much softer tone. 'No. I can't say that. Pym's a good man. If anyone else had asked me to get involved with this, I'd have told him to get stuffed.'

'Well, Bill,' said Milton decisively, 'if what you say is true, then it's pretty damned clear what we must do. Pym clearly thinks you're up to the job. From what I've seen, you've already shown you have considerable skill and judgement. So, we bloody well make sure that we succeed in our mission. Then you can stick two fingers to Dansey when we share our first beer back in London.' Looking squarely at Blake, he held out his hand and added, 'Deal?'

Blake stared at the road ahead, before smiling, turning to face his passenger and offering his hand in a quick shake, 'Deal!'

'Now that's agreed,' said Milton with a laugh, 'for God's sake keep your damned eyes on the road and both hands on the wheel, otherwise we'll be in that ditch and I don't want to get my feet wet!' Blake snorted and began to tap the steering wheel happily, as he whistled his way tunelessly through 'It's A Long Way To Tipperary.'

As they were approaching the small, spa town of Baden, some twenty kilometres from Zürich, Milton scratched his head and asked, 'Do you have any idea where we could go, while I get in touch with this Swiss officer?'

Blake responded decisively, 'Yes, I do. There's a safe flat in Winterthur that's hardly been used for years. In fact, we've lost so many people and the turnover's been so rapid, that I suspect not so many of our current lot even know of its existence. I think our best shot is to squat there for a few days and keep our heads down, while you contact your Swiss chap. You said the Professor rates him, so that'll do for me.'

'OK. You're the boss,' Milton agreed, before asking where the flat was located.

'It's pretty handy, only a few kilometres from Zürich. It'll be a perfect place to lay low for a few days.'

***

The top floor flat in the Haus zum Steineck, an imposing building located at the intersection of the Obergasse and Marktgasse in the centre of Winterthur was small, but perfectly adequate for a short stay. Blake knew exactly where the key was hidden on the landing and they were soon established in the flat. Later in the evening, Milton, covered by Blake, took a stroll down the Marktgasse to the main railway station, from which he dialled Graf's home number. As agreed, he left a message that his suit was ready for a further fitting, but also hinted at their location by adding that it was in the Winterthur branch. 'If he's as good as Pym thinks he is,' Blake had earlier said to Milton when making this suggestion, 'he'll know all about this place and it won't take him long to figure out where we are.'

***

Shortly after 10.30AM on the following morning, a sharp knock at the door roused Blake, who had been slumped in an easy chair reading the previous day's *Landbote* newspaper. He jumped quickly to his feet, his limp now almost gone, and stubbed out his half-smoked cigarette. 'You get in your bedroom and stay there until I give you the all clear,' he whispered. 'I'll see who it is.'

Milton was shocked to see Blake hastily stuffing a pistol into his jacket pocket and hissed urgently, 'Surely there's no need for that.'

'Better safe than sorry,' replied Blake offhandedly. 'Now, do as I say and get in that room.'

As soon as Milton was out of sight, Blake carefully opened the door, his pistol concealed behind his back. He was faced by the tall, lithe figure of Peter Graf, who smiled pleasantly, raised his hat and said, 'Good morning. I have called about a fitting for my suit. I'm so glad that I've caught you in. Allow me to introduce myself.' Graf then slowly and deliberately reached into the inside pocket of his jacket and produced an identity card for Blake's perusal. After carefully studying the card, the Blake's face creased into a smile and he gestured the Swiss into the flat.

'Please come in, Herr Graf. Herr Milton will be very pleased to see you. But, are you alone?'

Graf waited until the door to the flat had been closed, before answering with a shrug, 'Until I am fully aware of your situation, I judged it better to involve only myself. To my knowledge, I am one of only a very few people in my organisation who know of the existence of this flat.'

As soon as Milton had emerged from the bedroom, handshakes had been offered and coffee produced from the kitchen, the three men sat down facing one another around the oblong dining table. 'Now, gentlemen,' Graf began, after having declined one of Blake's cigarettes only to select one of his own and light it with an exquisite silver lighter. 'Perhaps you could tell me what's going on? I had expected you to be almost in Spain by now.'

Blake grimaced as he began his explanation of their journey through France and its eventual abandonment on the banks of the Rhône. 'Ah yes,' the Swiss said sadly, 'it seems that you were very unlucky. A few hours earlier and all would probably have been well.'

'But are you able to offer us any help, Herr Graf?' asked Milton hopefully. 'It's obvious that we can't get out through France now and, of course, the rest of Switzerland is bordered by Axis states. So, we're effectively trapped. And you should also know that Herr Blake is sure that, before we left Zürich, I was being followed by a Nazi agent.'

Graf's eyes narrowed at this intelligence and he turned immediately to face Blake. 'You are certain of this?' he demanded. 'Who was this man? Did you identify him?'

'I'm quite certain that Herr Milton was being followed. The German is called Schulz and he's an army captain, officially attached to the trade legation in Bern. But I strongly suspect that he's part of the Abwehr's Bureau F.'

Graf nodded his head rapidly and immediately cut in, 'I know very little more than you of this Schulz. But I agree with you that we must assume he is an intelligence officer and therefore dangerous. If you observed him, and he did not see you, then I should offer you my compliments, for it's clear that you are excellent at your work, Herr Blake.' Graf paused to light another cigarette, before continuing, 'But this is most unwelcome news, my friends. The involvement of Schulz and the Abwehr complicates matters. Your sudden disappearance from Zürich will probably have confirmed whatever suspicions he had of you, Herr Milton. In these circumstances, you did the right thing in keeping away from your home and not involving SIS. The fewer people who know you are back in Switzerland, the better.'

'I'm sure that the French border guards took down our details as we both entered and left France,' said Blake with a shrug. 'And while we had false passports, it's not impossible that the Germans will have been able to guess at least some of our movements.'

'Of course, they buy from those who are willing to sell,' shrugged Graf with distaste. 'And, regrettably, there are far too many of those. But all is far from lost. The Germans are struggling with a great deal of information from such sources and, in my opinion, it is highly likely that Schulz will not yet have linked you to the aborted escape through France. But, nevertheless, the sooner we get you out of Switzerland, the better.'

'So, you'll help us?' asked Milton quickly. 'Do you have any thoughts on how we might leave?'

'Well, my country isn't quite cut off from the outside world,' replied Graf enigmatically. 'I think I may have the germ of an idea. Now, would you be travelling as you are, with little luggage?'

'Ah well, that's another thing,' answered Blake, shaking his head in some embarrassment. 'I'm afraid that before our departure from Zürich, we didn't communicate with one another quite as well as we might have done. The upshot is, we inadvertently left behind something rather important. It would be better if we could take it with us, when we leave.'

After Milton had explained about the sacks of vital parts which were still located in the cellar of his flat, Graf smiled, 'Do not worry, my friends. The fog of war is dense sometimes. But I'm sure that the safe return of these sacks can be arranged. And I will ask my officers to retrieve your passport at the same time. It may well come in useful, where you are going.'

Graf took the two Swiss passports and it was agreed that he would make the necessary arrangements for the discreet retrieval of the materiel in Milton's cellar. Neither Englishman had any idea what he had in mind for their route out of Switzerland and he would give no further information. 'I must check out one or two things first,' he insisted as he prepared to leave. 'But you did the right thing when you contacted me, Herr Milton. I will notify Professor Pym of these developments and you may both rest assured that I will be in touch within forty-eight hours. In the meantime, gentlemen, please follow this advice to the letter. Herr Blake, you go out only when absolutely necessary and Herr Milton, you remain in the flat. With good luck on your side, you will soon be on your way back to Britain.'

***

The fugitive Englishmen followed Graf's advice and, apart from a couple of cautious trips by Blake to buy some fresh milk and bread from a nearby shop, they spent the next two days impatiently waiting in the Winterthur flat. Having pored frustratedly over various maps as they pondered their possible escape route from Switzerland, they eventually concluded that they had no idea what the Swiss might have in mind.

During a simple supper of bread, cheese, sausage and wine on their third evening in Winterthur, Milton again broached the subject of Blake's experience as an intelligence officer. He had been both intrigued by the brief references Blake had made to it and shocked by the vehemence of his outburst as they had driven past Bern. *It may be a risk, but we're going to have to work together, so I'd like to more about what makes him tick.* 'You know,' Milton began tentatively, 'I've never actually met a spy before and...' Blake immediately looked up from his food and fixed him with a hostile stare. 'No. Hang on a minute,' Milton hastily added, 'just tell me to shut up, if you like. But I've been thinking a lot about the difference between fighting a clandestine war and facing an enemy on the battlefield, or in my own case, on the high seas. We started to talk about this a couple of times, but somehow got side tracked. I'd like to talk about it some more.'

Blake finished chewing his Swiss sausage, refilled his glass of wine and took a mouthful, before replying, 'Look, Milton. I know you're a decent chap and, after a pretty poor start, we're managing to rub along together now. But what you don't seem to understand is that, once someone like me starts to 'discuss' what he's doing, he'd stop immediately and never do it again.'

'Why do you say that? It's not as if what you do is wrong. It's bloody essential, I'd say.'

Blake's initial reluctance to engage with the topic was overcome by his exasperation and he replied with resignation, 'You see, you desk jockeys and regular servicemen just don't get it. You've no idea what it's like. The sheer, undiluted terror. Of course, I accept all combatants face that, but usually it's in short bursts. The rest of the time military service is pretty bloody boring.'

'Yes,' Milton agreed , 'I can certainly see your point.'

'Can you? Can you really?' asked Blake not unkindly. 'Just imagine the constant feeling of threat and the absolute need to be on permanent guard. Think what it must be like always to be afraid of betrayal and, every second of every day, to remind yourself that you must, of necessity, trust absolutely no one. Of course, you may cooperate with some people. But trust? No. You must always be ready for the stab in the back. Even, or maybe especially, from those who you think are your comrades. And what if you do every bloody thing by the book? You make not one sodding mistake and all your comrades are honourable? I'll tell you, Milton. Even then, you live in the certain knowledge that, eventually, a damned bit of plain bad luck will end up with you being tortured and facing a firing squad. Try to comprehend the anxiety caused by every unexpected occurrence, whether it's a knock on the door, or simply someone asking you a question on the street. People who've never done it simply cannot envisage what it's like for field agents. Especially somewhere like Nazi Germany.'

   Milton could find no words that would not sound trite or, even worse, patronising. So he simply nodded in sympathy and poured him a healthy three fingers of the Grappa which he'd found in one of the kitchen cupboards. Blake smiled and savoured the liquid as it warmed his throat, before he continued. 'You just can't relax. When you're on a mission, there's no such thing as 'off duty' time. And it just plain grinds you down. Lord above, how it bloody grinds you down.' As he put the empty glass down on the table, Blake looked Milton directly in the eye and, without a shred of embarrassment, admitted with a shrug, 'At least, it definitely ground me down.'

Chapter Thirteen

Wednesday July 31st, 1940, Winterthur, Switzerland.

Graf was as good as his word. His characteristically brisk knocking on the flat door announced his return, shortly before 8AM on their fourth day back in Switzerland. 'There's a chance that you can leave, very early tomorrow morning,' he said as soon as they had shaken hands. 'If everything works out, you'll travel on what will probably be one of the last transport flights between the tiny Swiss airfield at Locarno and Belgrade in unoccupied Yugoslavia. These are special charter flights of Swissair, carrying a very valuable cargo of gold. Their flag of neutrality has so far been respected by all combatants. I think it will be the best way to get you both out of Switzerland. After that, however, you'll be on your own.'

Both Englishmen reacted with a mixture of astonishment and scepticism about the sense of flying even further away from London. However, as soon as Graf had unfolded a large map of the Balkans on the dining table, Blake began to see the possibilities. 'If we could just reach the Mediterranean coast,' he gabbled excitedly while pointing out a possible route with his smoking cigarette, 'somewhere in Greece, for example. There'd then be a good chance that we might get passage from a neutral port to one of our naval bases and get home from there.'

'Hmm. Maybe,' added Milton dubiously. 'But surely Gibraltar would be out of the question. So, it would mean either Malta or even Alexandria. Frankly, I'm not sure how realistic our chances of reaching one of those would be.'

'I'm no expert, of course,' added Graf, 'but I think the idea of Greece may be a good one. After all, the Greeks are by no means pro-German and they are a historic seagoing folk. I imagine you could pick up a passage on a freighter there.'

Blake and Milton looked at one another and simultaneously nodded, before the latter spoke for them both, 'Thanks very much for organising this for us, Herr Graf. We're both convinced it's the best chance we have of getting back to Britain. In fact, it looks like it's our only chance.'

After a round of celebratory handshakes, Blake asked pointedly, 'Are there likely to be many other passengers on board the flight? Because, of course, if there are Germans on board, that could be rather difficult.'

Graf drew deeply on his cigarette and sighed before wearily answering, 'Well, my friends, I cannot promise that there will be no other passengers. Indeed, the most recent flights have been full. However, my contacts at Swissair tell me that, to date, the Germans have shown little obvious interest in them.'

'And what about the sacks of materiel for the RAF?' asked Milton hopefully. 'I don't suppose you'll be able to retrieve them?'

'Everything has been arranged,' Graf answered urgently as he reached into his jacket pocket. 'And that reminds me. I have your passport here, Herr Milton. Now, gentlemen, I'll pick you up at midnight tonight and we'll drive to Ticino in good time for you to board the flight in the morning. The materiel you mentioned will travel with us. You and it are already booked on the flight, using your false Swiss passports which I also have here.' Having paused only to light a fresh cigarette, he concluded, 'We don't want to risk placing you in an hotel down there for even one night. It's very close to the Italian border and there is a significant risk of foreign agents. Also, tomorrow is the first of August, our Swiss National Day. There could well be a lot people travelling to the southern part of Switzerland in order to celebrate. So, I hope you understand, when I say that I will be relieved to see you on your flight and away. In the meantime, I advise you to get what sleep you can before I return.'

As soon as Graf had left, Milton poured two glasses of grappa, offered one to Blake and said with a broad smile, 'Well, I think you're pretty much off the hook now. This latest turn of events means that the reason for Pym's involvement of you – your knowledge of Western Europe and experience behind enemy lines - no longer applies. So, you could, in all honour...'

Sensing what the other man was about to say, Blake cut in sharply, 'Forget it, Milton. You don't get rid of me that easily. We've already decided that we're in this together and together we'll get the documents, you and those blasted sacks back to London, if it's the last thing we do. Agreed?'

'Agreed! Now let's hope this fire water sends us back to sleep. We could do with as much rest as possible before our lift is back for us.'

***

Thursday August 1st, 1940, Magadino, near Locarno, Switzerland.

The morning sun had yet to rise and bathe the beautiful, hilltop sanctuary of the Madonna de Sasso in its warm, golden light. Indeed, as Graf steered the large car expertly past Maggiore, the lake's silver and blue water glittered magically in the bright moonlight. The intelligence officer had been as punctual as the proverbial Swiss watch and the drive through the still night had been problem free. Indeed, Graf's confident control of the powerful saloon had got them to Locarno a comfortable hour before their scheduled 6AM departure. When they arrived at the small airport, Graf asked them to remain in the car while he made the final arrangements for their departure. He also took responsibility for checking in the sacks of materiel from Oerlikon, which he wheeled before him on an airport luggage trolley.

'Do you think we've managed to give the Germans the slip?' Milton asked, as he squinted at Blake's lined face.

'Your guess is as good as mine,' the agent replied with a shrug. 'Though I do think your Swiss chap is pulling out all the stops to give us the best chance possible of doing just that.'

'Have you thought any more about where we'll go after Belgrade?

'Not really,' acknowledged Blake. 'Look, let's get ourselves to Belgrade and maybe contact the British legation there. I know it's not what was originally planned, but they must have ways of getting chaps in and out. And at least the Jerries will never expect us to be heading to Yugoslavia.'

Milton smiled at the other man's encouraging wink and said, almost to himself, 'Yes, I suppose you're right. Let's look on the bright side.'

Blake was just about to light another cigarette, when Graf climbed into the car, 'Well, gentlemen, everything's arranged. Your sacks are being loaded as private cargo and you are safely checked in. We've been lucky, because there is a rumour that this is going to be one of the very last of these flights and demand for tickets was extremely high.'

'That's great,' said Blake 'Thanks a lot. Is it time to go?'

'Not quite yet, 'replied Graf, looking at his watch. 'The flight leaves in three quarters of an hour, so I think we should wait here for a few minutes.' Graf tried to ease the palpable tension in the car by explaining to the Englishmen that the airfield had opened barely a year before. 'It was for civilian traffic then, of course,' he said with a wistful smile. 'But last winter, the Swiss Air Force established a base here. It's very near the Italian border, so my guess is that it will be even more vital in the difficult months to come.'

At Graf's signal, the three men left the car and, to the surprise of the Englishmen, went around the side of the terminal building, rather than through the main entrance. 'It's better that we get you on board without mixing with your fellow passengers,' Graf explained. 'I'd prefer to keep you under wraps for as long as possible.' Blake and Milton followed him through a heavy gate and round the side of the airport building. Having reached the corner, Graf indicated that they should wait and, as they peered around the edge of the building's wall, Milton immediately understood his reason. A rather squat, stubby looking aircraft, silver coloured, but with the top half of its tail fin painted in the red and white Swiss flag, was standing patiently on the tarmac. The pre-dawn scene was illuminated by portable arc lights and a line of male passengers queued for their turn slowly to climb the steps into the plane's cabin.

'It's an almost new Douglas DC-3,' Graf said proudly as he carefully watched their sacks and other cargo being pulled towards the airplane on a rather simple looking wood and iron cart. 'I'm actually rather envious. They say the cabin is very comfortable. And just look at the size of those windows!' he added as he gazed at the seven rectangular windows which ran the length of the fuselage.

At last the column of men had disappeared into the body of the plane, leaving only a handful of ground crew on the tarmac. Graf immediately indicated urgently, 'Right, gentlemen, it's time for you to go. Your seats are at the front of the plane on the left side. Good luck!' With that, he led them out from their hiding place, onto the tarmac and towards the steps leading to the plane.

Just as Blake had climbed onto the first step, a wheezing man came rushing towards the plane. 'Thank God I'm in time!' he coughed as he stopped to catch his breath. 'Would've been the devil to pay if I'd missed it.'

As he recovered from his exertions, he looked straight at Milton, 'Why, it's Stephen isn't it? Stephen Milton. Didn't recognise you at first in this light. We met several times at Oerlikon. I'm Walford, Jimmy Walford. What a blessed coincidence!'

Panic crossed Milton's face as, frozen in his uncertainty, he didn't know whether to accept the outstretched hand of the other man who was fixing him with a curious look. 'I'm sorry, mein Herr,' said Blake in perfect Swiss-German as he turned to face the newcomer with some irritation. 'We are two Swiss businessmen. We do not know this person of whom you speak. You must be mistaken.' He then repeated the words 'Swiss businessmen' and 'mistaken' in broken English.

'Of course, I'm bloody well not mistaken!' shouted Walford, clearly outraged by Milton's refusal to acknowledge him. 'I tell you, this man is an Englishman, Stephen Milton and we have met several times.'

Realising that the situation could rapidly get out of control, Graf intervened quietly. 'Herr Walford? My name is Peter Graf from Swiss Military Intelligence. I'm afraid that I have some questions for you. Would you follow me, please?'

Walford quickly forgot about Milton's imagined slight as he studied Graf's identity card. 'But I must get on this plane.'

'The plane will wait for you, sir. This will not take long,' Graf lied smoothly as he guided the confused Englishman back towards the terminal building. Simultaneously, he gave a discreet nod to the head of the ground staff. No sooner had Milton and Blake fastened their seat belts, than the twin engines of the DC-3 roared into life and the plane began to taxi towards the start of the runway. Minutes later, the elegant, curved 'S' of the Swissair logo which was painted under the cockpit windows, adopted a steeper slope as the plane made its unfeasible leap into the gradually lightening sky.

Chapter Fourteen

Thursday August 1st, 1940, Belgrade, Yugoslavia.

The flight from Locarno more than lived up to its billing. The relatively new cabin was spotless and light, by virtue of the unusually large windows which had so delighted Graf; the leather seats were supportive, yet comfortable and the in-cabin service exemplary. On landing, the Englishmen were both a little surprised to enter what was obviously a recently constructed, airy and bright terminal building at Belgrade Airport. Milton was just taking delivery from customs of their postal sacks which Graf had affixed with official Swiss-post documentation, when Blake bustled towards him, cursing under his breath. 'God, these lot are total bandits! We'll soon run out of Pym's Swiss Francs at this rate. No more first-class travel for us! Anyway, I've got some local currency, so let's get into the city straight away.'

The airport lay around twenty kilometres from the city centre and, having hailed a taxi, Blake instructed the aged, cigar smoking driver to take them to the Hotel Astoria. Graf had recommended this, as, 'There are surprisingly few hotels in Belgrade. But the Astoria is relatively new and was recommended by my opposite number in the city. Of course, there are staff in every hotel who are open to bribery, but he says the owner is basically honest and tries to ensure his staff are. He believes that both yourselves and your materiel will be as safe there, as anywhere else in the city. Even for a few days, if necessary. It's also very close to the main railway station.'

It took rather longer than they expected to reach the hotel, but both men enjoyed the last ten minutes of the drive through the grand centre of the city. *I'd no idea that Belgrade was such a beautiful place,'* Milton thought with the enthusiasm of a genuine tourist. The driver recognised his enthralled expression in the rear view mirror and, frequently leaving the steering wheel to its own devices, began enthusiastically pointing out various landmarks and special buildings. As they pulled up outside the Astoria, Milton's face fell as he stared at the functional, concrete, five storey block. *My God,* he groaned inwardly as he helped unload all the luggage and sacks. *All those beautiful buildings and we end up in this monstrosity. It looks more like a commercial or industrial building than an hotel.*

Despite its bleak outward appearance, the hotel, which was built only three years previously, was very well appointed and was indeed very close to the main railway station. The sacks did occasion some quizzical stares as they were hauled through the hotel lobby, but the Englishmen, registering under their false Swiss identities, explained them away as 'important sample items for our business meetings.'

As soon as he had closed the door on their fourth-floor room, Blake turned and said, 'Right, I'll get myself off to the railway station for the gen on our possible routes out of here.'

A visibly surprised Milton looked up, confusion written all over his face. 'But I thought the plan was to go to the British Embassy and get them to help us.'

'I've been thinking about that,' Blake explained, 'and, to be honest, I'm not sure it's a particularly good idea. I've known enough chaps who had experience of these embassies in the Balkans and, to a man, they advised keeping the hell away from them. Leaky as old sieves, was the general consensus. No, we've got enough money and our Swiss identities. I'd say that we're safer staying under our own steam, at least for now.'

Milton shook his head in disagreement, 'Look, Blake, you've said you're in unknown territory here. As am I. I think we may need help from people who know what's what, otherwise we could end up making a fatal mistake.'

Blake readily acknowledged the point and suggested, by way of compromise, 'Look, how's this? I go to the station, get the info and then we have a pow-wow here and decide what to do for the best. If you're still dead against going it alone, I'll go to the embassy.'

Without delay, Blake left the Astoria and took a very circuitous route to cover the short distance to the main railway station. There, he bought a railway map of Yugoslavia and a timetable book. He had seen no indication that he was followed, but stopped to take a coffee in the buffet, before returning to the hotel by a similarly complex route.

'Have you had any thoughts on how we should try to get back to London?' Blake asked, while they both studied the railway route map alongside the smaller scale map of central and eastern Europe, given to them by Graf.

'As a matter of fact, I have,' replied Milton confidently. 'It seems to me that our best, perhaps even our only option, is to make for the Mediterranean, as we discussed with Graf. Greece would seem to be the logical choice. Once there, I'm sure we could get help. Here in Belgrade, we're still a bit too close to Germany for my liking.'

Blake smiled broadly, 'Excellent! Couldn't agree more. So, all we have to decide is the small matter how to get there.' With a rueful smile, he took the railway map and laid it carefully over the map of eastern Europe and both men squinted down at the spider's web of connections. Within five minutes, it was agreed that they should head to Nis, from where they could travel due south to Salonika. Once in Greece, it should be quite straightforward to get to Athens and to find help. Blake immediately returned to the station, where he reserved two tickets on the first available train. Some forty-five minutes later, he had returned with the news that they were unable to travel immediately and would leave Belgrade at just before 1PM the following day. 'With luck, we should arrive in Athens some time over the weekend and who knows?' Blake mused hopefully, 'we may actually be back home by the middle of the month.'

Buoyed by this thought, both men settled down to await their departure from Yugoslavia.

Chapter Fifteen

Friday August 2nd, 1940, Bureau F, German Legation, Bern, Switzerland.

Ulrich Schulz sat impatiently drumming his fingers on the folder lying on the desk in front of him. He had experienced a rising sense of frustration since losing Milton at the railway station in Zürich just over a week before. As each day passed, he recognised that it would be increasingly difficult to pick up his trail. Von Ilsemann had been extremely sympathetic, blaming understaffing more than any incompetence on Schulz's part, which only served to increase his determination to put things right. He had issued a description of Milton to Abwehr stations in Geneva, Lausanne, Lugano and Zürich, with the request that any possible sightings, however speculative, should be immediately reported to him. Having spent many hours reviewing what had happened, Schulz had been driven to the conclusion that Milton must have had a confederate in effecting his escape. A pick-up car was his favourite theory and he had, therefore, issued specific instructions for French border posts to exercise particular caution towards cars occupied by two men entering France from Switzerland. It was undoubtedly a very long shot, but probably his best chance of getting back on the scent of the Englishmen.

Finally, on Tuesday July 30th, he had received a report that two men had crossed the border into France at Le Châtelard, near Martigny on the previous Saturday. Even though these men were travelling with Swiss passports, the admittedly sketchy description of the passenger in the car bore some similarity to Milton. The driver, however, could well have been Swiss, as he spoke fluent Swiss German. Schulz was also told that this man smoked Murad cigarettes, the brand, coincidentally, being the favourite of the French border guard. There, however, the trail had gone cold. Schulz was aware that the German army had established check points on all the Rhône bridges that Milton could possibly use on his route to neutral Spain. Nevertheless, the two men in the report had not been seen again.

Perhaps the report didn't refer to Milton at all, but rather to two innocent Swiss businessmen. Quite possibly, he is still trapped in Switzerland. But in that case, he pondered irritably, *where on earth is he?* Schulz had kept under observation Milton's flat, the factory at Oerlikon and all known SIS houses in and around Zürich. But this had yielded nothing. Could he have found his way out of Switzerland by another route? Could he still be lying low somewhere? The whole situation was most unsatisfactory, especially if Milton was on the verge of getting the plans and franchise details back to Britain.

Schulz hated his enforced passivity and was lost in this uncharacteristically morose mood, when the latest intelligence reports from the various Abwehr stations in Switzerland were delivered to his office. With very low expectations, he began to glance through the twenty or so written reports. At last, his eyes alighted on a single sheet of paper, submitted by the Lugano station. This concerned a meeting between one of the resident Abwehr personnel and a regular Swiss informant, a flight mechanic based at the airport in nearby Locarno. *This might just be what I've been waiting for*, he hoped as he greedily read the report of an incident on the runway. *Best of all,* he realised excitedly, *this all took place on the first of August - yesterday!* As soon as he saw the name 'Meelton', he snatched the phone out of its cradle and cursed as the dial seemed to take forever to register the number of the Lugano station. 'Set up a meeting this afternoon with your informant,' he commanded. 'Tell him there's plenty of cash in it for him, if what he says rings true.' Certain that this was the breakthrough, for which he had been waiting so impatiently, Schulz leapt from his desk, briefly notified von Ilsemann's orderly of his plans and set off for the garage to commandeer a driver to take him to Locarno.

***

Hotel Astoria, Belgrade, Yugoslavia.

The tension was undoubtedly beginning to rise, as the steamy morning wore on and the two Englishmen became increasingly uneasy about the delay to their travel plans. To make matters worse, shortly after Blake's return from a brief foray to buy additional items for their now extended journey, their twin-bedded room had become an impenetrable fog of dense smoke. As Blake stubbed out yet another cigarette in the already overflowing ashtray, Milton scowled and resumed his previously failed attempts to open the heavy window which overlooked the avenue leading towards the train station. 'For pity's sake, Blake,' he pleaded, 'can you try to lay off the smokes for a little while? I like a cigarillo myself, but I'm not sure I can take much more of this.'

An unexpectedly loud knocking on the door brought both men to their feet. 'Room service has already been,' whispered Milton, hastily putting his briefcase containing the vital documents in the wardrobe as Blake reached into his pocket and produced his pistol.

'You stand behind the door, while I see who it is,' Blake ordered, as he unlocked and opened the door. The man standing before him was dressed in a smart suit and raised his hat, as if greeting a friend on the street. He then addressed Blake, in English, by his Swiss alias and asked if he could, perhaps, have a word. Blake estimated him to be in his mid-twenties and a fit, strong looking man. He was, therefore, reluctant to admit him, without first knowing his identity and his business.

'I'm sorry,' Blake replied in Swiss-German. 'But, as you seem to know, I am Swiss and do not speak English well. I cannot imagine what we have to talk about.'

The young man seemed not in the slightest perturbed by this rejection and simply smiled contentedly. He then checked that the corridor was empty and said softly, 'Bravo! That's exactly what Professor Pym said you'd say. So, now I have to mention the name Peter Graf to you. Pym was sure that would establish my bona fides.'

'Good God!' hissed Blake, frantically ensuring that they were still unobserved, 'do you want to blow the whole thing? You'd better come in and with your hands in the air where I can see them, if you please.'

Leaving Milton to close the door, Blake ordered the man to sit on the edge of one of the beds, but to keep his arms raised. 'Now,' he demanded, 'tell us who you are, why you are here and why I shouldn't just blow your head off and dump you in the Danube.'

'Look, old chap,' the visitor began calmly, 'do you mind, if I just put my hands on my head. Bit like at school, eh? More comfortable than holding them straight up.' Seeing Blake's brief nod, he continued, 'Thanks. Now, I'm Sandy Glen, Assistant Naval Attaché at the British Legation, here in Belgrade. First thing this morning, I received a private coded message from Professor Pym in London about your, how shall I put it? About your diversion to Belgrade. He gave me your assumed identities, your hotel and told me to offer you every assistance. Thank God, you're still here. The Professor's biggest worry was that you'd have already left Belgrade by the time I got here.'

'But how did Pym know that we're here in the first place?' asked Milton sharply, 'No one else knew about our flight here.'

'Except...' added Blake.

'Except this chap Graf,' interrupted Glen happily, 'which is why Pym told me to mention his name. Presumably Graf must have told him where you would be staying, because Pym was certain that I'd find you here. And,' he added with a beaming smile, 'so I jolly well have.'

A quick exchange of nods confirmed that Blake and Milton both accepted this as a reasonable explanation and

Glen continued breezily. 'I've also been told that, whatever it is you're doing, it's not an SIS operation, but more of a navy one. Which is why I'm here. You chaps can rest assured, no one else in Belgrade knows anything about this meeting. Or about you. And that includes the security services.'

'OK,' said Blake, 'let's say we believe you. What makes you think that we need your help?'

'Well, I do know the lie of the land here,' Glen replied confidently. 'If not perfectly, then certainly better than you two fellows. Look, do you mind if I…?'

'Yes, you can put your hands down now,' anticipated Blake. 'So, what do you want to know?'

Glen asked the obvious question about their onward travel plans and Milton explained that they had already booked train tickets to Athens, where they would seek help.

'Well, that's certainly a possibility,' responded Glen circumspectly. 'It certainly puts more miles between you and Jerry and you may well find help there. Nevertheless, I'd advise against it.' Noticing that a distrustful expression had returned to the faces of the other men, he hastily added, 'Look. I shouldn't really be telling you this, but our intelligence boys are sure that something's brewing in the border regions between Albania and Greece.'

'But Albania's been occupied by Italy,' Blake protested. 'Are you saying that Mussolini is planning an invasion of Greece?'

'We don't know for sure,' admitted Glen, 'but the last thing you want to do is get caught up in something like that.' Glen went on to explain that they could go to Nis as planned. But from there, rather than heading south towards Salonika and Greece, they could take a more easterly route, first to Sofia and then to Istanbul. 'Turkey, of course, enjoys neutrality, so there's no risk of jackboots getting control there,' he pointed out. 'And the Simplon Orient Express is still running. It would get you to Istanbul in twenty-four hours.'

'You can't be serious,' interrupted Milton dubiously. 'Surely since the fall of France that train has ceased to operate.'

'Actually, no,' replied Glen, shaking his head with an amazed smile and almost boyish enthusiasm. 'The section from Lausanne to Istanbul is still running. It goes through Italy, of course, which is why that stretch would've been too great a risk for you. But from Belgrade on, it should be fine.'

The Assistant Naval Attaché went on to explain that the train would leave Belgrade at 7.45AM and that he had taken the liberty of reserving two berths for the next day. 'You simply have to go to the station this afternoon, give them your names and show the passports you'll be travelling under. It's all paid. In fact,' he added while rummaging in his jacket pocket, 'here's the receipt. You'll need it at the station. Assuming you are in agreement and all goes to schedule, you'll be in Istanbul on Monday morning.'

'And what the hell do we do then?' asked Blake sharply. 'We've not much cash left and where are we supposed to go from Istanbul?'

'I've been told to make reservations for you at the Tokatliyan Hotel, on the Rue de Pera. Once there, you'll be contacted by Nesrin, one of our agents, using the code words 'mighty anvil.''

'What kind of name is that?' asked Blake pointedly. 'Would that be a man or a woman?'

'Unsurprisingly, it's Turkish,' replied Glen with a wink, 'and I can add this. By coincidence, a Turkish neighbour of mine here in Belgrade has this name and she's a woman. A damned attractive woman, at that.'

'A woman?' spluttered Blake, 'why on earth does our contact have to be a woman?'

'Couldn't say,' answered Glen with a lascivious smile. 'But I'd make the most of it, if she's anything like my neighbour.'

Ignoring Glen's crass remark, Milton turned to Blake, 'For goodness' sake, we are in the twentieth century. Women are every bit as able as men.'

'Maybe,' grumbled Blake, 'but I don't like it. That's all I'm saying.'

'Right, now that's settled,' said Glen, 'I'd better be on my way.' As he reached the door, he turned and suggested with some hesitation, 'hang on, I've just had an idea. You said you already have tickets for the train to Athens?'

'Yes, why?'

'May I know the names you used to make the reservations?' asked Glen thoughtfully.

'What the hell's that got to do with anything?' snapped Blake, before rubbing his chin, smiling and saying in a completely different tone, 'you navy types aren't all stupid, are you?'

'Would one of you mind telling me what's going on?' demanded a frustrated Milton. 'After all, I am involved as well.'

Glen grinned before explaining, 'Well, it occurs to me that you could use those reservations as a decoy. If, by some chance, Jerry tracks you to Belgrade, he'll be following the trail of your false Swiss identities.'

'So', interrupted Milton, 'we use our real British identities to travel to Istanbul and leave the false ones to lead any snoopers up the garden path? Very clever. Pleased I got there in the end.'

'And maybe it's better in Turkey not to be found travelling on false papers,' added Glen. 'I understand the Turks can come down pretty hard on that kind of thing.'

Taking his leave, he said, 'I'll make sure word gets to Istanbul that you're travelling under your real names. But now, I think that's all I can do for you gentlemen, other than of course, to wish you luck and God speed back to Britain.' With that, he reached into his inside pocket and produced a thick wad of Swiss banknotes. 'Pym did wonders organising this stash for you. Heaven knows how he did it, but don't spend it all at once.'

As soon as Glen had left, Milton puffed out his cheeks theatrically and said with feeling, 'Well, my friend, it really looks as if Peter Graf did us a huge favour in letting Pym know about our change of plans.'

Blake looked rather less certain, taking out and lighting a cigarette, before asking, 'Are you so sure? It all seems a bit convenient to me. This chap just turning up like that. But I have to admit that I can't think of any way that he could've known so much about our mission unless he was telling the truth.'

'I think so too,' replied Milton as he looked out of the window and down towards the hotel entrance. 'And there he goes now. He's completely alone and heading off down the street. You know, if he were shady, surely he would've tried to get us to walk into some kind of trap here? And I can't see the Orient Express being such an easy location for any sort of ambush. No, I have to say that on balance he really did seem on the level. And his arguments about going to Istanbul make sense, because we'll be moving well away from areas at risk of German invasion.'

'I suppose so,' responded Blake, before adding with a grin, 'and the money will come in very useful. So, I suggest that we keep our guard up, but that we follow his advice for now. I'll confirm our tickets at the station, then we'll set off for Istanbul tomorrow morning and await this Nesrin woman once we get there. I'm still not so happy about that, but we'll see. In the meantime, however, let's get as many of our grubby clothes as possible through the hotel laundry before we set off.'

***

Abwehr Station, Lugano, Switzerland.

From his car window, Ulrich Schulz surveyed the passing Swiss countryside, luxuriating peacefully in the warm sunshine. Wholly concentrated and reinvigorated, he knew instinctively that this was his most promising lead since losing Milton in Zürich. Always a man of action, he now felt the thrill of the chase and could sense that, at last, he had a realistic opportunity to get back in control of the situation. Relaxing into the journey, he pondered what Milton might have been doing at Locarno Airport. *Flying north, east or westwards would be wholly illogical,* he reasoned calmly. *So, it has to be south. But where on earth was he aiming for?* Unable to come up with a plausible solution to this conundrum, he postponed any further consideration until after his interview with the airport worker.

The car dropped Schulz at the corner of via Bertaccio and he began the short walk up the steps of the narrow street. The sun was very warm and he was grateful for the shade, as he walked briskly towards the town house which was home to the Lugano station of German Military Intelligence. He could sense something of the Mediterranean in the air, caused perhaps by the proximity to Italy. As he walked, he permitted himself a brief recollection of the week long honeymoon he had enjoyed, four years before, in Vernazza in the Cinque Terre. *We seemed so young then and so much in love*, he remembered fondly. *And so very happy to escape the hysteria surrounding Hitler's Olympic Games.*

Having found the house, Schulz rang the bell and waited, impatient to hear at first hand the mechanic's story. Within two minutes, he was addressing two men, seated around an oblong table in the meeting room. 'Good afternoon, gentlemen,' he began, with a smile of reassurance for the older, nervous looking airport worker. 'Now, I take it that you understand German?' Acknowledging the jerky nod of the head, he continued, 'Please, be so good as to tell me everything that happened. Leave nothing out. But be sure, if you exaggerate anything, I will find out and it will be the worse for you.'

The Swiss aircraft mechanic hastily told his story. How the two Swiss businessmen, accompanied by a third man who was obviously an official of some kind, had appeared very late at the boarding stairs for the flight from Locarno to Belgrade. 'That was the first thing that was odd,' he said, while fidgeting with his cigarette. 'You see, normally, passengers pass through the airport building and through a designated gate. These people just appeared from the side of the building and didn't go through the proper formalities at all.'

'Belgrade,' Schulz muttered to himself, 'very interesting. Please continue, mein Herr.'

The informer then described how a final latecomer, an Englishman, arrived. 'I'm not fluent in English, but I understand enough to know that this new man immediately recognised one of the Swiss as another Englishman. He called him 'Meelton,' or something like that.

'You're absolutely sure of this?' Schulz interrupted eagerly. 'This is most important. Think very carefully before you answer. You are certain that was the name he used?'

The man looked nervously at the Abwehr's Lugano agent, nodded his head several times and turned to Schulz. 'That's certainly what it sounded like, sir,' he wailed. 'You are not displeased with me? I am only telling the God's honest truth.'

A frown briefly crossed Schulz's face, before being replaced by another encouraging smile, 'Not at all, mein Herr. Not at all. Now, please continue.'

Reassured, the man explained, 'It was most strange. The one who was called 'Meelton' looked very shocked and frightened, but the other businessman quickly turned to this latecomer and said, just like a Swiss would, that he was mistaken.'

'You mean that he spoke Swiss German?' asked Schulz sharply.

'Very fluently,' the man replied. 'But not quite like a native. We all have our accents, you see, sir. The Bernese is very difficult, but nothing like the Walliser….'

'Yes, yes,' interrupted Schulz irritably, 'and this 'Meelton'? He said nothing? You are quite sure? He never opened his mouth?'

'No, sir. Not even when the Englishman persisted. He said nothing and the other one just said he was mistaken or crazy.'

'Is that all?' asked Schulz quickly, to which the informant replied tentatively, 'There was something else. I could've sworn that the Englishman said something about Oerlikon. That's a town near Zürich, isn't it, sir? Could that be right? It didn't make much sense to me, but I would swear that's what he said. I wasn't going to mention it, because it sounds so stupid. But you said that I should leave nothing out.'

Ignoring the questions, Schulz asked brusquely, 'and after all this, did everyone get on the plane?'

'That's another funny thing, sir,' said the informer, scratching his head as if some plausible explanation might fall out of his greasy hair. 'That's when the official looking man showed the Englishman some sort of identity document and took him back into the terminal building.'

'I see,' said Schulz as he rubbed his chin pensively. 'And this official looking man had not said anything before?'

'No sir, he hadn't,' answered the Swiss quickly. 'But before he led the man away, he gave us the nod to start the take off. Have you any idea what was going on, sir? It was all very unusual.'

'That need not concern you in the slightest,' said Schulz, a more menacing tone in his voice. 'In fact, when we have finished our conversation, you would do very well to forget the whole incident. Do you understand?'

'Oh, yes, sir. Of course, sir,' bleated the airport worker miserably, no doubt worrying that he had got himself involved with something that it might have been better to avoid altogether. *This German seems very pleasant*, he fretted, *but I bet he can be a nasty type, for all his politeness and fancy suit.*

'That is good,' declared Schulz, a supportive smile back on his face. 'Now, did the two men get on the plane and what happened to the Englishman?'

'Yes, they did,' stammered the informer, as if he wanted to end the conversation quickly. Heeding the warning not to embellish his story, he concluded, 'I'm afraid I don't know for certain what happened to the Englishman after the official took him back into the terminal building. But I did hear later that he was ranting and raving because he missed the plane. Did I do well, sir? Is the information worth anything?'

An enigmatic expression crossed Schulz's face as he tried to digest what he had been told. Finally, he pulled out a wad of Swiss banknotes, 'You did well. You may go now. Take your wife out for a slap-up meal and forget all about this business. Understand?'

The Swiss nodded his head quickly and with a muttered, 'Thank you, sir,' was hastily escorted from the building by the Abwehr agent.

'This man, is he reliable?' Schulz asked the other German, when he had returned from showing the informer out.

'Yes, I believe so, Captain Schulz,' replied the man deferentially. 'He doesn't give us much, but so far everything has been true and valuable.'

Schulz nodded his head in satisfaction and asked, 'tell me, what do you make of it?'

Pleased that his senior officer had asked his opinion, the agent replied carefully, 'With respect, sir, I'd say that this was definitely Milton, accompanied by another man. Despite speaking Swiss German, I'd guess that he's SIS. The mentioning of the name 'Meelton' and of Oerlikon is just too much of a coincidence.' Encouraged by Schulz's nod, he continued, 'My opinion is that the third man could easily have been a Swiss intelligence officer. I'd say that his job was to help them get out of the country.'

'Yes, on balance I agree with you,' responded Schulz.

'These Swiss officials definitely favour the Allies. But why on earth fly to Belgrade?'

The other agent replied with a confused shake of the head, 'I'm afraid that I've no idea, sir. After all, they would be going further from Britain. It makes no sense.'

'Indeed?' commented Schulz, a slight disappointment in his voice. 'They would, of course, also be moving further away from our sphere of influence. And from Belgrade, I imagine they could strike out for the Mediterranean; for Greece, for Turkey or even further afield. Don't forget, the nearer they get to the Middle East, the stronger would be the British and French influence, though the latter might not be of much help to them now.' A plan of action was already forming in Schulz's mind and he fixed the agent with a hard stare, 'This aircraft mechanic, is he your only informant at Locarno Airport?'

'By no means, sir,' replied the other man, relieved that he could offer something positive. 'I have two informants who work at check in and one who works in the main office,'

Schulz nodded and, handing over another healthy pile of bank notes, ordered the man to return immediately to the airport and find out the names, under which the two men in question had travelled.

'And book me a seat on the next available flight to Belgrade. If it's tomorrow, sort me out a hotel near the airport. I'll use the office upstairs to report back to Bern.

Oh, and send someone to tell my driver that he'd better wait with the car until further orders.'

Once Schulz had made himself comfortable in the deserted office, he rang Bern to explain to von Ilsemann that he was certain he had picked up Milton's trail and that he intended to follow him to Belgrade. Von Ilsemann was initially convinced by the mentioning of 'Meelton' and Oerlikon, but then began to doubt the story, arguing that the Englishmen would be 'travelling even further away from Britain.'

'But, with respect, sir,' replied Schulz, 'they would be moving closer to safety. Since the fall of France their options have been severely curtailed. It's my guess that they're trying to reach the Mediterranean and plan to meet a British warship there.' Von Ilsemann accepted this logic and both agreed that the Englishmen would probably be aiming for Greece or, less likely, neutral Turkey.

'Well Schulz,' von Ilsemann concluded, 'I'm still not certain about all this. It all hinges on the reliability of this ground mechanic. However, if you're convinced, I'll give the go ahead. But it's on your head if it all goes wrong.' Noting Schulz's willing acceptance of this condition, he continued, 'Make arrangements to go to Belgrade as soon as possible. When you arrive there, I'll ensure that staff from the German Tourist Office will meet you. That's the hub of our espionage activities there. I'll tell them that you're on your way and I'll also keep Colonel Kalz appraised of your movements. I need hardly stress that it's vital that you intercept Milton and his documents, so you have the full authorisation of Admiral Canaris to require any assistance at all from German nationals and officials. I know from your record that you are a credit to the army, Schulz. But, on this occasion you must do whatever is necessary to succeed, not what your scruples may tell you is the right thing to do. Understood?'

Chapter Sixteen

Saturday August 3rd, 1940, Belgrade, Yugoslavia.

Relief that their departure from the Astoria was so early in the morning coursed through Blake. Very few of the hotel guests made their way down to breakfast before 8AM and, as their train departed fifteen minutes before that time, he smiled at the welcome sight of an almost empty reception area. Milton was left in charge of their two small cases and, as ever, his own briefcase, while Blake went to the hotel luggage room to retrieve the materiel from Oerlikon. There always seemed to be a ready supply of taxis and the doorman found no difficulty in hailing one, which he ordered to take the two men to the railway station.

In contrast to the hotel, the station was a hive of activity, both men recognising that the arrival and departure of the Orient Express was something of an event. A low rise building with many terminus lines, the station lacked much of the grandeur and excitement which both men associated with long distance, international train travel. However, the arrangements for boarding, refined over decades of handling extremely demanding passengers, were exemplary.

As Blake and Milton approached the train, they were addressed by an official carrying a clip board. Having confirmed their names, they were directed to a small, swarthy man with a perfectly manicured moustache. He was wearing a knee length royal blue uniform coat with gold braid, black trousers, white gloves and shirt with a dark tie, all of which was topped off with a blue kepi. The man saluted briskly and smiled at their approach, 'Bonjour messieurs,' he beamed. 'Do I have the honour of addressing Monsieur Blake and Monsieur Milton?' The Englishmen nodded and the man continued, 'Bienvenue to the Simplon Orient Express, messieurs. I am Pierre and I will be your *conducteur* for the journey to Istanbul. Now,' he asked, indicating two trolleys pushed by station porters, 'is this all your baggage?'

Blake immediately answered, 'Yes, it is. And we would like it all to be placed in our compartment.'

Pierre's face immediately fell into a perfect expression of regret as he answered, 'Ah, monsieur, would that this were possible. Alas, I regret to inform you that it is not.'

'What do you mean?' insisted Blake, 'the items have all been paid for and appropriate labels attached.'

'Biensûr, monsieur,' explained the conducteur with a skill honed by years of dealing with such issues. 'The two sacks must travel in the luggage van at the rear of the train. I will accompany the porters myself and ensure that they are both safely on board. You may rest assured that they will be perfectly safe, while under the care of the Simplon Orient Express.'

Milton, suspecting that Blake was about to protest more vigorously and maybe create an unfortunate scene, rapidly intervened. 'That will be fine, Pierre. Now, could you please point out our compartment?'

'Of course,' the conducteur replied with a quick instruction to the porters to go to the luggage van with the sacks and wait for him there. 'If you would please follow me, messieurs. Louis, my attendant, will carry your suitcases.' Milton felt an undeniable thrill, as he admired the distinctive, dark blue carriages, all with the world famous 'Compagnie Internationale des Wagons-Lits,' written in gold just beneath a cream roof. They followed the diminutive figure, as he strode down the platform and entered the third carriage. The Englishmen exchanged impressed smiles, as they felt the deep pile of the immaculate blue and gold corridor carpet beneath their shoes. Finally, Pierre stopped by a finely polished wooden door which he opened and invited them to enter.

'Here is your compartment, messieurs. I trust that you will be very comfortable here. If you will permit, I will return shortly after we leave Belgrade to inform you of the arrangements on the train. But now, I must ensure that your additional baggage is loaded safely.'

'Wait!' called Blake, as the conducteur made his way down the corridor, 'I'll come with you.'

Pierre stopped, turned and with perhaps the slightest of exasperated sighs, said, 'That is not at all necessary, monsieur. Please leave me to supervise this. You will have no complaints. Of that I can assure you.' Milton touched Blake gently on the arm and unobtrusively shook his head to indicate that he should let the man get on with his job.

The last few passengers hurried along the platform through clouds of steam which billowed around the train as it stood, impatiently awaiting the station master's whistle and straining to be on its way. Alone in their compartment, the Englishmen surveyed their accommodation with undisguised pleasure. A padded bench, convertible into bunk beds, spanned the entire right side, from the corridor wall to the outside of the carriage with its large picture window. The far left hand corner, adjacent to the window, was taken up with a cleverly designed, and enclosable, wash basin and mirror. 'No excuses for letting ourselves go, Milton,' said Blake with a smile as he admired the quality soap and other toiletries. In the near left side corner, adjacent to the compartment door, stood a small, fitted wardrobe, where they could hang their freshly laundered and newly purchased clothes. Blake drew down the sliding window, just in time to hear a shrill whistle cut the air. This was followed immediately by a loud groan and lurch as the grand train began to steam out of Belgrade.

***

Locarno Airport, Switzerland.

As he buckled his seat belt on the dawn Swissair flight to Belgrade, Schulz felt more relaxed and confident that he would be able to fulfil his mission successfully and, despite von Ilsemann's last exhortation, do this in his own way. Having sent his driver back to his flat in Bern to collect sufficient clothes for a week and his Luger pistol with ammunition, he had spent an uncomfortable night in a small pension, not far from the airport in Locarno. But now, as the plane achieved its cruising altitude and he sipped a strong coffee, he could reflect on a job well done. His suitcase had been delivered to the pension in good time; he had sufficient funds; he had the commitment of assistance in Belgrade and, above all, he was hot on Milton's trail.

He had to assume that Milton was still accompanied by the British agent and that they already had some sort of onward travel plan from Belgrade. From the enquiries made by Bureau F in Bern, Schulz knew that the two most likely possibilities were Greece or Turkey. Moreover, Abwehr officers in Belgrade, operating on the reasonable assumption that the Swiss identities, used for the flight from Locarno, would have been used again, were busy trying to find out where the British agents were staying in the city. *With luck,* he reflected as he eased himself back into the extremely comfortable seat, *they should have some information for me when they pick me up at the airport.* For the next hour or two, however, there was little more he could do, other than settle down and relax for the rest of the flight.

Following almost exactly in the footsteps taken forty-eight hours earlier by Blake and Milton, Schulz collected his bag and immediately saw the burly young man, holding up a discreet sign, stating 'German Tourist Office.' Having introduced himself, Schulz allowed the other man to take his case and lead him to a black saloon car, parked outside the terminal building. The sun was beating down from a clear midday sky as Schulz removed his suit jacket, opened the rear door of the car and stepped inside.

'Welcome to Belgrade, Captain Schulz. I am Lieutenant Hartmann and I am here to offer you every assistance,' said the dark-haired man who was already occupying more than half of the rear seat. Schulz nodded, as a frown of disapproval at the enormous girth of the other man flitted briefly across his face.

'Thank you, Hartmann,' Schulz replied as the car edged out into the traffic which was heading from the airport towards the centre of the city. 'Did you have any success in tracking the two men down?'

'We think so, yes,' replied Hartmann ingenuously. 'Actually, there aren't so many hotels in Belgrade and we started with the ones that are closest to the railway station.'

'Good thinking,' Schulz acknowledged, 'though I suppose knowing their assumed identities was a help?'

'Maybe.'

'What do you mean?'

'Unfortunately, sir, it appears that they checked out this morning and, so far, we don't know where they've gone.'

Schulz suppressed his irritation at this development, suggesting, 'Let's go straight to interview the staff at the hotel. They may know something.' His face formed into an ingratiating smile, Schulz approached the reception desk at the Hotel Astoria, 'Good afternoon. I believe two of my compatriots are staying here? I would dearly like to invite them for dinner tonight.'

'Of course, sir. What would be their names?' As soon as Schulz mentioned the assumed Swiss names of the two Britons, the receptionist's face fell. 'I'm sorry, sir, but they checked out earlier today.' Further polite questioning elicited no useful information and Schulz, cursing this turn of events, began to turn away. 'You could try asking the doorman, sir,' the receptionist suggested. 'Perhaps they took a taxi. I know they had some large sacks with them.'

A look of confusion spread over Schulz's face. Sacks? Why on earth would Milton and the other man burden themselves with sacks? It doesn't make sense. Surely, they are just carrying the documents? A small bead of nervous sweat suddenly appeared over his left eye as he began to wonder whether, in coming to Belgrade, he had made another false move. But damn it! I'm certain I'm right. After thanking the receptionist, Schulz casually approached the doorman who had just closed the door of a taxi for a departing guest. Having elicited that he understood 'a little' German, Schulz asked about the two bogus Swiss who had left earlier that day. The Serb's face creased in a frown of mock concentration and, at the first sign of a shaking head, Schulz passed over a few local banknotes. He couldn't help but smile at the predictability of the doorman raising a finger in salute of his feat of memory. 'Ah yes, I remember,' he said as he pocketed the notes. 'They were going to the station and there were those sacks... pretty heavy, actually.

'Do you know where they were going and have you any idea what might have been in the sacks?' asked Schulz, perhaps a little too eagerly.

'Hmm, now you're asking...' the doorman hesitated, until a further few notes had been offered.

'Tell me first, then you get the money,' instructed Schulz, his expression beginning to show impatience. 'And do not mislead me or my friends will deal with you harshly.'

The doorman looked anxiously at Hartmann, lounging malevolently against the parked car and quickly decided that this was no innocent enquiry by a business friend. 'Don't misunderstand me, sir. I like Germany and Herr Hitler very much. I will not lie,' he gabbled. 'They definitely took a taxi to the railway station. But, as to what was in the sacks, all I can say is that they were heavy and contained several boxes.' Schulz nodded in thanks and slipped the doorman a bonus payment 'to help him forget about this conversation,' before climbing back into the car.

Hartmann's lips twisted in distaste as he asked pointedly, 'Did you give him money, sir? With all respect, I believe these Slav types react better to the stick, rather than the carrot. Five minutes with us and he would be singing like a bird.'

The steely glint in Schulz's eyes convinced the younger man to say no more and he listened as the older man instructed the driver to go to the station. Within fifteen minutes, Schulz had negotiated an interview with the manager of the station ticket office who confirmed that the two Swiss gentlemen had purchased tickets for Athens. Unfortunately, he could not confirm that those tickets had been used that day.

So, Schulz concluded, *it's Greece. They're heading for the Mediterranean to try to find passage back to Britain.* It was now imperative that he contact von Ilsemann, both to determine his fastest route to Greece and to alert the Abwehr there to prepare for the arrival of Milton. He hurried off to find Hartmann, but could not see him anywhere. Irritated, he looked carefully across the crowded station concourse. *Confound the man! Where on earth can he have gone?* Finally, he saw him in conversation with a tall man in the uniform of a platform master.

'Hartmann!' he yelled over the general noise, 'we must leave immediately!'

Hartmann swivelled round in surprise and immediately rushed over to Schulz. 'With your permission, sir,' he stammered, 'I think you might be interested in what this man has to say.' Seeing Schulz's dubious look, he continued, 'Since being a boy, I've always been fascinated by the Orient Express and it turns out that this man was responsible for this morning's departure.'

'And I'm supposed to be interested in that?' demanded Schulz incredulously. 'Come on, man, we've got to get a move on, not play toy trains.'

'With respect, sir,' gabbled Hartmann, 'I really think you should hear his story.'

'Very well,' agreed an obviously irritated Schulz, while staring at the increasingly nervous looking Serb. 'Tell him to get on with it!'

The platform master began in halting German, 'Please, your Honour, it's as I was explaining to your esteemed colleague. We were talking about this morning's departure of the Simplon Orient Express and I told him about a rather strange occurrence.'

'Yes, yes,' muttered Schulz, pointedly looking at his watch.

'Well, your Excellency, as I said, there were two gentlemen with the heavy sacks. Travelling all the way to Istanbul, they were.' As soon as he heard mention of the sacks, Schulz's entire attention was directed to the Serb. 'The funny thing was that one of the men tried to insist on seeing these into the luggage van personally. Most unusual, that was,' he observed, scratching his damp head after removing his gaudy peaked cap. 'Whatever was in them must have been very valuable. Still that's the British for you, eh? A bit fussy, I'd say.'

'What do you mean, 'the British'? These men were Swiss, surely?' demanded Schulz.

An expression of confusion mixed with suspicion clouded the Serbian's face. 'Well, I don't know about that, your Highness. But they were certainly speaking English with the conducteur of the train. Now, if you'll forgive me, I must return to my duties.'

Schulz had no option but to let the man go. Of course, if he'd been in Germany, it would have been a different story. But in Yugoslavia, he had no official status. He wasn't even in uniform. But what the man had said was a matter of some concern and Schulz tried to figure it out. *So, Milton and his comrade travel under false Swiss identities from Locarno and use these both to register at the hotel in Belgrade and to book train tickets to Athens. But now, this fellow says that two men, speaking English and with heavy sacks, boarded the train for Istanbul. What does it all mean? And what on earth could be in those sacks, that Milton would burden himself with them?* Shaking his head slowly, to rid himself of lesser issues, Schulz tried desperately to focus on the key point. *The two sets of tickets in different names with two destinations. That's what's really worrying me. Am I being played for a fool?* His reason quickly told him that it would be far too much of a coincidence for the paths of two unrelated pairs of men to cross in this way. *No,* he decided, *the Englishmen must be travelling to Istanbul rather than Athens. But are they still under the false Swiss identities? There's only one sure way to find out.*

'You did very well there, Hartmann,' Schulz congratulated the Lieutenant, 'but now it's vital that I speak with the ticket office manager again.'

A brown envelope stuffed with US Dollars soon afforded Schulz a glance at the list of the passengers who had boarded that morning's Simplon Orient Express at Belgrade, together with their destinations. There were only ten and, partway down the list, he saw the names Milton S. and Blake W. as sharing one compartment to Istanbul. Schulz tightened his fist in triumph. *I've got to get to Istanbul as soon as possible. And I'll ask Bern if anything's known about this Blake character.*

Schulz had no eyes to see the grand buildings of Belgrade, basking in the bright sunshine, as the car made its frustratingly slow way through the late morning traffic and back towards the German Tourist Office. Nor did he have time for conversation with Hartmann, however much he might be grateful for his contribution at the station. The cogs and wheels of his brain were trying to work out how best he could make use of his current advantage over the Englishmen. *I know where they will be early tomorrow. But they haven't a clue that I'm hot on their trail.* He began to consider why they were aiming for Istanbul, rather than Greece. *But where can they be aiming for?* Suddenly it hit him. *Egypt! It has to be! British controlled Egypt and then safe passage back home. But how can I catch them and stop them?* Schulz knew that Istanbul had no international passenger airport and, even if he could get a ticket for the next day's Orient Express, he would still be a day behind them. *Damn!* he cursed, *I must speak with von Ilsemann about the possibility of finding a faster way to get to Istanbul.* Having decided his strategy, his teeming mind turned back to the sacks. *What's in them?* he wondered hopelessly. *Milton definitely didn't have them when I lost him at Zürich, but they're obviously important.* He considered the possibility that they might belong to this Blake character and be nothing to do with Milton, but rejected that notion as unfeasible. *Think, man!* he commanded himself as the car plodded slowly on. *I know the Oerlikon factory produces all kinds of technical equipment and materiel for military and aviation purposes. And I was told that Milton has a very good relationship with Tröder, the Production Manager at the factory. Could the sacks possibly be full of items of crucial, military importance for the British? Especially after they lost so much equipment in the rout at Dunkirk? Could they be so valuable to the British, that they can't afford to leave them behind?* Suddenly, Schulz became aware that his mission could be even more vital to Germany achieving what surely must be the essential, quick victory over Great Britain. *Whatever's in those sacks,* he decided, *I have to stop them reaching Egypt. The key is to solve the problem of getting to Istanbul quickly. Then, for the first time, I'll really be ahead of the game.*

The German Tourist Office was located in a fine, classically designed building on one of the major boulevards in the heart of Belgrade's thriving commercial centre. The ground and first floor of the narrow premises were given over to the site's explicit purpose, the fostering of propaganda about Germany and the encouragement of tourist travel to the Reich. The second and top floors were the Abwehr headquarters for the whole of Yugoslavia. Perhaps in anticipation of military incursions towards Greece, the number of officers stationed in Belgrade had begun to increase sharply after the fall of France. As he passed through the bustling offices, Schulz detected an urgent, almost excited air about the place. He readily recalled the same atmosphere in similar offices in Prague and Warsaw in the months leading up to the invasion and defeat of Czechoslovakia and Poland. He couldn't help wondering whether these new recruits believed that they were the vanguard of a German takeover of Yugoslavia. Once inside Hartmann's small office, Schulz issued the order for an immediate phone call to be placed to Bureau F in Bern. *If I'm to have any chance of intercepting the enemy agents, it's imperative that I reach Istanbul as quickly as possible.*

***

Von Ilsemann sighed as he looked out of his office window, opened wide in an attempt to generate some air on an unusually hot afternoon in the Swiss capital. Outside, birds were singing in the leafy trees and the sound of an infrequent motor car was the only intrusion on a bourgeois scene that could have belonged in any pre-war, small German city. Having finished his call with Belgrade some minutes before, he shook his head to rid it of such happy memories of peaceful summers. Pausing only to mop his heavily perspiring face with a cool, cotton handkerchief, he then placed a call to his commanding officer in Berlin. Colonel Kalz was very interested to learn of Schulz's progress in Belgrade and promised that he would give urgent priority to finding a solution to the problem of reaching Istanbul as soon as possible, 'even if I damn well have to pilot him there myself.' Kalz had a reputation among Abwehr staff as a reliable and considerate commander and, reflected von Ilsemann, he was certainly living up to that today.

***

The Simplon-Orient Express.

Milton and Blake visibly relaxed as they settled into the long train journey through Yugoslavia. The track initially followed the Morava river as it flowed on towards Crveni Krst. After a short delay to allow those passengers who were heading for Greece to change trains, the express resumed its long journey towards the border with Bulgaria. Aware that their original plan had been to make for

Athens, Blake caught Milton's eye with a wry smile. 'Well, I guess that's it. It's Cairo or bust for us now!' Before a suitable riposte came to mind, the sound of the steward, announcing the first sitting of lunch in thirty minutes, was clearly audible from the corridor.

The conducteur had already visited them to explain the routine of the train and the facilities which were at the passengers' disposal. 'We are very proud,' Pierre had said, 'that this train actually has a bath car, with thermostatically controlled showers.' Gratified by the bewildered looks exchanged by the Englishmen, he went on to advise, 'Please contact me, in my office at the end of this carriage, and I will arrange to reserve the car for your use.' The conducteur had also, much to Blake's irritation, taken possession of their passports. 'It's standard practise, I can assure you. It eases the border formalities for all passengers.' He had also advised that he would be on hand to assist, if any questions about baggage were raised by customs officials.

Having risen very early that morning and foregone breakfast, the two men hurried along to the dining car, a long, narrow, though extremely elegant salon. They were quickly shown to a window table, at which they sat facing each another. Milton deliberately placed his briefcase on the chair next to him, in an attempt to discourage any other passenger from seeking to join them. Fortunately, the first was the less popular sitting and the fifty-six-seat restaurant was only just over half full. Having been reassured by Blake that the latest supply of Swiss Francs was more than adequate, Milton enjoyed himself, first studying and then ordering from the excellent menu.

'Well,' began Milton as soon as they had placed their order and were settled with a refreshing glass of white wine, 'It begins to look as if we might have got away from Switzerland without attracting the attention of any undesirables.'

'It certainly does seem so,' agreed Blake, 'but let's not congratulate ourselves too quickly. Sometimes, when one thinks everything is tickety-boo, it all goes pear shaped. And we've got a long way to travel before we reach safety. Don't forget, we're still travelling away from London.'

'I suppose you're right,' replied Milton, 'well, let's not dwell on that. We're on this train for a while and I'm conscious that I know little of your private background. Are you married? What about children?'

Blake shifted on his seat, reluctant to damage the better understanding that was growing between them, but equally uncomfortable in discussing personal matters. 'Oh, I'm pretty boring really. Not much to tell... I bet you're far more interesting.'

Milton didn't need a second invitation to chat about those things which were by far the most important to him; home, family and nation. As he spoke he realised with a jolt how easily the first two of these had slipped out of his thoughts over the past couple of weeks. Blake nodded politely and made the right kind of noises at the appropriate points, as the other man regaled him with how lovely his wife is, how delightful his daughter and how he missed his sublime existence in rural Kent. Each of the happy memories recounted, however, served to reinforce to Blake how bleak his own existence was, and it was something of a relief to him when lunch was finished and they could return to their compartment.

They had only just sat down when the train began noticeably to slow down as it approached the border with Bulgaria. The passport control was relatively straightforward, the documents having already been presented by Pierre. Indeed, a quick nod from the border guard, who peered through the compartment door, was the only check made. However, before the two men could toast their transit with a small brandy, a steward knocked gently on the door. 'I'm very sorry, sir, but you must come to the luggage van immediately. There is a problem with the border police. The conducteur is there to advise you.'

Blake immediately decided that he would handle the situation and followed the steward along the corridor, where an occasional inquisitive head appeared from the privacy of a compartment. Luckily, the border guard spoke some German and explained that it was irregular for such baggage to be transported on this train. Blake immediately acted on Pierre's discreet suggestion, offering a relatively small quantity of Swiss Francs, combined with a profuse apology. As soon as he'd handed over the cash, saying, 'I hope this will cover the justifiable fine,' the guard's frown was replaced by a broad smile and the train was quickly on its way towards Sofia.

'They have to supplement their very low wages, I suppose,' shrugged Pierre as the border guard left the train. 'Some unlucky passenger is selected every trip and this time, it just happened to be you.'

***

Belgrade Airport, Yugoslavia.

The sun was beating down relentlessly from an azure sky as the pilot eased the Heinkel He70 off the runway at Belgrade Airport. Schulz adjusted his seat belt and sat back to enjoy the last hours of peace before his arrival at Yesilköy Military airbase. Opened just before the outbreak of the First World War and some twenty-four kilometres to the west of Istanbul, this airfield was the only one to serve the sprawling city.

Matters had moved very quickly, once he had contacted Bureau F about the need to find a rapid means of transit to Istanbul. As luck would have it, a German paving specialist, who was under contract to improve the runway at Yesilköy, was due to return to Istanbul on the weekly service flight for the German diplomatic and military personnel stationed in Istanbul. He did not require too much persuasion to swap his seat in the drafty, noisy and uncomfortable transport plane, for a private compartment on the Orient Express, leaving the following day. A discrete change of passenger, when the Heinkel landed in Belgrade to refuel, saw both Schulz and the paver happy with the outcome.

Schulz was certain now that he would overtake the Englishmen as they steamed their way sedately towards Turkey. He recognised that his most important task on arrival would be to formulate a strategy to take full advantage of this. The situation sounded quite simple, but an earlier conversation with von Ilsemann had informed him of some of the sensitivities likely to be encountered in Istanbul. 'It's true that the city has a long history of being relaxed about the activities of foreign espionage organisations,' the Head of Bureau F had advised. 'But don't think that means anyone can do as he pleases. The Turks tolerate espionage to the extent that they can make some money out of it. So, you won't endear yourself to anyone if you start shooting bullets. Our Abwehr people in Ankara tell me that the Turkish Government is very impressed by the ongoing success of the army in France. However, it also worries that Yugoslavia, Greece and Bulgaria might be next in line for a Blitzkrieg. The Turks have even started to send out feelers about a Non-Aggression Pact with Germany, to which Berlin has responded positively. So, remember Schulz, respect their neutrality, but find a way of stopping the Englishmen. It's vital for the Abwehr that you succeed. Our people out there will give you every assistance.'

In light of this latest advice, simply to eliminate the Englishmen was, from a diplomatic standpoint, not an option. Schulz, of course, was not unhappy with this development. Even though Milton and Blake could be seen as spies and, therefore, not protected by the Geneva Convention, he saw himself as an army officer, not a professional assassin. Like many professional soldiers, he believed that violence and force were means to honourable and desirable ends, rather than ends in themselves. Indeed, he had seen significant active service in the Spanish Civil War and the Czech, Polish and Norwegian campaigns. He had seen at first hand and was, therefore, fully aware of the behaviour of which men in uniform were capable. Both the heroic and good, as well as the inhuman and brutal. Nevertheless, the injunction of his senior officer, regarding what was and what was not acceptable in neutral Turkey, did present him with a clear problem. *How can I make sure the Englishmen don't slip through my fingers? The obvious strategy,* he quickly decided, *is to delay them in Istanbul, discover their onward route and plan an ambush in a less diplomatically delicate location.* As he began to tease at this idea, he found himself repeatedly coming back to the sacks which the Englishmen were transporting. *I don't know why and I've no idea how, but I think these may be the key to unlock my problem. So,* he concluded, *I must prioritise the identification of their contents.*

Schulz used the last part of the flight to review the contents of a medium sized hold all which had been handed to him as he climbed aboard the plane. He smiled as he realised that Von Ilsemann had indeed arranged everything perfectly. The case contained a range of warm weather clothing, both civilian and military, various maps and information sheets, a money belt with what seemed like a great deal of Turkish and American currency, and a Luger pistol with a good quantity of ammunition.

If anything, it was even hotter when the cabin door was opened to the shimmering, early evening light at Yesilköy airfield and Schulz climbed down the steps onto the runway. Carrying his case and with the hold all slung over one shoulder, he squinted at the tiny, single storey building with its squat control tower which directed air traffic into and out of Istanbul. How very different it was from the grand, almost overpowering design of Tempelhof, Hitler's new airport in the centre of Berlin. As he peered down the runway, in the direction from which his aircraft had just approached the airfield, he could see evidence of building equipment and materials. He smiled at the thought of the Turkish labourers who would no doubt relish the extra day of rest, while their German overseer enjoyed his pampering on the Orient Express.

'It's an ill wind,' he muttered to himself, as with some relief he entered the shade of the building. There, he immediately saw a smiling man who was obviously waiting for him. Straight away Schulz noticed the empty right sleeve of his civilian jacket and hastily put down his case, in order to be able to shake with his left hand. 'Good afternoon, I am Captain Schulz.'

The younger man replied formally, 'Thank you, sir and welcome to Istanbul. I am Lieutenant Haller and my orders are to offer you all support and advice. Consider myself and my driver at your disposal during your stay in the city.'

A room had been booked for Schulz at the Park Hotel, 'It's in a lovely position,' Haller explained, 'and if you're lucky, you'll have a wonderful, view out across the Bosphorus. In any case, it's just across the street from the German consulate, so it's perfectly placed.'

Schulz used the forty-five-minute journey to the hotel to appraise Haller of the purpose of his mission and was immediately impressed by the younger man's quick grasp of the situation. Echoing von Ilsemann's analysis, Haller advised, 'The Turks are fine, as long as there's no violence. While the Abwehr is pretty understaffed here, Heydrich's SD security service is crawling with relative newcomers.'

Noticing Schulz's eyebrow rise in curiosity, the younger man continued, 'A lot of them are not too concerned if they throw their weight about a bit. For example, a couple of weeks ago a Jewish waiter was beaten to death on his way home from work. The word in the consulate was that a couple of SD were involved.' Raising his one arm in a calming gesture, he explained, 'Of course, the public view is that Germany condemns such violence, but the police remain very suspicious.'

'Sadly, that's quite normal for the SD,' commented Schulz, with an uncomprehending shake of the head. 'But do you think this will make my task harder?'

'Far from it, sir,' replied Haller to Schulz's surprise. 'The regular army has very strong connections with the Turkish military and this also applies to the police and the secret police. They see us as honourable, gentlemen even, in contrast to the SD.'

Reassured, Schulz then set out his plans. He wished first to visit the terminus of the Orient Express, to enable him to plan how the British agents could be put under surveillance. 'But we must be very careful not to be observed ourselves. The British know nothing of my presence here and I would prefer to keep it that way.'

The second priority was established as identifying the contents of the sacks transported to Istanbul by the British. 'That should be easy,' said Haller with a confident smile. 'Anything and anyone has a price here. It should be simple to bribe a porter and replace him with one of our men. He'd then be able to take a look at the luggage van when the train arrives, but before the passengers disembark.' Seeing the uncertain look on Schulz's face, he added, 'Don't worry, sir. We can find out the details of the compartment the two men are occupying from the ticket office at the station and we can bribe an official to keep them back for an few minutes extra.'

Schulz then explained that the final priority would be to devise a strategy to discover the next move of the British. It would then be necessary to find some pretext to delay them in Istanbul, while some sort of ambush is prepared in a suitable location. 'I may well need some extra muscle to achieve this objective, so give that some thought,' ordered Schulz.

Having checked into the Park Hotel and deposited his case and bag in the spacious room, which did indeed offer a view of the waters of the Sea of Marmara with the Bosphorus on the left and the Golden Horn on the right, Schulz instructed the driver to take himself and Haller to Sirkeci Station. The terminus of the Orient Express is squeezed into the hillside, below Seraglio Point, a stone's throw from the Topkapi Palace, where the Byzantine Emperors and Ottoman Sultans had located their royal households. As soon as he saw the station building, Schulz immediately understood that, while arriving in Istanbul by ship was reputed to be one of the world's most rewarding experiences, even to arrive by the legendary Orient Express was, in contrast, rather mundane. As they approached the scarcely grand station building, Haller turned to Schulz and, rather sheepishly, began to explain. 'I've liked railway architecture since childhood and, while this doesn't compare to St Pancras in London or the grand stations in

Paris, it does have its interest.' Grateful for the quizzical look which Schulz affected, he continued, 'The building itself was designed by a Prussian and I suppose it stands as a testimony to the closeness of links between our country and Turkey.'

Schulz studied the sunbathed building and had to agree with Haller. Sirkeci Station's exterior had some charm, with a central entrance which, with its Gothic and circular shaped windows and its two flanking clock towers, managed to look like a cross between a church and a railway station. Once inside, Haller turned to Schulz, 'It's a bit of a disappointment, isn't it?' The terminus of the great Orient Express was, in fact, little more than a large, provincial railway station. There was no light flooded and soaring arrival hall and no real excitement about the place at all.

Haller evidently knew what he was doing and, having excused himself for fifteen minutes, he discreetly gained entry through a door to the side of the main ticket office of the station. Some twenty minutes later, he returned to confirm that the British agents were occupying a compartment towards the front of the train, 'which is good for us, as it will take them longer to get to the luggage van at the rear.' He also verified that they had transported two sacks, stamped with Swiss postal markings, 'which should help our man to identify them.'

The two Germans then reviewed the platform, at which the train would arrive early the next morning and determined the most suitable place for Schulz to set up his observation point. One of Haller's best men would join the platform porters, shortly before the train arrived, and would be in position to examine the contents of the sacks. Haller would himself bribe the platform master to delay the two British gentlemen in their compartment. Finally, their driver would wait outside the station, to enable them to follow the British agents, should they leave by taxi.

A hot afternoon was now transforming itself into a sultry early evening, as the two men emerged from the station building. 'I've been cooped up all day in airplanes and cars,' Schulz said, as he stretched his back in an attempt to ease a slight ache. 'There's not much more we can do until tomorrow, so why don't you show me round this part of the city and then we can walk back to the Park Hotel and get something to eat there.'

Haller's even expression immediately creased into a frown.

'What's the matter? Have you something to do?'

'Oh no, sir, it's nothing like that,' replied Haller quickly, 'it's just…'

Schulz immediately recognized the other man's reluctance to speak. He was well aware of how the rise of the Nazi party, with its grotesque spider's web of informants, had caused mutual doubt and suspicion among normally straightforward military men. 'Come on man, out with it,' he coaxed. 'We're both just ordinary soldiers here. What's on your mind?'

Haller smiled, 'Well sir, it's just that the Park Hotel restaurant is pretty much full of Japanese in the early evening and later with people from the German consulate. They even say all the rooms are bugged by the Emniyet – the Turkish Secret Police – and that the restaurant waiters are very skilled at eavesdropping.'

'And you'd be more comfortable elsewhere. Is that it?'

'Well, sir, there are all kinds of inquisitive eyes and ears there.'

Schulz's curt nod was all the confirmation required and Haller, having dismissed the driver for the evening, led Schulz away from Sirkeci Station. With the calm waters of the Golden Horn glistening in the evening sun, they began their pleasant U-shaped route to Gülhane Park, situated just outside the walls of the Topkapi Palace. 'This area is the site of ancient Constantinople and the most noteworthy buildings in all Istanbul are concentrated here.' Haller indicated the minarets of the Blue Mosque, pointing like bright needles into the darkening sky and the cumbersome shape of the Haghia Sophia. 'It doesn't look much from the outside, but the inside is absolutely incredible,' he enthused. During their enjoyable stroll, Schulz temporarily forgot his mission as he listened attentively to Haller's informative and erudite introduction to old Istanbul. As dusk was falling and the plaintive cries from the multitude of minarets in the city began to carry on the balmy air, they turned into an extremely narrow alleyway, between the Grand Bazaar and the Blue Mosque.

Recognising a certain doubt on Schulz's face, Haller smiled and said, 'Don't worry, sir. It's perfectly safe. We're going to one of the best *meyhanes* in the whole city. By the way, a meyhane is an informal restaurant which serves alcohol and, typically, mezze and traditional Turkish food. It's a taste of real Istanbul and I must confess that I use them very frequently. It's such a relief to get away from the diplomatic and espionage communities.'

Haller was greeted like family by the moustachioed, fez-wearing proprietor and the two Germans were immediately led to a private table, next to a wall which was covered with dozens of framed black and white photographs. As soon as Haller had ordered a selection of mezze and two chilled beers, Schulz gave him a sympathetic look and asked, 'What happened to your arm? Active service?'

The younger man showed no sign that he found the question offensive. He merely sighed and said with a wistful smile, 'In a way, yes. I was a mathematics graduate and, when I joined up, I was sent to Spain to analyse the effect of mass bombing on civilian life. I just happened to be in the wrong restaurant at the wrong time and an explosion caused by the Republicans did the rest. So, no heroics for the Fatherland, I'm afraid.'

'Come on, Haller,' responded Schulz genuinely. 'We both know that stories of heroism are for folk tales and Herr Goebbels.' The two beers had arrived and, after quietly toasting the success of the mission, both men eagerly quenched their thirst. Schulz savoured the various vegetable, fish and meat dishes, served up with a selection of breads and was happy that the service was, as Haller had promised, discretion itself. 'I supply the proprietor with unimportant snippets which he sells to the British and Russians. He, in turn, leaves me to dine in peace,' Haller explained through a mouthful of wonderful aubergine dip. 'But there's something bothering me, sir. Do you mind?'

'Of course not, man. Come on, out with it.'

'It's just that I'm not sure why you think the sacks are so important? Why take the risk of having them investigated? If things don't go perfectly, there's a risk that we may just alert the British to our presence and lose the advantage of surprise. What do you think is in them?'

'I'd bet my last Reichsmark that it's war related materiel of some kind,' replied Schulz decisively. 'Whatever it is, it must have come from the armaments factory in Zürich. If I'm right, maybe we can use it to delay the British. After all, we're in a neutral country. The Turks may not take kindly to that kind of stuff being secretly transported and a word in the right ear might cause serious delays to them.'

Haller expressed doubt that there was anything fundamentally illegal in having such materiel in Turkey, 'but we have very good relations with the Emniyet. Their military has relied heavily on our army right back to the days of the German Empire. If we can prove that the sacks contain such stuff, we might be able to lean on the Turks to temporarily confiscate them. That might cause the British to stay in Istanbul longer than planned. But we'd have to be quick.'

Schulz's face creased into a broad smile and he raised his glass in a toast to his new found and extremely capable comrade. 'But tell me, Haller, you're obviously a bright fellow and you've been here a couple of years. You must have a good idea of the routes into and out of Istanbul. So, imagine you're the agent Blake. Where would you be heading and how would you leave the city?'

Haller rubbed his chin reflectively, took a long pull of the beer which Schulz had ordered refilled, and began. 'Well, given that they've travelled here from Switzerland, I can only assume that they're making for British controlled territory.'

'Egypt, you mean?'

'I'd say so. If they'd been aiming for the Mediterranean, in order to travel back home by sea, they'd have probably gone for Athens.'

'Yes. That's the direction we initially thought they were travelling. But, tell me, how would they get to Egypt from here? What options do they have?'

'The most obvious is the Taurus Express,' replied Haller enthusiastically. 'I've done it once all the way to Cairo. It's an amazing journey.'

Schulz's eyes lit up, 'That's very interesting. Let's get a bottle of raki and you can tell me all about it.'

As Haller was talking, the germ of an idea began to form in Schulz's mind. As soon as Haller had finished his account of the Taurus Express, he leaned forward to ask, 'This train, the Taurus Express? Does it run every day?'

'I don't think so, sir. I believe it runs only three times a week. Sunday, Tuesday and Friday, if memory serves.'

'I see. And your relations with the Emniyet, you say they're good?'

'Indeed, sir. Why, have you something in mind?'

'Possibly. Could you set up a meeting as soon as possible with the most appropriate officer?'

Haller pulled his diary from his inside pocket, saying, 'I can do that now, sir. The proprietor allows me to use his private phone when necessary. It's as secure as any phone line in Istanbul, including the ones in Abwehr HQ.'

Schulz's eyebrows arched in surprise, 'In that case, ring him, if you please.'

Five minutes later, Haller returned with the news that a meeting had been arranged for 11AM the following day. 'Excellent!' declared Schulz. 'Now, I need a team of four to be ready for deployment from 7AM tomorrow morning.'

Haller's face fell as he replied, 'I'm afraid Abwehr strength would not run to that, sir. But I could try to enlist the SD's help.'

Neither man relished having to work with that particular organisation, but Schulz shrugged, 'If there's no alternative.

Get them ready as soon as possible tomorrow. Is that likely to be a problem?'

'I can't see why it should be. There's so many of them that they're always underemployed and looking for things to do. I'll contact them tonight.'

'But you must make clear that this is an Abwehr operation and that we are in control.'

'Of course, sir. I'll explain that fully. I don't think that would be a problem. But what do you have in mind?'

It was just after eleven when the two Germans made their way across the Galata Bridge which spanned the Golden Horn and led towards Schulz's hotel. The train which was carrying the two British agents and their contraband was due at Sirkeci Station early the next day, so Schulz ordered Haller to have a car pick him up at his hotel at 6.00AM. He wanted to leave nothing to chance.

***

The Orient Express arrived in the capital of Bulgaria just after 4PM. As the train was grinding to a halt, with a screech of metal and hissing of escaped steam, Blake encouraged Milton to 'go and stretch your legs on the platform. It might be your last chance before Istanbul. We're here for fifteen minutes, so you've plenty of time. I'll just have a wash and brush up while you're gone. Take a few Francs, you never know what you might find.'

While Milton was gone, Blake both enjoyed a refreshing wash and seized the opportunity to do something which he had been wanting to do, ever since they left Switzerland. Satisfied, he had just opened the window to enjoy a cigarette, when Milton returned with a week-old copy of the New York Times. To both men's consternation, this reported that the RAF was in the middle of fighting a desperate battle for air superiority over southern England. 'Christ,' muttered Blake after reading the report, 'we'd better get a bloody move on, or it'll be too late by the time we get home.'

The news, while not altogether unexpected, acted as a dampener on the mood of the two British agents who retreated into their own thoughts until it was time for dinner. Hoping that they would not have to share a table with other passengers, they made their way to the dining car for the less popular first sitting. However, they had just settled down to study the menu when the waiter showed a middle-aged man to their table. 'Good evening, gentlemen,' the man said in good, though accented, English. 'I trust I am not intruding.'

'As a matter of fact,' Blake shot back, only to have his sentence completed by a smiling Milton, 'we're terribly bored with each other's company. It will be our pleasure to share a table with you, sir.'

Aware of Blake's instant irritation, the newcomer was charm personified. 'Thank you for your welcome. May I introduce myself? I am Mehmet Demir, a retired civil servant returning home to Istanbul.'

'Pleased to meet you, sir,' replied Milton brightly, as he studied the intelligent, dark eyes of the Turk. 'I am Stephen Milton and this is my colleague William Blake. We are British businessmen on our way to Turkey.' Blake persisted in alienating himself from the conversation and made it obvious that he preferred both his own company and that of a cigarette.

'Excuse me, Mr Blake,' enquired Demir with a playful smile, 'that is a Murad cigarette, if I am not mistaken.'

'What of it?' grunted Blake in reply.

'Oh nothing. I just wondered, if you like Murad, you may also like my preferred brand, Turmac. They are a mixture of Turkish and Macedonian and even richer and more aromatic than Murad.' Demir flashed a conspiratorial wink towards Milton as they both observed the rapid transformation in Blake. Inhaling the smoke from his first Turmac cigarette, he sighed with pleasure. 'My God, Mr Demir, that's a wonderful smoke.' The shared love of Turkish cigarettes was cemented when Demir produced half a dozen full packets from the briefcase which he carried. 'Then please, do me the honour of accepting these as a small gift.'

Demir was a fascinating table companion, sharing many interesting anecdotes of life in Turkey and offering a great deal of interesting information about Istanbul. In contrast, the Englishmen gave only the vaguest of indication of their reasons for travelling on the train and made every effort to redirect the conversation back to the Turk. As the evening wore on and he had run out of compliments to pay the magnificent food, Blake began to sense that there was more to Demir than met the eye. It was also evident that he was somewhat sceptical about their cover story. He was not surprised, therefore, when, over coffee and brandy, Demir asked, 'Is this your first trip to Turkey?' After receiving only silent nods in reply, he continued, 'Well then, please allow me to offer you some friendly advice.'

Blake looked uncertainly at Milton as the Turk continued, 'Forgive me for saying, but I have great difficulty in believing your story.'

Blake immediately began to rise from his seat, 'Well, sir, it's been a wonderful evening, but we should...'

'No, please,' interrupted Demir urgently. 'Let me explain. I was truthful when I told you that I am a retired civil servant. But, perhaps,' he added with a wry smile, 'I was a little economical with the truth.' Noting the expressions of concern exchanged by his dining companions, he went on to explain. 'You see, gentlemen, I did not tell you that I was a senior officer in the Emniyet, which, as you almost certainly know, is the Turkish secret police. I am very experienced in recognising those in a similar line of work. And I judge that you, Mr Blake, are anything but a straightforward businessman. Mr Milton, I have to confess, intrigues me. You do not have the demeanour of 'one of us', and yet....'

Milton's eyes widened in surprise and it was left to Blake to object, his palms facing the Turk in what he hoped would be interpreted as an expression of confused frankness. 'Look, sir, that's all very interesting and my colleague and I have thoroughly enjoyed our conversation. But I'm afraid you have us all wrong. I can assure you that we are, as we say, businessmen. Plain and simple. We are travelling to one of our trading partner countries on a commercial matter, the details of which I'm sure you will understand, we could not possibly divulge.'

'Very well, gentlemen,' replied Demir. 'But before we part, let me assure you that, unlike many of my countrymen, I do not favour Germany. I am what you might call an Anglophile. My love of Britain dates from 1920 when, as a forty-year old, I was fortunate enough to be able to participate in your wonderful Wimbledon Tennis Championship.'

Milton looked vaguely interested in this revelation, but Blake, as if totally wrong-footed, exclaimed in an uncharacteristically natural way. 'Good Lord! This is incredible! Do you know, ever since you introduced yourself, I was sure there was something familiar about your name. But, for the life of me, I couldn't think what it was. Wimbledon in '20! Of course! And you were 'The Turkish Treasure,' if I'm not mistaken. On account of your impeccable on court manners and graciousness in victory and defeat.'

For the first time, Demir looked totally shocked and merely lowered his eyes in something like embarrassment. 'You pay me far too great a compliment, Mr Blake.'

'Not at all! I remember that summer like it was yesterday. I was just about to go up to university and, believe it or not, I actually saw you lose to an Asian in the second round - don't tell me…. a Japanese wasn't he?'

'Indeed, he was,' confirmed a beaming Demir. 'Zenzo Shimizu went on to lose in the semi-final. I fought through the qualifiers, but lost to him in straight sets. He was far, far too good for an old man like me. But I must say that was one of the best weeks of my life and I've loved England ever since. So, my friends, do please let me offer you some well- meaning advice. I don't want to know what you are doing. I just want to help.'

Blake shrugged before replying, 'Look, sir, to make matters clear, I'm not for one second saying that you are correct in your assumption about our reasons for travel. Nevertheless, I'm sure that my colleague and I would be interested in what you have to say.'

This response seemed to please Demir and he lit up another cigarette before continuing. 'Firstly, it is important to recognise that Turkey is a hotbed of espionage. And Istanbul is its most information hungry city. So, one might ask, what does this appetite produce? Informants, my young friends, and plenty of them. And it is hotels which are at the centre of this intricate economy of information gathering and trading. You will be most welcome in Istanbul, because these battalions of informers recognise that the more foreigners there are, the more work there is for them. And the more money they can earn by selling the same information time and again.' Pausing to let the Englishmen exchange glances, he went on to advise, 'When you check in at your hotel, you will naturally allow your passport to be used to register your presence. Be certain that your details will be sold by the receptionist to the Turks, the Soviets, the Americans, the British, French and Germans. Everyone will be aware of your presence.'

'And we cannot do anything to prevent this?' asked Milton with concern.

'I'm afraid not, my young friend,' smiled Demir apologetically. 'You may pay a great deal for this promise. But it will never be kept. So, if you fear you may be of interest to anyone, the use of your real identity may not be advisable. You should also be aware that, while Turkey is neutral, there is a significant history of cooperation between the German and Turkish military. This goes back into the Ottoman period and it is still the case today that many educated and successful Turks sympathise more with Germany than with the Allies. Moreover, there is a large and very vocal German community in Istanbul, which is committed to Hitler and active in the interests of his Reich.'

Observing the nervous glances between his dinner guests, he hastily moved to reassure them, 'But please, do not view Istanbul as exclusively enemy territory. You will find others, like myself, who are on your side. But you must exercise great caution. Do you mind telling me where you plan to stay?'

Blake shrugged and murmured, 'Somewhere called the Hotel Tokatliyon, wherever that is.'

'That is most satisfactory,' smiled Demir. 'I'd have been worried, had you been planning to stay at the Park Hotel.

But the Tokatliyon was well chosen. Will you have assistance in Istanbul?'

'No,' replied Blake quickly, 'we'll be on our own. But our plan is to make immediately for the Aegean Coast.'

An unmistakable frown of disappointment crossed the Turk's face and, for a moment, it looked as if he would say something. However, he simply shrugged his shoulders, rose from his seat and wished them both a good evening. As he shook hands with Milton, the Englishman felt a business card palmed across to him and heard Demir whisper, 'Contact me if you are in trouble. I will do what I can to help.'

Milton said nothing to Blake about Demir's card when they were back in their compartment discussing the evening's conversation. 'I expected some degree of espionage and German presence in Istanbul,' Blake said wearily, as they prepared to retire for the night. 'But we're clearly going to be at risk, especially travelling under our own names. What he said about using false papers is a good idea. I say we use the French passports that Pym gave us. The Germans don't know about those.'

'I agree. Also, I think we should stay for as short a time as possible,' replied Milton. 'I meant to tell you earlier, but forgot with all the fuss about what we read in the newspaper. When I was out on the platform in Sofia, I joined in a conversation between a couple of Americans who were talking about the next leg of their journey to Cairo.'

Blake immediately stopped trying to take off a troublesome cufflink and stared at Milton, 'Excellent! After all, we've no idea how to get to Egypt. So, come on, what did they say?'

'They're travelling on something called the Taurus Express. It leaves from a station on the Anatolian shore of the Bosphorus and travels to Tripoli in the Lebanon. Apparently the railway track ends there and travellers go by road via Beirut to Haifa. Once there, the railway to Egypt and Cairo begins again. I'd say it sounds an interesting bet, don't you agree?'

Blake clapped his travel companion heartily on the back, 'I should say so, old man! That's great work! I'll make a spy of you yet! Now let's get some sleep and hope our contact is prompt and we can get quickly on our way out of Turkey.'

Chapter Seventeen

Sunday August 4th, 1940, Sirkeci Station, Istanbul, Turkey.

The main station on the European side of Istanbul was surprisingly busy when Schulz walked purposefully through the main entrance. He was reassured to see Haller, already deep in conversation with the platform master and an Abwehr officer, dressed in a Turkish Railways uniform, standing discreetly several metres away from them. A frown of uncertainty creased Schulz's face as he suddenly wondered whether the British agent, Blake, might have spotted him in Zürich while he was shadowing Milton. Cursing himself for his dullness in not having recognised this possibility previously, he now made sense of the unusual manner in which Milton had suddenly darted into and out of the main station. *Idiot!* he scolded himself. *It's blindingly obvious. Blake must have told him about the surveillance and planned the evasive manoeuvre.* This was a worrying development, as his whole strategy hinged on the British remaining ignorant of his presence in Istanbul until it was too late to help them. He quickly decided to modify his plans and to remain well out of the sight line of the passengers as they left the Orient Express.

'It's all agreed,' confirmed Haller, after joining Schulz in a corner of the station hall. 'A Turkish official will delay the British for a few minutes, which will permit our man to have a look at the contents of the sacks. He'll have no more than five minutes and he mustn't move anything.'

'And you're sure about this man?' asked Schulz with concern. 'It's vital we get a picture of what this stuff is.'

'He's the best I have, sir,' replied Haller confidently. 'He knows what he's about and I'm certain that, if anyone can, he'll get you the information you need. The SD has also placed a team of two officers at your disposal. They are awaiting your orders now, sir.'

***

Much to Blake's disappointment, the dining car had been detached from the Orient Express as it entered Turkey during the night. Consequently, a limited breakfast of bread rolls, honey and strong Turkish coffee was served in each individual compartment. The conducteur confirmed both that the train was due to arrive on time at 7.20AM and that they should await final passport clearance in their compartment, before attempting to leave the train.

Unusually, given their habitual dispositions, it was Milton who asked sharply, 'And what about our items in the luggage van?'

The conducteur patiently explained that both their luggage and their extra baggage would be brought out of the train and kept securely on the platform until they came to take possession of it. This would be after the completion of any passport formalities. Once the conducteur had left them alone, Blake sought to reassure Milton by suggesting that he, himself, would check the sacks 'as soon as possible.' Milton's job would be 'to keep that blasted briefcase safely in your hands.'

The train was now entering the final minutes of its journey, crawling rather than steaming along the coast of the Sea of Marmara, with the minarets and grand buildings of old Constantinople to the left. In the other direction, the views across the Bosphorus were breathtaking, as they inched around the Sultanahmet and made their final approach into Sirkeci Station.

***

Corporal Johann Held's heart was beating at an alarming rate as he watched the train hiss and groan to a halt at the station platform. A relatively new recruit to the Abwehr, he liked and respected Lieutenant Haller and was desperate not to let him down. Pulling his porter's cap low over his forehead, he immediately made for the luggage van at the rear of the train, urging himself to be as quick and careful as possible.

The two sacks, marked with the distinctive bugle of the Swiss Post Office, stood in the far corner of the large, but well filled van. The simple fastenings were relatively easy to open and he quickly saw that the first sack was full of smaller cardboard boxes, each of which carried both the sticker of the Oerlikon Machine Tool Company and a list of its contents. He eagerly made a written note of these, thinking to himself that the Lieutenant and Captain Schulz would be very interested in what he had to report.

***

For God's sake, how long is this fool going to take with our passports? fumed Blake silently, as the Turkish official laboriously scrutinised Milton's passport. *I wish to heaven I'd given him mine first. At this rate, it's going to be at least five minutes before I'm able to get out to the luggage van.*

Finally, the Turk returned the passports with an unctuous smile and the wish that the two men would have an enjoyable stay in Istanbul. He had barely finished speaking, when Blake pushed past him with a curt, 'Sorry, I have to get to the luggage van.' He rushed down the corridor and out onto the platform, just in time to see a porter wheeling the sacks down the ramp from the van. Having hastily rushed to claim the items, he noticed that the fastenings on at least one of the sacks didn't look quite the same as when they had boarded the train. However, it didn't seem that anything had been taken and he put this down to their rough handling by porters.

Reunited on the platform, Blake and Milton, accompanied by two porters, casually made their way towards the station entrance where they stood in the queue for a taxi. Lurking behind a group of bystanders, in a corner of the station's oblong entrance hall, Schulz recognised Milton immediately. As soon as it was clear where the Englishmen were going, he slipped away through the crowd, out of the station and through the open door of his waiting car.

'There they are. In the queue for a taxi. The two men with all the extra baggage,' he instructed the driver. 'Make sure you don't lose them.'

***

Even though it was barely 8AM as they wheezed away from Sirkeci station in their old taxi, the two Englishmen could see instantly that Istanbul was already a seething mass of people and all kinds of transportation. Sleek, polished saloons vied for space on the crowded streets with clanking trams and even horse drawn carts. To an enthralled Milton, this exotic cocktail of traffic seemed to dart and plod in all directions. Neither man had visited the city before and they stared wide eyed as the taxi crawled its way across Galata Bridge. The vista of the glistening waters of the Golden Horn to the left and the Bosphorus to the right was simply magnificent. Both stretches of water were teeming with all manner of smaller and larger craft, most carrying people or merchandise from one part of the city to another. The open aspect over the water soon disappeared, as the taxi made its laborious way towards Istiklal Caddesi, otherwise called the Grande Rue de Pera and the room at the Tokatliyan which had been reserved for them.

The building, in front of which the taxi heaved itself to a standstill, would not have been out of place on a grand Parisian avenue. Occupying a corner position, the classically elegant design of the hotel, with its grand dome and large windows facing out onto two sides, promised a light and comfortable place to stay. The Grande Rue itself was disappointingly narrow, before opening out, some hundreds of metres further on, into the vast Taksim Square. Like all Istanbul streets, it seemed a veritable bedlam and Blake and Milton were relieved to enter the calm and relative coolness of the hotel lobby. Having introduced themselves and handed over their passports, they were quickly shown to a bright and airy second floor room, which overlooked the Grande Rue.

As soon as they were alone, Blake lost no time in returning to the foyer, where he changed some Swiss Francs into local currency and obtained some information about the Taurus Express. 'I suppose,' he grumbled when he returned to the room, 'the waiting starts again now.'

***

Schulz was very impressed with his driver's ability to keep the taxi in sight. The chaos of trams, motor and horse drawn vehicles, together with droves of pedestrians, some of whom were pushing very large loads on handcarts, presented huge problems. Especially as the driver didn't know where he was going. However, the Abwehr man was able to keep the Englishmen under observation, even as they entered the imposing hotel entrance with their baggage. Speaking to the other agent in the car, Schulz ordered, 'You go and park yourself unobtrusively in the reception area of the hotel. If they both leave, make sure you keep them under observation. If only one leaves, wait and follow the second, should he also attempt to leave. Otherwise await further orders.'

Schulz occupied the vacated front passenger seat and ordered the driver to return to Abwehr headquarters, where he had arranged to meet Haller and Held. Confidently striding into the meeting room, Schulz immediately asked, 'Now, Haller, it's gone 9AM, so today's Taurus Express has already departed and our Englishmen are still in their hotel. How do you interpret this?'

'That they are awaiting a contact who will help them to plan their route out of Istanbul.'

'Exactly! So, today, we keep their hotel under close observation. Now, Held, what do you have for me?

'The sacks contained items called jewel centres and other stuff that sound like components. I read the contents of several boxes in both sacks and made a quick list, to which I added a few things from memory. All the packages were from the Oerlikon factory.'

'Excellent, Held,' praised Schulz. 'Now, get yourself out of that ridiculous railway uniform and report to the foyer of the Hotel Tokatliyon on the Grande Rue. Until further notice, you are to help Ackert with the surveillance duties there. Should either of the two suspects attempt to leave the hotel, one of you is to follow. The second is to report what has happened and keep his eye on the second man. Understood? Good, off you go, then. So, Haller, what do you make of Held's report?'

'I believe jewel centres are vital for aircraft instruments. As to the components, I can only imagine that they are connected with the weapon the British want to start making.'

'Exactly! Now I can see why Milton wanted to take the materiel with him. In their current beleaguered state, the RAF must be desperate for such replacement parts. Very well, now tell me, when do we set off to meet our Emniyet colleagues?'

'We should leave immediately, sir. There has been a change in plan.'

'Really? To our advantage, I trust.'

'I think so, sir. My contact rang me earlier to say that we should not meet at Emniyet headquarters, as I had imagined.' Noticing Schulz's immediate frown, he continued, 'Oh, they're not trying to put us off. Far from it. The Deputy Head of the whole service would like to meet you in person.'

'But that's excellent, Haller. So, what's the problem?'

'Well, maybe it's not so great a problem, but he wants to meet us at his family's summer villa on Büyükada island. It will take us a couple of hours at least to get there.

Having initially reacted with some irritation to this news, Schulz soon relaxed. His assumption was that the Englishmen, because they had not taken that day's Taurus Express and had clearly checked into a hotel, had no immediate plans to leave Istanbul. Rather, they were awaiting a contact of some kind, probably at the hotel. Moreover, he had left officers in charge of surveillance at the hotel and they knew to keep Blake and Milton in their sights.

Indeed, as soon as he found himself standing on the shaded deck of the ferry, his mood continued to improve as quickly as the pleasant sea breeze replaced the intense heat of the city. Büyükada was the largest of the Princes' Islands, which form an archipelago in the Sea of Marmara, off the coast of Istanbul. Originally a place of exile for Byzantine princes and other royalty, since the nineteenth century the islands had become a popular place for Istanbul's wealthy to build their summer houses.

Büyükada was the last of the islands to be served by the ferry and, as the sturdy white steamer approached its destination, Schulz gazed at the magnificent hilltop villas, nestled among the bright green leaves of the varied trees. Lower down, almost at the water's edge, stood a terrace of older, triple storey buildings. Many of these had balconies which offered a splendid view, both of the sea and of the land-based fishermen who were throwing huge nets into the water.

'I don't think I've ever seen fishing done like that done before,' said Schulz, shaking his head and smiling. 'The sea here must be absolutely teeming with fish.'

At last, they were tied up at the single jetty and, having disembarked, they made their way through the grand ferry building with its impressive cupola. All around, happy people, almost all dressed in fashionable western style clothes, were sitting at pavement cafés, enjoying the warm sunshine. As he gazed, open mouthed, at the glamorous scene, Schulz could easily imagine himself transported back to those happier, more innocent, pre-war days on the Côte d'Azur, where he had holidayed with his wife. At that moment, in this beautiful, romantic location, her absence from his side felt utterly unnatural. Indeed, he felt an almost physical pain of longing for her. Pulling himself reluctantly back to the present, Schulz noticed with surprise that, despite the crowds of people and bustling atmosphere, he could see only horse drawn vehicles waiting to transport the passengers to their various destinations.

'No cars are allowed on the islands, sir,' explained Haller. 'For myself, I must say that this is a big part of their charm.'

After a short wait in the queue, the two Germans climbed into a covered carriage, pulled by two fine looking chestnut horses. Haller instructed the driver to take them to Çankaya Avenue and the passengers made themselves comfortable on well cushioned, wicker sofas which faced one another. Schulz had chosen the forward-facing position and thoroughly enjoyed the cooling breeze as it soothed his skin and raised his spirits. As they moved slowly away from the lively harbour area of the island, with its many guest houses, hotels and cafés, the buildings became much more spaced out. After several minutes' ride, he was able to admire the large, wood framed houses, all with whitewashed verandas and louvred doors. These exclusive villas were invariably set in extensive, wooded grounds which offered a perfect retreat from the fierce strength of the summer sun. After so many days of travel in hot weather, he relished the perfumed air, spreading from the garden walls which were covered in white and purple oleander and bougainvillea. His eyes began to close as the carriage, whispering its way over a thick carpet of pine needles, began to rock like a cradle. He was just beginning to dream of returning to this heavenly place with his beloved wife when Haller coughed and announced, 'Excuse me, sir. We're almost there.'

Schulz blinked and immediately saw that Çankaya Avenue consisted of a series of massive villas, many of which seemed to have smaller guest houses overlooking the turquoise sea of the Anatolian coast. 'The road winds down to a small ferry landing. It's quite a place,' Haller said, almost to himself. Finally, the carriage turned into the shaded driveway of one of the most beautiful villas Schulz had ever seen, before stopping smoothly at a shaded entrance. Fully awake and eager to get to work, Schulz climbed down athletically from the carriage and strode towards the entrance, leaving Haller to instruct the driver. 'Please wait here. We are not sure how long we will be.'

The two Germans were greeted with a low bow by a tall, muscular man, dressed in loose, white cotton clothes and a red fez. They were shown into a cool entrance hall, with a broad staircase, marble floor and, on a sideboard, a bust of Atatürk. A man of middling height, informally dressed, in a well-tailored, cream linen suit and open neck white shirt, walked confidently through an opened set of double doors. Both his arms were outstretched in greeting, 'Welcome to my family home, gentlemen. I am Ender Sakarya and I am very happy to meet you.'

Schulz judged the Turk to be in his early fifties and a man who was used to being in control of a situation. Impressed both by his general appearance and the fact that he spoke excellent German, he answered, 'Thank you very much for agreeing to meet with us Herr Sakarya. I am Captain Schulz and this is my colleague Lieutenant Haller. We are both assigned to the German Military Intelligence Service.'

Sakarya nodded in acknowledgement and smiled warmly, 'Lieutenant Haller, I have heard of. But I have to confess, Captain Schulz, your name has never been mentioned to me.'

'I am only temporarily here in Istanbul, sir,' replied Schulz confidently. 'I am normally based in Bern.'

'Ah! Switzerland!' Sakarya beamed, thereby showing a fine range of gold teeth. 'A splendid country indeed. But you will surely not be interested in my memories of that beautiful place. Please allow my servant, Levent, to look after Lieutenant Haller, while we speak more fully.'

'Of course, Sakarya bey, that will be our pleasure.' The Turk's face creased into a delighted expression at Schulz's use of the correct Turkish form of address. Leaving his servant to offer Haller refreshment elsewhere, the host deftly put his arm around Schulz's back to guide him through the opened double doors. A refreshing breeze was billowing the floor length, thin, cotton curtains as Schulz entered a spacious, bright room, furnished in a sophisticated mixture of modern Western and traditional Turkish styles. Such cocktails frequently clash and contradict one another, but Schulz recognised immediately that great care had been taken to choose items that blended together perfectly. 'What a beautiful room,' Schulz enthused as he turned to survey the entire space.

'Yes, isn't it?' Sekarya agreed with evident satisfaction. 'Although I can claim no credit. It is all the work of my darling wife, Pinar. Are you married, Captain Schulz?'

'Yes, I am. And very happy to be so.'

The Turk nodded and smiled again, as if Schulz had passed some sort of test, before indicating that he should sit on one of two sofas which faced one another. As soon as he was seated, Sekarya reached to the tray which had been placed on the low table between them, saying, 'It is very warm. Perhaps you would care for some refreshing Ayran?'

Schulz had no idea what was in the creamy looking concoction which rose precipitously above the rim of the thick goblets. Sensing the other man's confusion, the host laughed in reassurance, 'I'm sure you will like it. It contains chilled yoghurt, salt and cool water. You have my word that it is a most refreshing beverage. Especially on such a warm, summer afternoon.'

Schulz accepted the goblet with a smile of gratitude and was duly amazed at how much better he felt as the rehydrating drink started to do its vital work.

'Is this your first visit to Turkey?' enquired Sekarya, after delicately wiping his mouth with a crisp cotton napkin.

'It is, sir,' replied Schulz enthusiastically, 'and I must say that I am most impressed.'

This reply also seemed to satisfy Sekarya who went on, 'There is, of course, so much still to do. But we have made great progress. Handcarts and donkeys still far outnumber trains, trams and motor vehicles, but things are improving. Did you know, for example, that it is less than ten years since the Surname Law, which requires everyone to adopt a fixed surname, was passed here?'

Gratified by the evident shock on Schulz's face, the host continued, 'Yes. That suggests we are a pretty backward lot. But on the other hand, women were granted full political rights only fifteen years after your country and we now have female members of parliament. The education of girls and young women is recognised by law as being of equal importance to that of boys and young men.' Sekarya suddenly stopped and smiled bashfully, 'But come, my friend. I have lectured you for too long. I'm sorry that my pride in my country is so obvious.'

'Not at all Sekarya bey,' replied Schulz graciously. 'The more I learn of your country, the more fascinated I become.'

'You are too kind. But now we should take a stroll in the garden. We have much to discuss, if I am not mistaken.'

The two men left the villa by the French windows and emerged onto a wide stone terrace, overlooking a glorious lawn which swept invitingly down to the shade of a grove of cypress trees. Through the foliage, Schulz could see the sun, glinting off the sea and breathed deeply, 'It really is a perfect spot.'

'Yes, we are fortunate indeed. My father fought very bravely at Mustafa Kemel Atatürk's side at the Battle of Sekarya. In fact, he saved the Great Leader's life, during a counter attack on the Greeks. My family took the name

Sekarya in honour of this and the Turkish Republic offered this home to my father in gratitude.'

As they moved towards the tree line, Schulz caught sight of an idyllically placed retreat, perched right on the cliff edge and asked, 'What is that building? It looks exquisite.'

'Indeed, it is, my friend. I can see you have a good eye for such things. This is our guest house. It's a splendid place. It was even rented for a short time by Leon Trotsky.'

Laughing at Schulz's start of surprise, the Turk explained, 'but I'm afraid that my family's relationship with the great revolutionary ended badly. There was a fire which severely damaged the house and threats of legal proceedings on both sides. Suffice to say, the family has never been tempted to offer hospitality to such a celebrity again. Indeed, I hope that your country's new-found friendship with Trotsky's homeland does not end as poorly.' Schulz was no great supporter of the Führer's 'masterstroke' in forging the Non-Aggression Pact with the Soviet Union, but judged it politic to react by simply staring away over the calm waters, towards the Anatolian coast of Turkey. 'A poor joke, my friend,' admitted Sekarya sadly. 'But come, tell me. What is it that you wish to discuss with me?

Ninety minutes later, Schulz and Haller found themselves on the return journey to the ferry to Istanbul. Sekarya had graciously invited Schulz to stay the night. However attractive an idea that was, the German recognised that his mission demanded that he return to the city, as soon as possible.

'Was the visit a success, Captain?' asked Haller, as soon as the carriage had pulled away from the villa.

'Oh yes, Haller. Very much so. I think we will be working quite closely with our friends from the Emniyet.'

Chapter Eighteen

Monday August 5th, 1940, Istanbul.

The hours since their arrival the previous day had really dragged for both Blake and Milton. The former was extremely anxious that, by early Monday afternoon, they were still awaiting news of their contact Nesrin, whereas the latter was railing at having to remain cooped up in the hotel, when there was a fascinating city to be explored. 'We're not here on a bloody sightseeing tour, you know,' Blake spat over breakfast, in response to the suggestion that they could enjoy at least a couple of hours' break from their increasingly smoky and oppressive hotel room.

In the end, they agreed that if Nesrin had not made contact by 3PM, Blake would enquire at the hotel reception about reserving tickets for the next departure of the Taurus Express. 'It leaves tomorrow morning, so we couldn't get going any faster than that, even if our contact turns up right this second,' Milton had reassured him.

Shortly after 2.30PM, there was a gentle knock on the door, which Blake opened to reveal a beautiful, dark haired, brown eyed woman in her twenties. The Englishman gaped in surprise as she said in reasonable English, 'Good afternoon, my name is Nesrin and I am to say, 'mighty anvil' to you.'

Milton pushed past Blake to open the door wider and responded with a smile, 'Then you'd better come in, Miss. We've been expecting you.' The young woman indicated her thoughts on the state of the room by coughing loudly and Milton rushed to open the window. 'I'm very sorry that it's rather foul in here,' he apologised.

'But we have been stuck here for more than a day, waiting for you,' protested Blake.

'Yes, I know and I'm very sorry for that,' the woman replied with a winning smile, as she took off her wide brimmed, straw hat to reveal luxuriant wavy hair. Smoothing her bright floral dress, she sat down on one of the two armchairs. 'But your trick of changing to French passports threw us, I'm afraid. Given the way things are with informers in Istanbul, it was a very good idea, but we weren't expecting it.'

'And we, as sure as night follows day, were not expecting a….' countered Blake.

'Woman as young as I am?' she said, arching her eyebrows and crossing her legs demurely. She had expected a certain initial scepticism from the two Englishmen and was ready with her argument. 'Has no one told you that in today's Turkey, girls are increasingly brought up to see themselves as the equals of boys? Surely it's the same in Great Britain?'

'Well, if it isn't, it dashed well should be,' answered Milton supportively.

'Very well. Point taken,' conceded Blake, his face creasing into a grin. 'I've no problem with you being such a young woman. It was just a bit of a surprise, that's all.'

In response to the immaculate appearance of their visitor, both men busily ran their hands through their hair and tried to make themselves look a little more presentable. Nesrin relaxed at this clear sign that both felt somewhat off balance and her initial doubts about the wisdom of her ability to take on this mission began to dissipate. Smiling warmly at both men, she asked, 'Have you already made any plans of your own to leave Istanbul?'

Milton quickly answered, 'Nothing definite. We were, of course, waiting for you. But we had decided that, if you hadn't shown up by 3PM today, we would reserve tickets for tomorrow's Taurus Express,'

'That's an excellent idea,' confirmed Nesrin empathically. 'In fact, it's good that you didn't do that already, as it would have been a waste of money. You see, we have already reserved tickets for all three of us on the train which leaves Haydarpaşa Station at 9AM tomorrow. We'd better get used to one another, because we'll be together, at least for a couple of days.'

Milton immediately looked doubtful, 'Look here, miss, I've checked the duration of the journey to Cairo. If you are to be with us for only a couple of days, it doesn't sound like you are going with us the whole way.'

Nesrin looked up sharply at the younger and more handsome of the two Englishmen. What he had just said was an important lesson to her. She should not underestimate this man. 'That's right. I'll explain why later.'

'It also seems that the train doesn't run all the way to Cairo. Is that correct?'

'I'm afraid it is. There's a section between Tripoli and Haifa which must be covered by road. However, rather than risk travelling in the bus which is provided by the train company, we have arranged for our own hire car and we'll make the journey independently. This will be easier and less conspicuous, given that you have some extra sacks to be transported. Is my information correct?'

'Yes, it is,' confirmed Milton eagerly, 'they're down in the hotel's store room. The Duty Manager assured us that they would be safe there.'

One immaculately groomed eyebrow raised in doubt as the young woman said, 'Well, let's hope he's right. For my money, it will depend what's in them. What is it, by the way?'

'Oh, it's just ...' Blake started, before Milton cut in and lied, 'engineering samples and simple components. Nothing too exciting. All rather boring, I'm afraid. By the way, will the road journey take long?'

For a couple of seconds, the young woman seemed slightly disturbed by Milton's answer to her question. However, she soon recovered her smile and replied, 'We will arrive in Tripoli early in the morning. We'll have all day to reach Haifa, from where you'll leave for Cairo by rail at 8PM and I'll return to Istanbul.'

'You seem to have thought of everything,' approved Blake. 'So why are you not coming the whole way?'

'Before I explain that,' Nesrin hesitated, as if unsure whether now was the best time to broach what could be a tricky subject, 'I suppose I should tell you that there's one important thing to bear in mind. For the first thirty-six hours of its journey, the Taurus Express shares its route with the Berlin-Baghdad railway. This has been a huge undertaking and was, in fact, opened to an express service less than a month ago. As you can imagine, it's still a novelty and, unfortunately for us, very popular with German officers.'

'You can't be serious,' shouted Blake in alarm. 'You mean we'll be sharing the train with a load of Nazis?'

Nesrin moved quickly to reassure the Englishmen, 'Don't worry. Remember, Turkey is a neutral country, so there should be no danger there. Moreover, the train we will be catching goes on from Aleppo to Tripoli, whereas anyone wanting to go to Baghdad would have to change at Aleppo. So, the Germans will leave our train there.'

'But surely, once we leave Turkey we'll be in the French controlled part of Syria and Lebanon,' interrupted Milton authoritatively. 'Now, that was fine as long as they were our allies. But we all know that's no longer the case. If the French there have sided with Pétain, that could be quite problematic for us.'

'Shit,' muttered Blake in agreement, 'it's looking more and more like one hell of a risk, isn't it?'

'Oh, the latest intelligence we have,' Nesrin responded breezily, 'is that the situation there is somewhat confused. The French are basically in chaos after their rapid defeat. Neither do we have reports of a significant German presence in their Mandate. Besides,' she continued with an enigmatic smile, 'there are precautions we can take to head off the risk.'

'Such as?'

'Firstly, we will all be travelling on German passports. I will take your photographs now and bring the passports with me tomorrow. And we have one final trick to play to keep any inquisitive people off our track.'

Relishing the look of confusion on the faces of both men, the young woman swept her hair back behind her ears before looking directly at Milton with her limpid eyes. 'It has been decided that you will be my husband for the duration of our journey together.'

During her briefing for the assignment, she had agreed that Milton was by far the more important of the two men. He carried the vital documents and was the gunnery expert. Above all, she somehow had to keep close to him. She had asked whether an alternative strategy could be used, but had eventually been convinced of the necessity of playing the part of his wife. 'Don't forget, he's a married man,' she had been reassured, 'and, of course, British. The British are frightened of forward, confident women. So, you know what to do, if you want to establish your position.'

Nesrin tried not to look too complacent as Milton reacted with exactly the degree of discomfort which had been predicted. Shaking his head violently, he stammered, 'Now, look here miss. Would that mean we would ...'

'Have to share a compartment on the train' asked the woman blithely. 'Well, that's what married couples normally do, isn't it?'

The Englishmen responded to this development in totally different ways. The very happily married Milton was horrified at the prospect of any possible intimacy with another woman and protested vigorously.

'I must say, young lady, that I find this arrangement totally unnecessary. We both have perfectly good French passports, on which we can travel. I really don't see the purpose of this subterfuge.'

Blake, whose experience of marriage was altogether less positive, initially felt a surge of resentment against Milton. *Damn it all, the woman's exceptionally good looking and the logical thing would have been to put her together with me.*

Nesrin realised that this was a crucial moment for her to establish her role as a leader and guide and said uncompromisingly, 'I'm afraid that the decision has been made, gentlemen. German nationals are hardly a priority for the Abwehr or the SD, of whom there are many here in Istanbul. Our departure would not, therefore, be the subject of any real interest from that quarter. And, in the unlikely event that it was, we all have the language to fool them. That's another reason why it's best to undertake the road section by car. You can show your British passports at the border with Palestine and I my Turkish one.'

The young woman could see that these arguments were beginning to win the older man round. Her putative husband, however, still seemed troubled and she judged that further persuasion was required. 'Consider this. Anyone interested in you would be looking for two men travelling together. But on the train, we will be a young couple and a single man travelling alone. Even if the Germans are looking for you, we will attract little attention. I have your tickets here. It's too late to change them now, even if I would agree to it. So, you see, the decision is not only correct, it's also final.'

Blake was warming more and more to the arrangement as, for the first time since the mission had started, he would be able to operate on his own. By far his preferred method. *Let the two love birds look after themselves,* he thought happily, *I'll be free to run things, as I want.* 'Well, Fräulein ...er...' Blake began, 'you really seem to have thought of everything.'

'It's Vogel. And it's Frau Maria Vogel,' corrected Nesrin before blowing a kiss towards Milton. 'And this is my dear husband Werner.'

Milton squirmed as Blake laughed and demanded, 'and what's my name? Not Josef Goebbels, I hope.'

'Hardly,' replied a stony faced Nesrin. 'It's Uwe Lehmann and I have here some background information, with which you should familiarise yourselves by tomorrow.' As she handed over two type written sheets to each man, she explained, 'I already know my false identity to the last detail. I hope you will be like that by tomorrow.'

'Understood,' Blake shrugged. 'We get the picture. Now, how long are you staying here and when and where shall we meet in the morning?'

'It's better that you remain here tonight, still in your guise as Frenchmen. But I would caution against leaving the hotel. Please reserve a taxi for tomorrow and pick me up in Taksim Square at 6AM. Tell your driver to approach the square from Tarlabaşi Boulevard, drive around the Attatürk monument and I will be waiting for you there. I will leave here as soon as we are all sure of what we have to do and I have the photographs.'

The young woman stood and smiled warmly at Milton, 'This is as awkward for me, as it is for you. If we behave like professionals, we will get you safely to Cairo and, surely, that is all that matters.'

'Well, I'm not happy, miss, but...' began Milton with a shrug, only to be immediately and angrily cut off.

'From now on it's Maria or, even better, darling. We must start living our parts now. Even minor false moves may be dangerous.'

'Don't worry, Frau Vogel,' confirmed Blake. 'I'll make sure that we both know our lines. There'll be no fluffing from us.'

The woman took a selection of portraits of the two men before replacing her hat and checking her appearance in the mirror. Just before opening the door, she turned and grimaced, 'Now I will leave you to your cigarettes.'

Blake issued a quiet wolf whistle as he watched Nesrin walk confidently out of the hotel, her hips swaying in a most provocative manner. 'I must say, I quite envy you, Milton. Being 'married' to that honey for a couple of days sounds like heaven to me.'

Milton simply grunted and sat down to study the papers left by the Turkish agent. Impatiently, he began to leaf through the type-written sheets of paper, 'My God! Look at the state of this stuff. I can hardly understand it.'

Blake picked up his notes from the side table, on which he had left them. Scratching his chin, he replied with a wry smile, 'Well, it's not the most fluent English I've ever read, I'll grant you that. But hang it, they are Turks and I suppose they've done their best at such short notice.'

'Really? I would have thought that Pym would've arranged for the British to be involved somehow. You know, I'm not really so sure about all this.'

'Oh, come on, man!' scowled Blake. 'They've only had a day or so to put all this together. It looks acceptable to me. And let's face it, we're going to have a much better chance of pulling this off with the protection of German identities and with us being split up in the way she suggests. I must admit, I'd not really considered the problem of the French Mandate at all.'

'You may be right,' grumbled Milton, 'but I'm still not happy. And it isn't just that I have to play footsie with a stranger for two days.'

'And nights, don't forget,' laughed Blake.

'Enough! All right, I don't see we have much choice and you may be right about posing as Jerries. But, whatever she says, let's keep in touch on the train and the first sign of anything suspicious, we bail out and take our chances alone. I've rather come to think that you and I make a decent team. So, is that agreed?'

'Anything you say. Now, let's get to work on these damned identities.'

In anticipation of the very early start the next day, the two men decided to take an early dinner and followed Nesrin's advice to stay in the hotel. Blake reserved a large taxi for 5.45AM the next day and arranged for their mail sacks to be brought from the store room in good time.

There was a certain tension in the air, as they sat, almost alone, in the hotel dining room. Milton reacted irritably to Blake's constant ribbing about the arrangements for the upcoming rail journey. 'For goodness' sake, man. Just put a sock in it, will you. I'm quite happy to hand over the role of Herr Vogel, you know.'

'Relax, old chap. It's just a bit of harmless banter. You know it makes sense. Splitting us up and putting someone as gorgeous as herself between us will surely throw anyone looking for us off our scent.'

Milton had to admit that Blake was right, but he remained somewhat sceptical about the arrangements. Between the starter and main courses, he suddenly stood up and muttered, 'Sorry. Must pay a visit. All that coffee I drank this afternoon, I imagine.' Blake watched him with an amused expression as he made his way towards the hotel reception.

Chapter Nineteen

Tuesday August 6th, 1940, The Taurus Express.

As the taxi drove slowly into Taksim Square, the Attatürk memorial, which looked to Milton like a Turkish Cenotaph, loomed on the right hand side. Blake and Milton were once again amazed at the volume of traffic on the roads and the driver had to take care to avoid unlit, horse drawn carts in the early dawn light. It was just as he had braked hard to avoid such a contraption, which suddenly bolted in front of him, that Milton caught sight of Nesrin. She was waiting on the kerb, with a medium sized suitcase at her feet. Even in the poor light, she was a stunning sight, dressed in a smart, knee length coat and a pretty matching hat, from beneath which her rich, wavy hair flowed. 'Stop here!' he commanded the driver and Blake leapt out of the car to retrieve her case and make room for her in the rear of the car with Milton.

As soon as she had settled in the seat, the taxi became a battleground for the delicate, floral scent of her perfume and the old, stale tobacco smell which had greeted the two Englishmen five minutes earlier. Smiling brightly, she issued instructions to the driver who simply nodded and pulled out, amid horns of protest, into the slowly moving traffic. 'We're going to the pier at Karaköy. There is a private boat waiting there to take us across to Haydarpaşa Station.' It very much impressed the professional in Blake that, in keeping with her cover identity, she spoke German in the taxi and he turned to nod at her, in recognition and appreciation.

As soon they arrived at the quayside, Milton, as always neurotically keeping hold of his brief case, helped his 'wife' into the boat, while Blake paid the taxi driver and organised some men to retrieve the post sacks and other luggage to place in the boat. By this time, dawn had broken to a rather misty morning. Seated in the motor launch, Milton looked wistfully back towards old Constantinople as the boat pulled away from the jetty, causing the city's many minarets to be gradually lost in an opaque grey swirl. As their journey across the Bosphorus progressed, the sun rose higher, causing the fog to disperse and Milton was astonished by the scale and beauty of what he imagined must be Haydarpaşa Station. 'Is that it?' he said in bewilderment. 'But it looks just like a noble château on the River Loire!'

'Yes,' replied Nesrin, smiling proudly, 'that is Haydarpaşa. I'm so glad you think it beautiful.' Blake merely glanced at the grand design, with its two circular towers and long classical frontage, before shaking his head in bafflement. *It's just a bloody station.*

The powerful, German built engine was already standing at the platform, steam hissing from its valves as if it wanted to emphasise that it was ready to begin its mammoth journey across Turkey and onwards into the Middle East. The Taurus Express proper comprised three sleeper carriages, one dining car and a luggage van, but there were also three classes of regular Turkish Railways coaches attached to it. 'These are for people who wish to take shorter journeys to stations between here and Adana,' explained Nesrin in response to Blake's perplexed expression. 'They'll all be decoupled there.'

In scenes reminiscent of their embarkation on the Orient Express in Belgrade, they made their way along the platform between galley hands feverishly taking huge ice blocks and great baskets of fresh fruit on board. 'Herr und Frau Vogel?' enquired an official in very good German, 'it is a pleasure to welcome you on board the Taurus Express. I am your conducteur for the whole journey and I am here to make sure that you have everything you desire. Please, let me show you to your compartment.'

Nesrin linked arms with Milton in the natural gesture of a young wife in love and nestled her head into his shoulder saying, 'Oh, darling. Isn't it wonderful?' Blake felt a temporary surge of irritation as he admired the woman's perfectly shaped legs climbing into the carriage. Part of him railed inwardly that it was Milton, rather than himself, with the Turkish woman draped all over him. He soon recovered his composure, however, as he remembered with a smirk that, essentially, he was now unencumbered by the necessity to consider Milton. *He's her responsibility now.*

'Herr Lehmann?' enquired the conducteur on his return from settling Milton and Nesrin in their compartment. 'Please allow me to show you to your accommodation.' A surge of near panic rushed through Blake as he realised that he may actually have to share a compartment with someone else. *For God's sake,* he fumed silently, *why the hell did I agree to this damn fool charade? I might even have to bunk up with a damned Nazi!* He imagined that the obsequious Turk would be up for a bribe in return for giving him a compartment to himself and was glumly contemplating how much of his remaining money he would have to offer, when the man opened the door to an empty compartment and smiled. 'I am pleased to inform you that the train is not quite full and I have managed to provide you with a compartment to yourself. I trust this will meet with your satisfaction. We are always happy to be of special service to our German guests.'

'Indeed it will, my friend,' beamed Blake, handing over an excellent tip. 'Indeed it will.' Blake was delighted that he could now come and go as he pleased. He had decided that this newly granted freedom would permit him to keep a close eye on his fellow travellers and deal with any problems, should they arise. Having kept his eyes open on boarding, he estimated that there might be more than fifty people travelling on the train and resolved to make a brief assessment of each person he saw.

Bang on time at 9AM, the train eased its way out of Haydarpaşa Station and was soon steaming its way along the coast of the Sea of Marmara. It passed quickly through leafy suburbs and flashed by gorgeous villas, with beautiful gardens which overlooked the water. Milton was idly looking out of the window, contemplating how domestic matters would be organised with Nesrin, when a curve in the track offered him a wonderful view of Istanbul, basking in the morning sunshine on the far side of the glittering water. Moved by its beauty, he spontaneously said, 'Just come and look at this view. It's simply magnificent.'

Nesrin joined him at the window and gasped with pleasure at the grand vista. Just then, the train lurched over some points and she fell into Milton's arms, her unfathomable eyes looking directly into his for several seconds before he released her from his embrace. An unwanted surge of desire pulsed through his body and he turned away from her, embarrassed and more than a little guilty. 'Look,' he blurted out, 'I'm just not sure this is going to work. You see, I'm very happily...'

'Married?' added Nesrin, with an enigmatic smile which showed her perfect white teeth. 'Of course I know that already, Werner. As I said yesterday, we are professionals doing a job that needs to be done. No more. No less. The fact that you are a most attractive man and that you may find me just a little bit desirable should not come into it at all. We are both adults and we must behave as such.'

Milton had never been in such a situation before. His mind was racing in all kinds of directions. He thought, naturally, of Helen and how she was waiting patiently and loyally for him to return to her in Britain. But he also noted with a thrill that this beautiful young woman had described him as 'a most attractive man.' Riddled with contradictory feelings, he smiled shyly and, shaking his head replied, 'Of course you're right. I'm sorry. I'm making a bit of a hash of this aren't I?'

Nesrin laughed, in part to conceal the confusion she was also beginning to feel. She was a fairly experienced agent, who, over the past years and without too much hesitation or regret, had suppressed her own emotional life to such an extent that it barely existed any more. She had actually welcomed and enjoyed his embrace and, even more unaccountably, had told this gentle Englishman that she found him a most attractive man. *What on earth was I thinking?* she demanded of herself. *Was it just a slip of the tongue, to be forgotten as soon as said?* She then tried to convince herself that she was continuing to put the Englishman at a disadvantage by playing the forward female. *Or am I? Could it signify something about myself and my feelings?* Whichever way Nesrin looked at it, this type of inner confusion was not what she had planned or wanted.

Milton looked at her with concern, 'I say Maria, are you feeling unwell? You look rather flushed. Please, sit down and I'll get us both a nice cup of tea.' Determined to regain control of her thoughts, she thanked him and replied flatly, 'Yes, please, Werner, that would be wonderful.

***

Having located Milton's compartment, Blake had spent as long as he reasonably could, hanging around the corridor of their carriage. He had been smoking by an opened window in the hope that he could at least make contact with Milton to reassure himself that all was well. Eventually, the curious looks he was receiving from a middle aged couple forced him to move. They had been returning to their compartment from the dining car, having seen him in the same spot, when they passed him some thirty minutes earlier.

He decided to visit the dining car himself and was directed to a table, from which he could observe the other guests. As Nesrin had suggested, the predominant language was German and many of the passengers were either military or security service personnel, probably on their way to Baghdad. *Perhaps the plan to put a 'wife' between Milton and me wasn't such a bad idea after all,* he pondered as he savoured his coffee and cognac while gazing out of the window as the train turned away from the coast and began to steam through the swampy terrain on the banks of Lake Sabaudya, before it entered the more fertile land of the Sakaria Valley.

***

Milton and Nesrin had planned to use their cover as a recently married couple to spend as much time as possible together in their compartment. Milton's German, although good, was certainly the weakest of the three of them, so it had been decided that he should expose his cover story, only if absolutely necessary. As the morning wore on, and for ironically similar reasons, they both began to see the disadvantage of this strategy - they would be thrown back almost exclusively on their own company. They therefore decided to risk lunch in the dining car as the train made its painstaking way, via a succession of bridges, tunnels and cuttings, up the seven and a half mile ascent of almost one thousand feet, finally to emerge onto the vast Anatolian Plateau.

A navy man, Milton had a reasonable grasp of geography, but he was shocked at the sheer size of Turkey. 'It's a huge country, isn't it, darling?' he smiled as they enjoyed a post meal coffee.

Even though she knew that he was correctly playing his allotted role, Nesrin's heart fluttered at the sound of the endearment from Milton's lips. She sat in silence, trying desperately to comprehend what was happening to her. *Why am I so attracted to him?* she asked herself. *It's true that he's very different from all the young, and some not so young Turkish men who have made approaches to me. How brutishly self confident and unromantic they were! He seems so masculine, but at the same time sensitive and understanding. His wife,* she concluded ruefully, *is definitely a lucky woman.*

Lost in her thoughts, she had barely heard Milton's question and had offered no response. The silence between them eventually caused her to look away from the window to see that he was staring at her. She hastily covered her embarrassment, saying, 'I'm sorry Werner, I feel a headache coming on. Perhaps we could return to our compartment.'

The guests at the adjacent tables smiled in sympathy as the young couple quickly left their table. Just as they reached the dining car door, Milton was startled to hear a deep voice, 'Herr Vogel. A minute, if you please.' Turning, he saw that it was merely the head waiter who wanted to know if he and Madame would still like a table reservation for dinner. 'Of course,' replied Milton, 'I'm sure it's only a slight headache. My wife will be fully recovered by this evening.'

***

'Calling you Maria seems a bit silly to me, now that we are in our compartment,' Milton said, as soon as he had closed the door. 'After all, no one can hear us. I'd rather call you Nesrin. It's a beautiful name. I've heard all Turkish names have meanings. Perhaps you could tell me what your name means.' Her unmistakable flinch surprised him, causing him to hastily reassure her that, 'it was a silly question and you should forget it.'

'No, it's fine,' replied Nesrin with a smile. 'It's Persian and means wild rose. But, really, we should not mix ourselves up by using more than one name.'

'Of course you're right' concluded Milton and busied himself by opening the week old German newspaper he had bought at Hydarpaşa.

'Is all the news bad?' asked Nesrin with a sympathetic frown.

'It's certainly been better. It appears that that upstart Hitler has had the audacity to order Britain to surrender. The man understands nothing of the British people.'

'But surely, your army was defeated and you have no allies. I fear for your country.'

'Britain's not finished. Not by a long chalk,' replied Milton with perhaps more confidence than he really felt. 'But that's why I've got to get back there as soon as possible. You know, I really do appreciate your help.'

Nesrin turned away at the sight of his earnest face and pretended to search for something in her handbag. 'You know, Werner,' she said after producing her nail file, 'I'm so glad that you are not a heavy smoker. That would have been very difficult for me.'

Milton laughed, 'Yes, Herr Lehmann's a bit of a demon with the ciggies. As a sailor, I used to smoke a pipe, but now it's just the odd cigarillo, nothing more.'

'Ah yes, you said you were in the navy. It must be wonderful to go to sea.'

'It certainly has its moments,' agreed Milton, before going on to tell her about some of his adventures and mishaps at sea and some of the salty characters with whom he had served.

***

At 9PM Milton and Nesrin were still seated in the dining car when the train pulled into Ankara station, where it had a scheduled fifteen minute pause. Their dining companions, a pleasant, retired couple from Chicago who were fulfilling a lifetime's dream of visiting the ancient sites of Egypt, had left some minutes earlier and they were enjoying a post dinner coffee with cognac. Suddenly, out of the steam which billowed along the platform, they both caught sight of Blake. He was strolling along the platform, smoking one of his now favourite Turmac cigarettes, of which he had bought a huge supply before leaving Istanbul. Milton immediately excused himself and descended onto the platform, where he casually walked past Blake, before innocently asking him if he had a light for his cigarillo. The two men restricted themselves to a discreet acknowledgement that everything was running smoothly and Milton quickly returned to the dining car. He only realised that he had left his briefcase under his chair at the table when he was climbing aboard the train.

'It's still there, don't worry,' said Nesrin reassuringly. 'I suppose that its contents are quite important.'

Milton did not respond directly, but invited Nesrin to return to their compartment. As soon as the door was closed, he turned to her, 'You mean to say that you don't know what this is all about? You're quite possibly risking your life and you don't know the reason?'

Nesrin shrugged in response, 'Sometimes, in this line of work, it's best not to know too much.'

Milton laughed harshly, 'Now you sound more like our 'friend' Herr Lehmann. That's the sort of stuff he spouts all the time.'

'Whereas you are something of an innocent?'

Milton stared into her dark eyes, 'If you like. I'd rather see myself as just trying to do my duty. But that doesn't mean I forget that I'm a human being. If I ever forgot that, I'd have to ask why I'm bothering to fight this damned war.'

'Sometimes a war has to be fought in ways that none of us really like.'

'Ah well, that's where I part company with you. We must each retain the responsibility for the way we fight our own war. Both as individuals and in our countries. That's one of the big differences between us and the Nazis.' Nesrin nodded thoughtfully, before suggesting that she would like to go to bed. They had already agreed that Milton should enjoy a cigarillo in the corridor and return to their compartment only when she was already in her berth.

As the three of them lay in their respective beds, sleep would not come easily. Milton could not stop worrying that he was increasingly unable to live up to his fine words of earlier in the evening. It was only when his thoughts turned to his wife, safe back in Britain, that an uneasy sleep enveloped him.

Blake lay awake, struggling to rid himself of the feeling that his life was a hollow shell. When he had pleaded with Pym and Dansey to let him return to Britain, he had hoped that, somehow, once he was there he would be able to rebuild his life. Perhaps even become as happy as Milton obviously is. But now that their goal was coming closer with each passing minute on the train, he actually began to fear what would happen once he was back, in what he used to, but could no longer call home.

For her part, Nesrin felt a rising sense of confusion. She had been perhaps naïvely excited at taking on her first, very important mission. But now, she feared that she was becoming increasingly attracted to Milton. Such a development would clearly have potentially far reaching consequences and it took a long time for her finally to subside into a deep, dreamless sleep.

Chapter Twenty

Wednesday and Thursday 7-8th, August, 1940, The Taurus Express.

After a surprisingly restful sleep, Milton awoke to the sound of the steward's knock on the compartment door. 'Good morning, sir. I have your coffee and croissants.' Milton struggled out of his berth and opened the door to receive the tray with mumbled thanks. As he lifted the window blind, he could understand why, over dinner the previous evening, Nesrin had described this section as the most dramatic part of the journey in Turkey. 'We'll pass through Konia while we're asleep,' she had explained, 'and it's there that the German designed and built Baghdad railway really starts. The first hundred and twenty odd miles are uninspiring, but the section from Bulgurlu to Yenice is a wonderful feat of their engineering. You may not like to hear this,' she had teased, 'but I can assure you that it's true. With luck, we'll see it as we wake up tomorrow.''

'Yes, I believe that it's pretty incredible,' Milton had replied, 'but didn't I read somewhere that originally they'd wanted to simply cut through the Taurus mountains with one long tunnel?'

'That's right,' she had answered, impressed at his knowledge and interest. 'But they were in a rush to complete the line, because of the Great War, so they decided to create a series of twelve shorter tunnels, over an eight-mile stretch. Apparently they did this, so they could work at many locations at the same time and speed things up.' Now that he could see what Nesrin had described, he recognised that, if anything, she had undersold the Germans' achievement. He gazed in amazement down into gorges a thousand feet deep, spanned by magnificent, arched bridges and bordered by very steep river banks.

Just as the conducteur came down the corridor to announce that breakfast was being served in the dining car, Nesrin stirred from her slumber. Her hair spread over the pillow in rich dark brown waves as she opened her eyes to Milton, who smiled and offered her a rather cold cup of coffee. 'I'm afraid the steward brought it some time ago,' he laughed as she screwed up her face at the taste of the cold and bitter beverage. 'By the way, you were right about the spectacular passage through the mountains. If you hurry up, we can enjoy what's left of it while we're having our breakfast.'

Milton left her to get dressed and made his way to the dining car. He found Blake lurking in the unstable section between two of the sleeper carriages. 'How's married life,' he smirked. 'A night of pure bliss, no doubt. Though I see you still have sufficient wits about you to keep hold of that briefcase.'

'As a matter of fact,' replied Milton sharply, 'I think Nesrin is doing an excellent job. So, what have you been up to?'

Blake explained that he had spoken to several of the passengers, observed many more and was as certain as he could be that they had not aroused any suspicions. 'Indeed,' he added appreciatively, 'I heard more than one or two old biddies, expressing concern about her sudden departure yesterday with a headache. She's a real pro.' The two men agreed that they should continue to keep their distance from one another, but perhaps meet a couple of times before their arrival in Tripoli, early the next morning. With a curt nod, Blake lurched off down the corridor without a backward glance.

After breakfast, Nesrin and Milton enjoyed a pleasant morning in their compartment. He was very interested in the development of Turkey, especially over the seventeen years since Atatürk's revolution. As a young woman who had grown up during this period, Nesrin was understandably eager to point out the extent of her nation's progress.

'I know it sounds awful,' admitted Milton, 'but I really had Turkey marked as a pretty backward sort of place. It certainly looks like I was wrong.'

Nesrin smiled happily, 'Well, perhaps it's not entirely your fault. After all, your Royal Navy doesn't spend much time near my country.' She continued to be surprised at how easily and spontaneously she could talk with the Englishman about all kinds of things. It was strange how she felt a natural connection with him, even though they had only just met and, in truth, had so little in common. Over a mid-morning cup of fruit tea, served in the compartment, she suddenly said, 'I've been thinking about what you said yesterday. About it being good for me to know what this mission is all about. Maybe it would help.'

Why on earth did I just say that? I must stay in control and not get any closer to him.

'Well, it's not too fanciful to say that what we're doing might be of very great importance to the development of the war,' Milton began. He then went on to explain briefly about the Oerlikon cannon and its potential significance.'

'And are the papers in your briefcase? Is that why you keep it by you all the time?'

'Best I say nothing about that, I think.'

'It must have been very difficult to send your wife back to Britain, while you had to stay in Switzerland,' she prompted wistfully.

'Yes, it was. It was one of the lowest moments of my life. But, with luck, we'll be reunited before the end of the month.'

Nesrin nodded pensively, while he simply sat with his eyes fixed to the floor. In some way, the mention of his wife had had a sobering effect on both of them and, each in their own personal way, locked firmly away what might have passed between them, never to be thought of again.

***

Shortly after midday, the train reached Adana. There, during a twenty- minute halt, the Turkish Railway personnel were replaced by a French crew which would staff the train for the leg of the journey to Aleppo in Syria.

Many of the passengers took the opportunity to leave the train for a breath of air and some exercise. Among them, Blake and Milton ventured briefly outside the station which, for all the world, resembled a desert fort. Its two squat towers, linked by a single storey entrance area, looked exceedingly bleak and uninviting. Moving well away from earshot of anyone, Blake whispered, 'Well, this it, old boy. We're passing into more dangerous territory now.'

'How can you be sure?' asked Milton with concern. 'Have you heard something?'

'You could say that. I was talking over breakfast with an old buffer from America. He travels this route frequently and was certain that the French Army of the Levant will throw in its lot with Vichy.'

'So, until we reach the British Mandate, must we treat ourselves as being in enemy territory again?'

'Not necessarily. From what he says not much has changed just yet. He has been told by the US Embassy in Berlin that, for the time being, the Germans don't want to tread on too many toes. This is especially the case in the French Mandate, where nationalist feelings are still strong among the Arab population. But, nevertheless, we'd be wise to be as careful as possible. So, I suppose it might, after all, be better to consider ourselves in enemy territory.'

'My God, Blake. I'm so sorry. I had hoped the Free French might have exercised some authority here. I know you didn't want to be in that situation again. I never dreamt...'

'It's fine, Milton. I'm on top of things. I just keep telling myself that, masquerading as Krauts, the French will be desperate not to irritate us. I must say, your Frau did a good job getting us those papers.'

'We'll see. Anyway, how long do you think it'll take us to reach Palestine?'

'I think we should discuss this with Nesrin in your compartment. I'll slip along when everybody else is taking afternoon tea.

To Milton's eye, Nesrin had not received the news of the proposed meeting well. Nevertheless, at 4.30PM, when the dining car was full of teapots, sandwiches and cake, Blake knocked sharply, before entering the compartment without waiting for an invitation. Nesrin's eyes flashed with irritation as she looked disdainfully at him, 'I thought we'd agreed no contact until we are safely off the train in Tripoli.'

'You might have said that, my dear,' Blake retorted. 'For myself and Herr Vogel here, I think we need some idea of what lies ahead of us tomorrow.'

Nesrin heaved a bored sigh and explained that a large hire car would be waiting for them near the railway station. They would drive towards Haifa, where they would board a train to Cairo and she would return home to Istanbul.

'We were trying to estimate how long the car journey will take,' explained Milton calmly. 'We know the connecting train leaves Haifa for Cairo at about 8PM, so we want to be sure we have enough time to make it. Otherwise we might be better travelling on the Taurus Express bus connection.'

'That's right,' interrupted Blake. 'I've been told that they hold back the train if the bus is late. They certainly wouldn't do that for us, if we are travelling under our own steam.'

Milton was taken aback by the force of her reaction, 'It was clearly agreed that it would be far safer to travel alone. And I'm absolutely certain that we'll have plenty of time to make the connection.'

'Well,' reasoned a still dubious Blake, 'as far as I can make out, it's about fifty miles from Tripoli to Beirut as the crow flies. By road, it's sure to be further and, given that we have no idea what state the road's in, I imagine it could take us between two and three hours. Perhaps even a little longer. I suppose we'll take a break there. Is that the plan?'

Recognising that, at this stage of the operation, the last thing she wanted was the Englishmen to lose confidence in her, Nesrin forced what she hoped would be a convincing smile. She then produced a battered old road map from her handbag, like a magician producing a white rabbit out of a top hat at a children's party. After opening it out on the bench seat next to her, she replied. 'Yes, it is. And then we'll complete the slightly longer journey to Haifa. That will take about four hours, assuming a modest speed and allowing for any border checks as we enter Palestine.' Pointing at the route on the map with an elegant finger, she concluded, 'As you see gentlemen, we arrive in Tripoli at around 7AM and the connection leaves Haifa at 8PM. So. we'll have over twelve hours to complete a journey that should take only six or seven hours.'

'Very well,' accepted Blake grudgingly. 'I assume we'll travel in the Lebanon under our false German papers, but enter Palestine with our authentic British passports. That would make sense.'

'Exactly,' confirmed Nesrin. 'The Vichy in Lebanon are now, of course, your enemies. It would obviously be better not to give them any chance to arrest you.'

'So, really,' concluded Milton, 'the drive to the border with Palestine may well be the most dangerous part of the whole journey.'

'Yes,' agreed Nesrin. 'But our German papers and cover stories should be more than enough to hoodwink any inquisitive Frenchman.'

As an uneventful day began to draw to a close, Milton sensed an increasing air of excitement and anticipation as he and Nesrin made their way to the dining car for their final evening meal. 'It's because so many passengers will be leaving us at Aleppo,' the waiter explained, in answer to Milton's question about the strange atmosphere. 'We'll be there at 10PM and they must change for Baghdad.'

'So, many of my German countrymen will be leaving the train there?' prompted Milton.

'Some, certainly. A majority even. But some will undoubtedly remain to keep you company to Tripoli.'

I doubt that many of them will be facing the kind of journey we'll have tomorrow, pondered Milton later as he and Nesrin made their way back to their compartment.

***

All the passengers, including Milton, Blake and Nesrin, were up very early the next day as the train steamed into Tripoli, the harbour city situated on the Mediterranean coast of the Lebanon. Milton, as ever carrying his briefcase, had organised a couple of porters dressed in flowing Arabian robes, to take charge of the Swiss postal sacks and he stood, scanning the station concourse for any sign of Nesrin and Blake. The place was bustling with all kinds of activity and he was propositioned numerous times by dark faced men with crafty eyes, who offered all kinds of delights for the effendi, if he 'would just care to follow me.' At last he saw Nesrin pushing her way through the crowd, a piece of paper held tightly in one hand. 'This is the authority to collect the car. They say it is parked at a garage very close to the coach station.'

'It's best that I go alone to collect it,' decided Milton. 'Frau Vogel doing that would seem very odd. I'll get these sacks in the boot and drive straight back to pick you up at the entrance. You find Herr Lehmann. He can't be far away. I imagine he's buying more of his infernal cigarettes. When you've located him, get the rest of our luggage and wait outside for me.'

Milton obtained directions to the coach station from a French policeman, dressed in a light beige uniform but with the normal black kepi. *How strange to regard the fellow as a potential enemy,* he thought as he led the porters down the hot, crowded street. The 'garage', if it could be called that, was little more than a dismal shack with a number of cars, many of dubious vintage, parked haphazardly in front. Milton approached the opened door and peered into the gloom. Eventually, through the dust and flies, he was able to make out an old man in a dingy *galabiya*, enjoying a small cup of treacly coffee in between sucks on his hookah.

'Bonjour, monsieur,' began Milton in his halting French, only to be interrupted impatiently.

'Papers please, monsieur.'

As soon as he had the paper in his hand, the old man scrabbled around on his chaotic desk and eventually found some pince-nez, which gave him a bizarrely studious air. 'Good. Your car is waiting for you.' Milton followed his shuffling gait to a somewhat battered looking Citroen. 'It's a C4 Berline!' the old man enthused, claiming that it would be as reliable as a camel in the desert. As he laughed at his own witticism, Milton saw his remaining, stained teeth and caught an unwelcome flavour of his breath. He decided to leave quickly and asked if the car had sufficient petrol. As far as he could understand, the old man told him that there was some petrol, but that he would be well advised to fill up at the petrol station on the Beirut road.

As he was approaching the car, Milton saw the large coach, which was to transport rail passengers to Haifa, pull into the coach station. Suddenly an idea struck him and he hastily made his way to the driver who was climbing down from his cab.

***

Nesrin was not happy at having to let Milton out of her sight, but she could find no convincing counter argument to his eminently sensible proposal. Indeed, after waiting in vain for ten minutes with a surly porter and two suitcases, she had finally found Blake, as her 'husband' had predicted, stocking up with his favourite brand of Turmac cigarettes at the station kiosk. This delay was definitely not something that she had wanted and she nervously urged Blake to leave the station as soon as possible. 'After all, you were worried about having enough time for the journey.' Blake followed her and the porter out onto the station entrance where, amid the hustle and bustle, they saw a large Citroen approach. It had obviously once been a fine automobile; royal blue up to the window sills and black thereafter. The colours had, however, been badly faded by the sun and, no doubt, by the dust which seemed to be everywhere. Indeed, the air was a not altogether pleasant cocktail, combining a heady aroma of the sea, exhaust fumes and animal and sewage smells. As soon as Milton had parked the car, Blake made for the box-like rear boot, only to be warned off, 'Sorry, old chap. That's already got 'you know what' locked away inside. No room at all for anything else. There's plenty of room on the back seat for all our cases, so hop in and we'll be on our way.'

Blake looked uncertainly at the faded and dented bodywork of the car, only to be berated by Milton. 'True, she wouldn't win a beauty contest, but the old chap let me have a look under the bonnet when we started her up. First time as well. No messing! Anyway, I know a thing or two about engines and this one'll do for me. Runs as sweet as a nut. So, what are you both waiting for?'

Nesrin took her rightful place in the front passenger seat, while Blake squeezed into the rear seat alongside the three cases and Milton's briefcase. She immediately opened her road map and indicated the correct route.

Situated on a u-shaped promontory, jutting out into the Mediterranean Sea and dominated by the ancient Citadel of Raymond Saint-Gilles, the French influence on Tripoli was immediately recognisable. Grand Catholic churches and Basilicas coexisted with a multitude of mosques, their minarets glinting in the already bright summer sun. Low rise, whitewashed buildings huddled beneath much larger and more impressive stone constructions and wide, cedar lined boulevards spread languidly in various directions. Not a few hundred yards distant, however, narrow, teeming alleyways, into which the sun never shone, jostled with one another for space. History seemed to live in the ruins of buildings, which dated to the time of the Crusaders and contributed significantly to the exotic feel of the city.

'Quite a place,' Milton murmured to himself, as he fought to avoid the trams, other motor vehicles, mule drawn omnibuses and countless pedestrians, none of which had any inkling of conventional road sense. After a hectic fifteen minutes, they eventually reached the Beirut road, which hugged the coastline and disappeared into the heat haze in the distance. Having been forbidden by Nesrin to smoke in the car, Blake took the opportunity to wander away from the car and ostentatiously enjoy one of his cigarettes, while Milton and Nesrin lounged in the shade of a nearby tree as an attendant filled up the car. They soon approached the small town of Chekka, where the road became narrower and hugged the rocky coastline. Just as Milton had negotiated a bend in the road, with the sea breaking onto rocks some fifty metres below, and a fearsome looking cliff looming above, he braked hard at the sight of a French policeman. The uniformed official had his hand raised in the universal sign that they should halt .

Sensing Blake's immediate reaction behind him, Milton said confidently, 'Relax. It'll just be a routine check. We'll be fine.'

While his comrade remained in the shade, the Frenchman asked Milton to hand over all the passports. As soon as he saw the Nazi eagle perched atop the garlanded swastika and the ominous words 'Deutsches Reich: *Reisepass*' he made a perfunctory check of the photos and handed them back to Milton.

'Where are you going and why is this man travelling with you?' the Frenchman asked, with no great enthusiasm. It was clear that he was irritated at being the one standing in the burning sun and kept throwing envious glances towards the other policeman who was lounging in the cool shade of a nearby tree.

'My wife and I met him on the Taurus Express. We got on and so we offered him a lift to Beirut as we're all going there,' replied Milton in a rather broken French

'Eh bien!' the officer saluted vaguely, 'Then I wish you a safe journey, messieurs, madame.'

Milton had just put the car into gear and was about to move off, when the policeman turned, as if something had suddenly struck him. Rubbing his chin, he remarked, 'It's very odd that you have your suitcases on the rear seat when the Citroen Berline has a wonderful boot. What's back there, if all your suitcases are here? Maybe you should open it for me.'

Milton felt a surge of panic, while Blake began to feel at his feet for his revolver. Before he could take what might well have been disastrous action, Nesrin smiled coquettishly and said in charmingly halting French, 'Oh, officer, my husband did not tell you that we are on our honeymoon.' Fluttering her eyes delightfully, she complained, 'surely you would not expect me to travel with just one suitcase?'

The Frenchman grinned and winked conspiratorially at Nesrin, 'Of course not madame. I understand. Goodbye and have a safe journey.'

Once through Chekka, the landward side of the road gave out to huge, dusty fields, occupied by Arab peasants working in the same way as they did at the time of Jesus Christ. Milton had to stop frequently, while a herd of goats, or some wayward camel was brought back under control. It was during one of these halts that Nesrin, complaining of a headache, asked Blake if she could sit in the rear of the car. The Englishman surreptitiously slid his revolver into the glove compartment as Milton got them underway again. They had been on the road for a little over two hours and had just passed through the delightful, ancient site of Byblos when, in the distance, Milton thought he could see an obstruction of some kind. 'Good grief, not another Froggie checkpoint,' he muttered to himself as he began to slow down. The road was deserted in both directions, apart from a sole car which appeared to have suffered a breakdown. A man in a pale cream suit was waving his straw hat in a desperate bid to ask for help.

'Poor buggers,' sympathised Milton, 'I suppose we should stop and see if we can help.'

'We'll do no such bloody thing! It's far too risky!' exploded Blake. His voice changed almost immediately as he said, 'Wait a minute…. I think I recognise that chap trying to flag you down. Yes, I'm damned sure I know the bastard. Put your foot down and let's get out of here fast.'

The faint click behind them was unmistakable, as was an altogether hostile steeliness in Nesrin's voice. 'That's not a good idea, Mr Blake, as I have a loaded revolver pointed at Mr Milton's head. I can assure you that I am a good shot.' Seeing Blake reach for the glove compartment she added, 'and you're wasting your time with that. I unloaded it back at the petrol station while you were both distracted. Just be sensible and pull over please, Mr Milton. I hope you believe me, when I say that I would be very unhappy to see you both shot dead.'

Chapter Twenty One

Thursday August 8th, 1940, South of Byblos, Lebanon.

The smile on Schulz's face concealed a cocktail of emotions which whirled around his mind. Pleasure at having finally run his quarry to earth was certainly present, but there were also more muted feelings. Relief, exhaustion and, in a way that he couldn't quite fathom, perhaps even a hint of sadness. 'Guten Morgen, meine Herren!' he greeted them with an ironic smile. 'Or, perhaps it would be more accurate to say good morning, Mr Milton and Mr Blake. It is indeed a pleasure to renew our brief acquaintance.'

Blake flinched at the mention of his real name. *How long has the German known of my existence? Has he just been playing with us, like a cat with a mouse, awaiting the perfect moment to strike? And what about the woman? How could I have allowed myself to be so totally taken in?*

The two Englishmen had been forced out of the stationary car at the point of Nesrin's gun and were now covered by two further armed men. They had been stopped just off a wide curve in the road, from one side of which the land rolled down gradually to the sea. To the landward side lay a series of low sand dunes, partially covered by tufts of thick, desert grass. These served to block the breeze, causing the heat to be overpowering. There was little sign of agriculture and Blake had to admit that they had chosen an excellent place for the ambush. He had counted three men, all in civilian suits. Schulz, he had already identified and, from their general appearance, he judged the others to be German officers of some kind. He couldn't be certain, but he instinctively felt that there was a fourth man sitting in the car. Given that he and Milton were unarmed and, especially with the damned Turkish woman's betrayal, they were clearly outnumbered. *Overpowering them is out if the question. The priority has to be to stay alive, maybe by keeping Schulz talking, and to be prepared for any chance to turn the tables on him.*

'I'm sorry,' answered Milton, squinting into the sun and unable to see Schulz's face clearly. 'But I fear you have the advantage of me. Have we met before?'

'Our paths crossed once at the machine tool factory at Oerlikon. It was only a second. Perhaps you do not remember.' Just as he finished speaking, the beating sun disappeared, somewhat improbably, behind a lone cloud. Milton was able to make out the German's features as he dabbed away perspiration with a damp handkerchief.

'Ah yes. Now that I can see you, I most certainly do recognise you. You will forgive me, if I do not share your happiness at our re-acquaintance.'

'You were following Milton. But we gave you the slip in Zürich. How the hell did you find us again?' demanded Blake, his face working as he struggled to find a solution to this conundrum. 'Even we didn't know where we were going!' He then loosened his tie and ran his finger round his gritty collar before clicking his fingers and answering his own question. 'It was that stupid arse at the airport in

Switzerland, wasn't it? Blabbing on, just as we were about to get on the plane. Some bastard there sold us out for thirty pieces of silver.'

'Believe me, my friends, you made it very difficult to find you,' replied Schulz, almost kindly. 'And, yes, I have to acknowledge that you had great misfortune at Lugano. But first, please tell me, why on earth did you choose this route back to Britain? Surely to aim for Spain would have been far easier?'

Blake was reassured by the approach adopted by the German. Had he been one of those fanatical Nazi swine, he and Milton would have been dead already. *Maybe there's still a slight hope that we can at least escape with our lives.* Wiping his brow very obviously, Blake chose to reply obliquely, 'Look here, it's very hot here. Do you think we could have a drink of water?'

'Of course,' smiled Schulz and indicated that Nesrin should offer them a water canteen. The woman was unable to return the looks of disappointment, betrayal and, from Blake, even hatred as she offered water to the prisoners.

'Thank you,' replied Blake, civilly. He was determined to try to dominate the conversation and explained with candour, 'We damned well nearly made it, you know. We were probably less than an hour too late to get across the Rhône at Valence. The bloody German army turned up, just as we were reconnoitring the bridge.'

'Bad timing again, gentlemen,' murmured Schulz, with a sympathetic shake of the head.

'And what about you?' Milton asked Nesrin sadly. 'Did you do it all for the money as well? You played a fine role, I must say. Fooled both of us, that's for sure.' The eyes of the young woman glistened with unshed tears as she stood to one side, unable or unwilling to defend herself and clutching Milton's briefcase tightly.

'There you are wrong, Herr Milton,' interrupted Schulz. 'Fräulein Benli is a loyal officer of the Emniyet. Like all of us, she has merely been carrying out her duty.'

Blake looked at her sharply, 'What happened to our real contact? He or she was expendable, I presume?'

Nesrin looked away uncomfortably, again leaving Schulz to answer. 'She is quite safe. I have an undertaking from the Turks that she will not be harmed. Imprisoned, perhaps. That is, after all, up to them. But she will not be harmed. We are not barbarians, Herr Blake.'

After the initial shock of the ambush, Milton had begun to focus on the approach being adopted by Blake. *Why is he being so bloody pleasant to the Hun? Why's he not railing and screaming at him.?* It then dawned on him that, perhaps, Blake had reasoned that their best chance of escape lay in keeping the German talking. He remembered a conversation that the two of them had had, whilst waiting at the flat in Winterthur. When asked about the weaknesses of the Germans, one of the characteristics that Blake had identified was that 'their mentality cannot resist boasting about its own superiority.' Perhaps he was trying to prolong the conversation for so long that a passing vehicle may be alerted to the situation and offer some slim opportunity for them to escape. *Righto,* he concluded, *if that's your plan, boss, I can play along as well.* Trying to support Blake's strategy, Milton asked with as much sincerity as he could muster. 'I understand how you got onto our track, but how on earth did you manage to get ahead of us?'

Schulz merely smiled, like a teacher leading a student through a challenging exercise. 'While I am perfectly happy to explain this to you, gentlemen, please do not hope that by delaying me, you will perhaps be able to summon help from a passing vehicle.' Milton flashed an irritated glance at Blake as the German continued, 'You remember that nice French policeman who stopped you a little while back? Well, he notified us by radio of your imminent arrival, so we could set up this dramatic little scene. He and another colleague, to the south of where we are now, are kindly holding back all traffic until notified by us that our business here is concluded. You see, gentlemen, you British are very much the outsiders here. This has been a cooperative operation of German, French and Turkish allies.' Schulz seemed to tire of the conversation, which was taking place in the full glare of the baking sun, and indicated to Nesrin that she should pass him the briefcase. 'But I'm sure that you will both agree that we should not delay the public from engaging in its lawful activity any longer than necessary. I imagine all the relevant documents are in this case, are they not? I believe that it has not left your side since you left Switzerland, Herr Milton?'

Milton tried to make a rush for the German, only to be struck on the side of the head by one of the armed men.

Nesrin screamed and Blake immediately tried to reach Milton's side, only to be held back by the other German.

'The Englishmen were not to be mistreated,' screeched Nesrin as she knelt by the side of the groaning Milton. 'You gave your word.'

Inwardly cursing at the ill luck which had injured Held and Ackert in a car accident on Istanbul's treacherous roads and caused him to have to rely on SD officers to support this operation, Schulz reacted as if he, himself, had been struck. Furiously, he rounded on the two Germans, 'I told you there was to be no violence! My orders are to intercept the documents and any relevant materiel. Whatever you do in the SD, you are now under my command and you will restrain yourselves and conduct yourselves as soldiers of the Reich.' The armed men sullenly backed away, leaving Schulz to speak to the injured Englishman, 'I am very sorry, Herr Milton. I have no wish to harm you. Fräulein Benli, there is a first aid kit in our vehicle. Please do your best for him.' While Nesrin carefully tended to Milton's head wound, Schulz asked Blake for the key to the case.

'I'm afraid we don't have it,' he smilingly replied. 'It's normal practice to lock the case and throw away the key. Avoids all kinds of problems, you see.'

'I would advise you most strongly not to overplay your hand,' Schulz said softly, but with great menace. 'Do not provoke me with such childish replies. Now, where is the key?'

Blake simply smiled at Schulz and, fearing another, perhaps more violent attack, Nesrin raised her head to Schulz. 'Milton keeps it taped underneath his left arm.' Wincing at the nature of Blake's renewed look of betrayal, she added bitterly, 'As his 'wife', he has few secrets from me.'

Milton had not yet fully regained consciousness and the key was easily retrieved from its hiding place. Schulz greedily opened the case and quickly scanned the first few pages of the documents, nodding his head and smiling with satisfaction. 'Excellent. Everything seems to be in order. Thank you, gentlemen. I do not think I will need to detain you much longer.' Having replaced the papers, he turned his attention to the boot of the car. 'And now, I fear that I must confiscate the gifts you received from the Swiss. I'm sure that the German armed forces will put them to good use.'

As a visibly weakened Milton tried to struggle to his feet, Blake placed himself between the car and Schulz. 'You'll have to kill me before you open this boot.'

The German merely pushed him aside and into the firm grip of the armed officers, saying. 'Please, Herr Blake, no pointless heroics. I have no desire to hurt either of you. You have run a good race, but you have lost. Please try to calm down and you will soon be on your way to Cairo.' As soon as he opened the boot, the smile disappeared from Schulz's face, to be replaced by a look of incomprehension. Slamming the roof of the car with his hand, he turned and demanded, 'Where are the postal sacks? What have you done with them?'

Blake wrenched himself away from his captors and gaped in confusion at the empty boot. 'What do you mean? I don't understand.' Turning to the still groggy Milton, he shouted, 'What the hell's going on here, you bloody fool? What've you done with them?'

Milton's eyes registered shock as he looked over Blake's shoulder. 'But that's not possible. How can this have happened?' he moaned softly.

Leaving the Englishmen to glower at one another, the German turned threateningly to Nesrin. 'You! How do you account for this? You were with these men the whole time?'

The colour had drained from the woman's face and she struggled to retain her composure, 'Of course. Yes. No. Let me think. Milton went to collect the car while Blake and I retrieved the luggage.'

'And the sacks? Where were the damned sacks?'

'Milton took them with a couple of porters.'

'And did you actually see them in the boot?'

Nesrin could not face another look of betrayal from Milton and swiftly decided to say. 'I'm not sure. That's to say I think so.'

A furious Blake had, by this time, noted the pleading look discreetly cast in his direction by Milton and quickly added, 'Of course we both saw them in the boot. That's why I had to sit in the back with all our other bags. You must remember?'

'That's right, I remember distinctly now. That's what happened,' confirmed Nesrin. 'But what could have happened to them?'

'Those blasted Arabs, when we stopped to fill up the car on the outskirts of Tripoli,' cursed Milton. 'They must have got them out while we were all distracted. You remember there were lots of them milling all around the car?'

'Christ,' muttered Blake glumly. 'We've made a right royal cock up of this mission. The Jerries get the papers, the Arabs get the materiel and we get bugger all.'

Schulz fixed Nesrin with a piercing look and demanded, 'Is this possible? Could it have happened as he says?'

Without blinking, she replied firmly, 'I'm afraid it could, yes. It's the only possible explanation.'

'Very well,' Schulz accepted, though the doubtful glint in his eyes was unmistakable. 'It's regrettable, but we can call into the petrol station on our way back to Tripoli. With luck, we'll be able to track down the sacks. But, if we cannot, we at least have the main prize here in this case. And we do know that the materiel won't be finding its way to the British.'

The older of the two SD officers approached Schulz and saluted, 'With respect, sir. Would it not be better to eliminate the British spies? We could easily make it look as if they had an unfortunate accident?'

Nesrin's heart accelerated sharply as she awaited the German's response. 'This is an Abwehr operation and will be conducted according to the highest standards of the German army. We will ensure that they have no weapons in their vehicle and then we will be on our way.'

Nesrin asked Milton to sit on the ground while she checked the dressing on his head. As she leaned over him, hiding her face from the others, she mouthed a silent 'I'm so sorry.' He saw the tears in her eyes and responded with a wistful smile and a nod of his bandaged head.

'Good luck, gentlemen,' wished Schulz as he climbed into the large vehicle. 'I do hope that you finally reach Cairo.'

Milton stared at the desolate expression on Nesrin's face as the car swept down the road back towards Tripoli. 'Why do you suppose she lied for us?' he asked quietly. 'After all, she betrayed me about the case key.'

'Oh, come on man,' replied Blake, clapping him on the back with surprising joviality. 'She was terrified that the Hun would have beaten up her darling hubby even more. She was sweet on you, old son. No question. And never mind her, what did you do with the blasted sacks? I thought I caught a sign from you about them. But I've no idea what you meant.'

'Oh, I can't really explain,' murmured Milton. 'There was just a nagging doubt in my mind about us travelling independently. So, at the last minute I decided to take some of our eggs out of this basket and send them with the coach service of the railway company. They're addressed to Professor Bernard Pym, care of the British Legation in Haifa. I couldn't think of anyone else to name as the recipient. I'm sorry, Blake, I just didn't have the time to tell you.'

'Well, matey,' beamed Blake, 'it was bloody clever of you, well done.'

'Clever?' shouted Milton. 'It wasn't so damned clever to stand here while the German took the papers. They were the important thing, after all. I just can't understand why you're so infernally happy.'

'Come on. Let's get out of here. And then I've got something to tell you,' replied Blake with a cheerful guffaw as he led Milton back towards their car.

Chapter Twenty Two

Thursday August 8th, The Lebanon.

As they drove back towards Tripoli as quickly as safety permitted on the patchy desert road, the mood in the Germans' car was decidedly mixed. Schulz sat back in some satisfaction, the vitally important brief case clutched tightly under his arm. *But I'm disappointed,* he mulled, *that I couldn't put the icing on the cake by intercepting those damned sacks of equipment. That would have rounded things off perfectly. And I must admit that I was far from convinced by the woman's endorsement of the Englishmen's explanation of what happened to them. In fact I'm sure there was something going on between her and Milton. But at least I know the sacks are not in their car and therefore, not in the possession of the enemy. And I've fulfilled the key purpose of the mission by seizing the franchise documentation and technical information on the Oerlikon cannon. Without these, the British cannot possibly begin production of the weapon.* As he glanced up at the rear-view mirror, he caught sight of the driver's eyes, looking directly at him. They shifted away sharply, but were unmistakably hostile. During and after the invasions of Czechoslovakia and Poland, he had witnessed the extremes, to which the more politically motivated sections of the armed forces were eager to go. Like many in the Abwehr, he found such atrocities contrary to the correct rules of war. *Very well,* he resolved, *if these two SD oafs think that they can show such obvious indiscipline, it will go badly for them as soon as we return to Istanbul. I'll see to it that they are both disciplined.*

The SD officers Schmidt and Draxler, the first driving and the other sitting in the rear, between Schulz and the woman, were still seething with frustration. They burned with resentment that their request to eliminate the British had been frustrated by such a 'gentleman soldier.' When they were 'loaned' to the Abwehr, however, they had been given very explicit orders. If Schulz managed to achieve his objective, then they should defer to his authority. But if he should fail, or it should seem that there was a good risk of failure, then they should take over, by force if necessary. They had been chosen deliberately by their commanding officer as two of his most experienced, battle hardened and committed men. His message had been clear, 'If Schulz makes a mess of it, eliminate anyone and everyone who gets in the way of getting the papers.' *Well,* they reasoned simultaneously, *the one-armed officer presents no problem and we can easily take Schulz by surprise.* Both men continued to stare ahead, stony faced and determined to await any chance of enjoying a sweet revenge.

Nesrin had become increasingly unhappy about her role in the mission, especially since she had fully understood what the Englishmen were trying to achieve. *I just don't see,* she worried, *how their success could possibly damage the interests of Turkey. And I despise the kind of 'gentlemen's deal' which led to my involvement. It's simply unworthy and demeaning.* Miserably, she tried to avoid any physical contact with the brutish SD man by pushing herself further and further into the corner of the car. The cracked and well used leather seating was far from comfortable as she squeezed herself harder against the door and wheel arch. Now that it was all over, she could admit to herself that she had grown to like Milton. *He was gentle, considerate and amusing and fiercely loyal to his wife, unlike most Turkish men I've met. Even Blake, for all his asocial tendencies and strange shifts of mood, grew on me in the end. I hated betraying Milton's hiding place for the key, but it probably saved him from a harsher beating. I just couldn't have borne that. The Captain and the one with only one arm seem to be decent and civilised people, not like the other two absolute brutes. And in any case, the Germans would undoubtedly have searched him and found it easily.* Resenting more and more the success of her part in the mission, she stared out at the passing countryside, desperate to return home to Istanbul. *At least,* she finally consoled herself, *the Englishmen survived and I did help them to keep the sacks away from the Germans. Milton even acknowledged that with that look. But I do wonder where on earth they might be.*

They had been driving for around thirty minutes when Haller twisted to look towards the rear seat, 'I have some interest in technical drawings, sir. I'm certainly no expert, but I'd be very interested in having a look at the documents in the briefcase.' Schulz saw no reason to deny the request and handed the case over Haller's shoulder. It took the one-armed man a little time to extract all the papers, but as soon as he had them out on his lap, he began leafing carefully through them. 'Ah,' he said with real pleasure,' that's got rid of all the legal mumbo jumbo. Now let's have a look at the technical stuff.' Within a few minutes, it seemed to Schulz that Haller had some concerns. The feverish way in which he kept checking the documentation, shuffling backwards and forwards, mopping his now heavily perspiring brow and shifting uncomfortably in his seat, all betrayed his obvious sense of unease.

Eventually Schulz broke the silence, 'What the hell's the matter with you man? You look like you're sitting on an ant hill, you're so twitchy.'

'There's something a bit odd about this stuff, sir,' Haller croaked. 'Something very strange indeed. Would you mind if we stop for a minute, so we could compare notes on it?'

Schulz noticed the quick glance which passed between Schmidt and Draxler via the rear-view mirror and felt a sudden unease in his stomach. *For God's sake*, he worried, *nothing could have gone wrong, could it?* 'Very well, Haller,' he replied in what he hoped was a confident and decisive tone. 'Let's take a short break. Schmidt, pull over!'

The two SD officers left the car and, having found a little shade underneath a lemon tree, enjoyed a much needed cigarette. Nesrin moved to the front passenger seat and Haller settled himself in the rear beside Schulz. He fidgeted around with the papers for a minute before Schulz barked, 'Come on man! Out with it. Is there some kind of problem?'

'Well, sir,' replied Haller hesitantly, 'these are definitely plans for some kind of artillery gun. But, from what I know of it, they don't look very much like the Oerlikon cannon.'

'What do you mean?'

'For a start, the whole thing looks too heavy. I know the Swiss cannon is light and easily manoeuvrable. And the diameter of the barrel looks a bit too large.'

'Are you saying that the plans are false?'

'That's not the only thing, sir. I'm no legal expert either, but this contract has the right partners, but the text looks standardised. Like it might have been copied from a commercial law textbook.'

'So, what's your opinion?'

'I think someone has put together a very clever and plausible dummy contract and franchise agreement with some equally believable plans. They could easily fool any non-expert.'

'Like me, you mean?' said Schulz bitterly, before turning his attention to Nesrin, who had been listening to the conversation with a mixture of rising alarm and exhilaration.

'You. Tell me. Are you sure he kept the papers in his briefcase?'

Nesrin stared at the German, wide eyed. 'Of course I am! The case never left his side. And I mean never. Blake used to joke about it. There would have been nowhere else that he could have kept them safely. I searched his suitcase several times.'

'Could he have given them to Blake? In return for these dummies? Just to confuse us?'

'Categorically not. He was most insistent. It was his task to carry the papers back to Britain and he took that duty very seriously. He told me that he'd already had to give up an active service career. He'd have never passed that responsibility to another person. And besides, you saw how he reacted back there, when you took the case key from him. He looked like a broken man. Either he's a very good actor, or he believed the papers were in the briefcase.'

'And yet it damned well appears that they're not,' shouted Schulz, as he punched the back of the driver's seat. 'There's nothing for it but to turn around and chase them down before they escape to the British Mandate. Do we have sufficient time?'

***

'You did what?' bellowed an outraged Milton, as he stared out towards the coastline. 'Why, you conniving, cheating bastard.'

Blake had expected some hostility, when he revealed that the genuine franchise and plan documents had been in the false bottom of his case ever since he had encouraged Milton to leave the Orient Express for a few minutes in Sofia. *But this is just plain hysteria*, he moaned to himself. *Damn it all, I actually prevented the bloody papers falling into the Germans' hands.* 'Now, come on, old chap,' he tried to reason as he approached a furious Milton from behind. 'After all, we still have the papers and, as one of our famous countrymen once said, all's well that ends well.'

This attempt at humour seemed to enrage Milton even further. 'You had it planned from the start, didn't you? Was Pym in on it too? You'd have dropped me like a hot brick, had the occasion presented itself. You, you...' Just as Blake touched Milton on the shoulder in a vain attempt to pacify him, he turned round and punched the unsuspecting agent full on the nose. Blood poured all over Blake's shirt and jacket.

'You damn fool!' hissed Blake through his bloodied fingers, with which he was trying to stem the flow. 'We're not operating in a school playground, y'know. Did that knock on the head from the Jerry cause you to lose all common sense? You think you can stand on your honour out here? You think anyone gives a shit what happens to you or me, providing the papers get back home? Just count yourself bloody lucky that the German in charge seemed a decent sort. The other two would have shot us out of hand.'

Milton seemed wholly unconcerned by the other man's arguments and was shaping up to hit him again. The pent-up anger of his compulsory demobilisation from the Navy and now, his belief that, at last, he was actually doing something important for Britain was being snatched away from him. All his fury concentrated into one clenched fist which he drew back.

Fearing the worst, Blake said quietly, 'And what about you with the sacks? You did what you thought was best and how did I react? I bloody well congratulated you! I didn't all but break your blasted nose.'

Milton held back his second punch at the last moment and sank to the dusty ground with an anguished groan. 'God, what a prize fool I am.'

Blake went to pat him on the back, but seeing his bloodied hands, withdrew them and said softly, 'No you're not. You're just behaving as any decent man would. Now, let me get myself changed and try to stop this nosebleed. You get in the passenger seat. The Jerries aren't total idiots and those false papers aren't that brilliant. It might not take them long, before they realise they've been had. And then they're sure to be on our tail. And I don't think they'd be so honourable, if they catch us again.'

Aware that he was withholding one final secret, Milton felt even more wretched at the generous tone of Blake's response.

***

As soon as they heard Schulz's urgent call for them to return to the car, Schmidt and Draxler hurriedly stamped out their cigarettes. 'Something seems not quite right with some of the papers. We need to find the Englishmen again. They have more than half an hour start on us, so, let's step on it.'

The two SD men exchanged a meaningful look as Schmidt climbed behind the wheel of the car and Draxler got into the rear, alongside Haller and Schulz. Haller quickly estimated that they had nearly fifty kilometres to Beirut and then a further hundred or so to the border with British Palestine. 'From what I could see of their sedan, our vehicle is better suited to this kind of terrain and road. So, if we have luck and guess correctly that they will stay on the coast road, I think we still have a chance to catch up with them.'

'Was your plan to travel by the coastal route?' Schulz asked Nesrin sharply, his eyes indicating an increasing degree of scepticism about her loyalty.

The Emniyet agent had no desire to help the Germans further and paused, as if trying to recall the details of some past conversations. In reality, she was desperately trying to think of something plausible that would put them off the scent. 'Now that I think about it, we did talk about taking an inland route from Tyre towards Dibbin and then crossing the border at Metula. They thought there might be less chance of running into the French military than on the coast road to Haifa. Perhaps they'll take that route.'

Over the past days, Schulz had come to have a high regard for the judgement of Haller and asked his opinion. 'Well, sir, of course whatever we do is something of a gamble. But I really cannot believe that, with a car such as they have, the British would risk crossing that difficult terrain. They'll obviously think that their ruse with the false documents will have given them sufficient head start to go for the faster, coastal route. I believe we should go that way. We could also ask any French police we encounter, if they have seen Milton and Blake. That would help us to judge whether and where we might intercept them.'

'Good idea. Haller. Draxler, keep your eyes open for any passing gendarme.'

Very well, the SD officer thought, *you might think you're in charge for now. But if we find those spies again, things will be very different.*

***

After a quick roadside change of shirt and rinse of his face and hands, unavoidably using some of their precious water, Blake climbed into the driver's seat alongside Milton. The blow had evidently not broken his nose and he had managed to stem the bleed by tearing strips off his handkerchief and stuffing them up his nostrils. Milton's head wound had been well patched up by Nesrin, though he was still suffering from a headache. 'By God,' mumbled Blake, 'we look a splendid pair, you and I. Still, we only lost a few minutes with our little bust up. Next stop Beirut.'

'I think it's just under thirty kilometres to the city,' said Milton. 'Maybe we could get some more water and petrol there, if necessary.'

'I imagine we'll run into more traffic as we hit the outskirts,' Blake said, as he put the car into gear and moved off towards Beirut. 'So, we should make as much progress as we can on these quiet stretches. You get your head down and I'll wake you when we're approaching the city.

As he drove further south, the glinting Mediterranean continued to beckon on the right side, while to his left, he was surprised by the increasing quantity of land under cultivation. In the more fertile sections, fields of cereal crops alternated with land given over to fruit orchards and huge vegetable gardens. As a consequence of this land usage, he frequently met mule drawn vehicles, being driven by traditionally clad Arabs and loaded to the brim and beyond with produce for the cities and towns. About half way to Beirut, he began to feel desperately thirsty. While Milton gently snored next to him, he stopped and bartered five of his beloved cigarettes for half a dozen of the juiciest oranges he had ever seen. As the Arab pocketed his payment, Blake was treated to a view of the Arab's gleaming white teeth, which suggested that he had been hugely overcharged. However, once he had peeled the first orange, he was able to get under way again and refresh himself with each successive succulent segment. Swaying camels, stoically carrying people and goods, were a common sight on the edges of the road, preferring as they no doubt did, the more natural feel of the earth under their hooves. Unexpectedly, the sheer exhilaration of driving in such exotic surroundings enabled Blake temporarily to escape from the threat of their current situation every bit as successfully as his sleeping comrade.

It was now some time since he had seen the last, ancient looking goatherd, crook in hand, directing his assorted animals. Without really being aware of it taking place, the agricultural land, at least near the road, had increasingly given way to housing. Initially, this was rough and ready, traditional, low rise buildings which probably housed animals as well as people. Gradually, and to Blake's relief, the quality of the road had improved, but countering that, the volume of traffic had significantly increased. This resulted in progress being easier, but infuriatingly slower and he began to wonder whether the Germans might be in with a chance of catching them up.

He passed a huge shanty town sprawling between the road and the sea. The random mixture of tents, wooden shacks and ramshackle buildings, put together using waste construction materials, was clearly home to hordes of ragged children, accompanied by packs of feral looking dogs. These amused themselves by dodging in and out of the traffic as it made its way towards the city centre. Finally, the wretched housing of the poor and the city's refugees petered out and Blake had an unobstructed view towards the ninety degree turn in the coastline. He could now see clearly the peninsula, on which stood the capital of the Lebanon and, further inland, two hills, onto which the city had spread in the previous decades.

As he approached the peninsula to his right, he decided that it would be unwise to attempt to take the shortest route across its neck. This, he reasoned, could involve trying to find his way through a dense maze of crowded, narrow streets. His plan was to stick to the coast, a route which was longer, but which would minimise the chances of getting lost and thereby wasting more precious time. Beirut harbour gave shelter to a wide range of sailing craft, both pleasure and trading and including some traditional dhows. Further out to sea several steam freighters wallowed lazily at anchor in the sun. To the left, he passed the grand port building, standing proudly like a classic town hall in some regional city and guarded, he noted, by a detachment of French troops. While the war certainly did seem a long way from here, he was conscious that, as he passed close to the city centre, he had seen a far more significant police and military presence. He was acutely aware that, even so close to success, he would be foolish to rely on the French offering them any consideration. *Best we keep the Frogs in ignorant bliss.*

As he continued to make slow progress because of the heavier traffic, he could see that Beirut itself was a charming coastal city. The architectural influence of the French was very apparent, though with an appealing middle eastern edge. The promenades, along which he was driving, were thronged with people, many looking very much like tourists. *The modern world at war is a damned peculiar place*, he reflected, as he saw many couples and families, seated at pavement cafés, enjoying refreshment and shade from the strong summer sun. Just as he was beginning to think that he would never escape Beirut's clutches, the road became much straighter, quieter and bordered by low rise whitewashed buildings. To his relief, he realised both that he was finally leaving the city behind and that Milton had begun to stir from his sleep. Suddenly, Milton opened his eyes and blinked in the bright sunshine. 'Where the hell...?'

'Relax, Milton. It's me, Blake. We're just leaving Beirut behind. So far, so good as there's been no sign of the Jerries. Glad to see you back in the land of the living.'

Their original plan had been to stop in Beirut for something to eat, before tackling the last part of their journey to the border with Palestine. Sensing this missed opportunity, Milton groaned that he was hungry and thirsty.

'Help yourself to those oranges on the back seat. Never tasted anything like 'em before. By the way, how's the head?'

'Oh, it's much better thanks,' replied Milton as he greedily tore off the peel from an orange and sighed with contentment as he savoured the sweet flavour of the fruit. 'Where on earth did you get these? They're bloody delicious!'

'Nice chap at the roadside. But let's just say that my bargaining skills weren't the best. You'll be glad to know I'm a few cigs down.'

'I thought the car was oddly free of smoke. How long before we reach Beirut?'

'That bash to the head must have scrambled your brain more than I thought. I've just said that we're leaving the city. Probably under a hundred kilometres to the border now.'

Refreshed by his orange, Milton coughed uncertainly, as if he had something to get off his chest. 'Look, Blake, about punching you back there. I was totally out of order and behaved like a spoilt brat. I'm sorry. You were just doing your job and I now realise that it was a damned good job you did.'

Blake shuffled in his seat, as if embarrassed by the comment. 'Forget it. No harm done, eh? Probably that blow from Jerry scrambled you a bit. You can buy me a cold beer as soon as we get to Haifa!'

'You're on! I can taste it already.'

Because the Citroen was fairly old and had a great many kilometres on the clock, Blake was not pushing it too hard. He reasoned that the Germans would be a good distance behind and that the greatest risk of recapture lay in them experiencing a breakdown or accident. *Milton*, he reflected, *did a bloody good job giving the car a once over in Tripoli.* Apart from the odd spell of minor overheating, when it was forced to climb away from sea level, the car had performed better than Blake would have thought possible and certainly carried sufficient petrol to take them across the border into Palestine.

About half way between Tyre and the border between the Lebanon and Palestine, the road left the coast and was increasingly covered with sand. Over time, this had been moulded into a rather rutted surface and the Citroen protested noisily as it bounced along over the uneven track. Suddenly, as if in protest at the indignity of having to negotiate such a surface, rather than the more acceptable one of the Champs Elysées, it lurched off to the side of the road. They had just rounded a broad bend and to their left, low bluffs crowded around them on the landward side. The area here did not appear so fertile and there was no sign either of buildings or people. Worse still, for the last half hour, they had seen only a very occasional truck or car drive carefully by.

'What the hell's happened?' shouted Milton, 'did we hit something?'

'I don't think so. You're the technical chap. You get out and have a shufty. I'll watch the road. They left me my empty pistol. Good job I hid some bullets under the driver's seat. It's not much, but we don't want to risk Jerry catching us here.'

After a brief inspection, Milton shouted to Blake, who was standing guard twenty metres away in the middle of the road and looking back in the direction from which they had just driven. 'It's just a flat tyre. I checked the spare before we left Tripoli. It shouldn't take too long before we'll be on our way again.'

Given the strain of the past few hours, Blake was feeling increasingly queasy, especially as he was standing hatless in the excessive heat of the midday sun. As he stared at the road, it seemed to flicker and dissolve disconcertingly in the haze. Almost too late, he spotted a car approaching them and raised his pistol in preparation to fire.

***

'That's Blake,' shouted Schmidt in triumph as he slowed down and stopped the car some fifty metres away from the British agent. 'We've done it! We've caught the bastards up. Draxler, you jump out and take care of him. There's a rifle in the boot.'

'Now wait a minute,' interrupted Schulz. 'I am the ranking officer here. Draxler, you will obey my orders.'

Schmidt took out his revolver, turned in his seat and pointed it straight at Nesrin's head, 'I think not Captain. My orders were to obey you, if you were successful in getting the documents. You`ve clearly failed, so we'll do it our way this time.'

***

What the hell are they doing? Blake asked himself, as he frantically wiped the sweat from his fevered brow. *It looks like they've stopped Why the hell would they do that? Now he's rummaging in the boot. Maybe they've broken down as well. Christ, it's so infernally hot, I'm not sure I'm seeing things right anymore.* As he squinted into the sun, a single rifle shot pierced the still air and his chest exploded in a shower of blood and tissue. The force of the bullet twisted his body and he slumped, face downwards, onto the ground. The front of his new shirt rapidly darkened as his blood started to flow out of the entry wound and into the surrounding earth. He lay, still as death, on the dusty ground.

'My God, Blake, what was that?' shouted Milton, getting up from his work on the other side of the car. As he wiped the sweat from his eyes with a ringing wet handkerchief he shouted, 'I could have sworn that was a bloody rifle shot.' His eyes finally focused on the body lying in the road, some metres away and it was too late when he noticed an ominous shadow cross his line of vision.

'Indeed it was, mein Herr,' grinned Schmidt as he raised the rifle directly at the Englishman, 'Hands up, if you please.'

'What the hell,' shouted Milton as he fought to understand what had just taken place. 'Where did you come from? Is that Blake? What've you done to him, you bastard? If you've harmed him, I swear I'll...'

'I'm afraid that he's probably beyond your help now. But don't worry, you'll soon be joining him.'

Draxler had forced Schulz to drive the Germans' car to the scene of the shooting and Milton gaped in disbelief as the Abwehr captain, Nesrin and Haller were led from the vehicle at gunpoint. *What the heck's going on?* he wondered, *Certainly looks like Schulz is no longer in command. What does that mean? It just doesn't make sense.*

As soon as she saw Blake, prostrate on the ground, Nesrin's hand covered her mouth to stifle a sob and without thinking, she ran to kneel by his side.

'Never mind him, you fool,' shouted Draxler. 'He's already dead. Or he soon will be.'

Nesrin's face stared with open hostility as she turned to confront the German. 'No, he's not! He's still alive. You must let me help him.'

'You and the cripple can help him, if you like,' replied Schmidt with a contemptuous glance towards Haller. 'But the captain and Milton stay with us. Any funny business and they die.'

Nesrin rushed back to the Germans' vehicle and once again took out the first aid kit. With horror, she recognised immediately that it would be pitifully inadequate to treat a wound of such severity. Nevertheless, with Haller's limited assistance, she turned Blake over onto his back and urged, 'I'm here, Blake. It's Nesrin. You've been hit. But it's not so bad. You're going to be fine. Just do as I say.'

Milton had been moved to the far side of the British car and could not see his fallen friend, but he could hear Nesrin's desperate words and Blake's coughing and gurgling, as streams of blood flowed from his chest and his mouth. Sickened to his core, he resolved to tell the Germans nothing of the whereabouts of the documents.

'Now, mein Herr,' gloated Schmidt, 'you are once again in our hands. But this time, it is the SD which will decide what happens to you. You will soon discover that we are a very different proposition to Captain Schulz. I strongly advise you to make this easy on yourself and tell me where the documents are hidden. If you save us time, it will go easier on you.'

Milton looked him in the eye, spat at his feet and replied, 'Go to hell, you Nazi bastard.'

The blow from the German's Luger caught Milton on the side of his jaw and he reeled back in pain. 'Now, that was not very intelligent. I will ask you one more time, tell me where the papers are.'

Milton simply stared ahead and the German nodded briskly, went over to where Blake was lying and, having pushed away the woman, took his revolver and placed it down onto the open wound. Blake's body convulsed in agony and his attempted shriek of pain was drowned in a gurgle of blood.

'I command you to stop such appalling behaviour, Schmidt,' ordered Schulz as he moved towards the SD officer.

In response, Schmidt raised his gun and shot Schulz in the left arm, 'You are no longer in charge here, Captain. You will do as I command.' In shock, Schulz struggled back to his feet, his right hand attempting to use a handkerchief to staunch the blood from the bullet wound in his arm.

Milton still couldn't make sense of what was happening. *Why did Schmidt shoot Schulz? They're both bloody Germans. Has the world gone completely mad? And whose side is Nesrin on? She led us into this trap, but now she seems to be trying to help as much as she can.* It was all too much and Milton slumped to the floor. As all people must at some point, he had simply reached his limit and could not countenance being responsible for the further torture of his friend. *How strange it is that, after all our ups and downs, I now regard Blake as a firm friend.* 'They're in a false bottom in one of the cases,' he confessed flatly.

At a nod from Schmidt, Schulz struggled to take out the first of the Englishmen's cases, which he put on the ground and opened. He carelessly threw the clothes onto the dusty roadside, before finally looking up to Schmidt and shaking his head grimly. Schmidt responded that Schulz should take out the second case and he once again littered the surrounding area with its contents, before looking sharply up at Schmidt. 'It's here. There's a false bottom. I can tell by looking at the depth of the case.'

It didn't take the wounded Schulz long to pull out the false bottom and extract the files. Just as he raised the papers to show them to Schmidt, the first shots rang out. The side of Schmidt's head disappeared, as the bullet exposed the naked whiteness of his skull and the greyer colour of his lifeless brain. His body twitched and jerked grotesquely as he sank to the ground. Despite his wound, Schulz immediately ran back around the bend in the road, in an effort to escape. He had no idea who the attackers might be, Jewish nationalists or perhaps Arab bands, but his one thought was to keep hold of the documents. *I've got to destroy them. At any cost.*

On hearing more shots, Milton's first reaction was to throw himself onto the dusty roadside. But he quickly remembered that Schulz had the documents. *I've got to find him, but I daren't bloody move until this shooting stops.*

Draxler, cursing loudly, ran behind the Germans' car, using it as cover, in order to return the fire which seemed to be coming from the top of the bluffs above the road.

Nesrin and Haller were both caught out in the open as they tended Blake. Without thinking, the woman lay on top of the Englishman, in an attempt to use her body to shield him from further harm. The German officer tried to move towards Draxler and the cover of the car, but his body was riddled with machine gun fire before he had taken three steps. The fire fight continued for another thirty seconds, before a shot struck the petrol tank of the car, behind which Draxler had taken cover. The resulting explosion and fireball blew the German into the air, before he fell back into the roadway, his lifeless body smoking hideously.

Milton took advantage of the explosion and resultant heavy smoke to escape in the direction Schulz had disappeared. He could see no sign of him, other than a trail of blood which led back around the bend in the road. His mind set firmly on retrieving the documents, he finally caught sight of Schulz, stumbling along the road, some fifty metres away. The German realised that he could not outrun Milton and stopped to try to find his cigarette lighter. *If only that idiot Schmidt hadn't shot me, I'd have destroyed the documents by now,* he railed. He had just pulled out his lighter when Milton brought him down with a flying leap. The wounded Schulz was helpless and unable to fight back effectively and was swiftly subdued.

Breathing hard, the documents safely in his hands, Milton bent double to try to catch his breath. In was then that he sensed, rather than saw the shadow of a man, peering down at him. Milton squinted into the sun and could just about make out the Arab headdress, incongruously combined with worn and dusty khaki shorts and shirt. 'Mr Milton, I presume,' a voice said in a perfect Home Counties accent. 'May I offer you our assistance?'

Chapter Twenty Three

Thursday 8th August, 1940, Near the Lebanon Palestine Border.

'I think we should make every effort to leave here as soon as possible, sir,' the young officer said as he nervously looked up the road towards Tyre. 'Our operations here are, well, a little unofficial and that car exploding like that was rotten luck. It's bound to attract the attention of the French and I'd rather we were well away from here before they turn up. I'm Captain Frobisher, Royal East Kent Regiment, by the way. Pleased to meet you.'

Milton nodded in gratitude as the British officer helped him to his feet, leaving Schulz face down on the ground. 'A handshake can wait until I've checked these,' said Milton with a grin, as he nodded towards the folder of documents which he had taken from the prostrate German. 'Now I have these in my possession again, I'm ready to go. But what of my friend, the wounded man? And what about the woman? Is she unharmed?'

'I'm sorry, sir, I'm not sure what the exact situation is back there. I know that there were some casualties, but I've no idea who was hit.' As he pointed a pistol at Schulz, he asked, 'What do you want us to do with him? One of the Jerries who were giving you such trouble, I presume? Still, he's in civvies, so we could treat him as a spy.'

Milton stopped, turned and fixed Frobisher with a determined expression. 'His name is Captain Schulz and he is a German army officer. While he is our prisoner, I'd be very grateful if you would extend to him the courtesy due to his rank. And get someone to help him with his wound, please.'

Recognising the explicit rebuke, the shamefaced officer replied, 'Of course, sir,' before leading them both back towards the scene of the firefight. The Germans' car was still burning fiercely and Draxler's smoking body lay several feet away, where it had been blown by the explosion. Several British soldiers, dressed in the same odd uniform as their commanding officer, were dragging Schmidt's lifeless body to the side of the road. The oldest of the group, a wizened, little sergeant suggested, 'We could put both bodies into the wreck, sir. It's still burning enough to make identification difficult. It may even temporarily fool the French into thinking it was an accident.'

'Good idea, sergeant. No sense in advertising our role here.'

Milton had no interest in what happened to the SD officers. He was much more concerned to see Nesrin, on her knees, between two seemingly lifeless bodies. Blake lay to one side, a gaping chest wound livid in the sunshine and Haller, lying face up to the far side, his body riddled with bullet holes. Milton crouched down by Nesrin and gently touched her arm, 'Is he alive?' He waited for several seconds for a response, before shaking her gently and repeating. 'Nesrin. It's important. Is Blake still alive?'

Her distraught face turned towards him and she cried, 'I'm not sure... I think he might be....'

'For God's sake, Captain Frobisher,' shouted Milton, 'get your men to leave those bloody Germans and give what help they can here.'

The sergeant hastily left his comrades to push the bodies of the SD men into the burning wreck, while he ran back to one of their armoured vehicles to retrieve the first aid kit. As soon as the sergeant reappeared, his anxious and tentative manner made it obvious to Milton that he had little idea how to treat such wounds. *Christ! After coming all this way, it finally looks as if there's no hope for Blake.*

'I know something of how to give immediate treatment to this kind of injury,' volunteered Schulz. 'I've seen some action in the past two years and have dealt with a few bullet wounds. Admittedly,' he concluded glumly, 'nothing as bad as this.'

'Look, Mr Milton, I really think...' began Captain Frobisher, only to be cut off by Milton's angry voice. 'I couldn't care a monkey's what you think, Frobisher. If Captain Schulz is willing to help my friend, then we will give him the time to do so.'

Frobisher exchanged an uneasy glance with his sergeant, before conceding grudgingly, 'Very well. You can have ten minutes. Then my men and myself will leave, with or without you.'

Even the most cursory examination of the wound convinced Schulz that there was little he could do for the stricken Blake. 'It looks very, very bad,' he murmured to

Nesrin, 'and because of my own wound, I can't do much myself. But, if you are prepared to follow my instructions, we can clean him up a bit and try at least to stop the bleeding.'

Nesrin's delicate hands carried out Schulz's instructions with surprising skill and Milton acted as her fetcher and carrier. Once the wound had been cleaned and dressed and a shot of morphine administered, Schulz thanked Nesrin and turned to Milton, a resigned look on his face. 'We've done all we can now. It's a very bad one and he is very, very weak. He has lost a great deal of blood and I think that one of his lungs has been damaged. But at least the wound was on the right side. On the left, it would have pierced his heart and he would have been dead instantly. Can we fashion a stretcher for him?'

The sergeant had anticipated this request and had somehow managed to remove a bench seat out of one of the armoured cars. Milton, the sergeant and two privates then carefully lifted Blake and placed him as gently as possible onto the wooden bench. To Milton's despair, his face remained deathly pale, he looked feverish and his breathing was extremely shallow as they loaded him into the rear of the vehicle. The sergeant shook his head gravely at Milton's questioning look, 'You never know, sir. I've seen men survive worse and others succumb to much lesser wounds. It's all about the fight they have inside, if you ask me.'

The casualty having been treated to the best of their ability, Frobisher reassumed command, distributing his soldiers between the two unusual vehicles. To Milton, they looked the same general shape as the front half of a single decker bus, but painted in desert camouflage. The rear half of the vehicle was covered only by framed canvas and a machine gun was fixed to the roof of the cab. Six soldiers were to be in the first vehicle, with Milton, Schulz, Nesrin and Captain Frobisher occupying the second vehicle with Blake and three soldiers. Just as a private came to lead Schulz into the vehicle, he turned in appeal, 'Herr Milton, I have a request for you. Is it possible to take Haller's body with us? He was a good and honourable officer and does not deserve to be left as food for the desert wolves.'

In response to Milton's questioning look, Frobisher replied with a sigh, 'Why not? We seem to be breaking all our rules on this mission. I'm sure we can fit his body in.'

Schulz saluted Frobisher, saying, 'Thank you, Captain. In return, I offer you my parole that I will not attempt to escape, nor to cause any disruption to your progress.'

'I'm picking up some Frog traffic on the radio, Captain Frobisher,' called out a voice from the cab of one of the vehicles. 'I don't understand it all, but they've been talking about the fumée and even I know that means smoke.

'Right, chaps,' ordered Frobisher. 'Saddle up! We'd best be on our way, sharpish! And make sure those gun positions are manned!'

Once they were underway, Frobisher turned to Milton and said, 'We're about ten kilometres from the border with Palestine. We'll take the back roads and do a bit across country. We should have you over the border in half an hour or so.'

Milton was relieved to hear Blake's breathing had become calmer and more regular and he smiled at the young captain, 'That's the best news I've had for some time. But tell me, what on earth are you doing out here in Lebanon? And how did you know where to find us?'

'Oh, we had an alert to keep our eyes open for you and we were lucky. We tend to keep off the major roads, as our presence here in the French Mandate is somewhat unofficial, especially since their armistice with Jerry. We were just making our way parallel to the main coastal road, on the other side of the bluffs, when we heard the shot. Once we had a look, it was pretty clear who were the good guys. Anyway, while we're getting you safely back to Haifa, maybe you could tell me something of what you've been up to.'

Chapter Twenty Four

Wednesday 18th December, 1940, The Army and Navy Club, Pall Mall, London, England.

On the same day that Adolf Hitler signed Directive Number 21, which instructed the German army to make preparations for Operation Barbarossa and thereby changed irrevocably the trajectory of the Second World War, Stephen Milton was looking forward to lunch. Professor Pym had invited him to the Army and Navy Club and, despite the dismal weather and the even gloomier prospects for Britain 'standing alone' against Nazi Germany, it was with a spring in his step that he approached the fine building. In common with most public buildings in central London, its fine, classical design was now hidden behind dozens of sand bags and the glass of its beautiful windows was protected by metre upon metre of unsightly tape. Nevertheless, Milton bounded up the central of three elegant porticos and entered 'the rag', for the first time in more than four years.

After the events of the past few months, he was now able to look back with some embarrassment on the utter lack of motivation and purpose that he had felt in those dark days after his forced retirement from the Royal Navy. Indeed, he felt that he owed a considerable debt of gratitude, both to Louis Mountbatten and to the Oerlikon gun itself. As he passed the magnificent stone staircase, leading up to the library and the apartments beyond, he was reassured by the sense of quiet calm displayed by those, mostly in uniform, who were going about their normal business in the club. *Britain might well be standing alone against the Nazis,* he reflected, *but, since I got home, I've seen no sign of defeatism or fear.*

Pym had arranged to wait for him in the glorious 'Morning Room', whose fine, arched windows and shining mirrors amplified the light, even on such a dull day. He saw the Professor, seated at a side table in the company of another, slightly built man, who seemed to be sitting rather uncomfortably. Pym's companion had noticeably greying hair, was dressed in a smart, dark blue suit and was listening attentively to the Professor. Unaccountably, Milton felt a pang of disappointment that he was to be forced to share his time with the Professor.

'Stephen!' Pym beamed, as he stood and advanced to greet and shake hands with Milton, 'it's very good to see you again.' Noticing Milton's glance at the other man, Pym took him by the arm and laughed. 'If I'm not mistaken, I do believe you two know one another.'

As the man slowly rose from his seat and turned to face Milton, his face creased into a broad grin, 'Well, Milton, I seem to remember promising you that you could take a free swing at me, if we ever got back to Blighty. Well, old boy, now's your chance.'

Milton staggered back in astonishment, before moving with outstretched arms to embrace the other man, 'Bill Blake! By all that's holy! It's really you. I can't believe it. It's, it's wonderful to see you again, my friend.'

Pym chuckled at the warmth of the reunion, before encouraging the two old comrades to join him in the famous old dining room. 'I'm sure you've both got a lot to talk about, so let's go to our table straight away.'

As soon as they were seated, Milton looked Blake squarely in the eye. 'Until I saw you just now, I actually thought that you were dead. Nobody would tell me anything about you. It was bloody annoying. Even the Professor here would say nothing.'

'Well, I damn well nearly didn't make it. When I came round, the sawbones told me that Nesrin and Schulz saved my life. I wonder, whatever happened to them?'

'Never mind them. How long were you in hospital?'

'Oh, my story's pretty tedious. The wound was on the right side of my chest, otherwise I'd have been a goner. As it is, I just had to lie about for two months, letting those gorgeous nurses fuss over me. Now I'm as good as I'll ever be. A bit out of breath too easily, muscles still wasted and the damned docs say that on no account may I smoke again. Only got one fully functioning lung, you see. The other`s pretty useless.' Blake had to stop to catch his breath, before continuing, 'But no bugger would tell me what happened to you all. I don't remember anything after the moment that Nazi shot me. So, come on, you two, spill the beans.'

Milton, aware as ever of security issues, glanced quickly at Pym, who gave the slightest of nods. 'Well, basically we were rescued by a British Army patrol.'

'You're joking! What the hell were they doing there? We were still some miles away from the border with Palestine.'

'You're right, Bill, and it was a bit of luck really. You remember that Turk who we had dinner with on the Orient Express? Mehmet Demir?'

'Of course. The gentleman tennis player. He introduced me to those marvellous Turkish cigarettes.'

'That's the chap. Well, he slipped me a card with his phone number on it as we were breaking up that night. Whispered I should call him if ever we needed any help. Turns out he was a big noise in the Emniyet in his day and knows the Professor here quite well.'

Pym nodded in agreement, 'A fine man, Demir. You were deuced fortunate to come across him, I'll tell you. By no means all Turks are as pro-British and honourable as him.'

'Anyway,' Milton continued, 'I can't explain it really. I just had a bit of a feeling about it all. I can't say that I suspected Nesrin of working with the Jerries, but I did figure a bit of insurance couldn't do us any harm.'

'So, you rang this chap before we left Istanbul?'

'That's right. From the hotel, the night before we left. You remember I said I'd been caught short over dinner and had to disappear to the gents. Well, I rang him from the hotel lobby and told him our travel plans. He said he'd do what he could to make sure we had a 'guardian angel.''

'So, he got in touch with our top man in Haifa,' interrupted Pym, 'and he contacted me immediately. Of course, I vouched for Demir, and realised pretty quickly that it was you two he was talking about. Our border patrols were alerted to keep an eye open for you. As it turns out, they were about as far into Frog country as they would have wanted to go, so again you were rather fortunate.'

In the circumstances of wartime, the food was very good and Milton tucked in with relish. He couldn't help noticing, however, that Blake merely toyed with his meal. 'I say old chap, are you not hungry?'

'I've not had much of an appetite since I was shot. The medics say it's pretty normal and I should pick up in time. But, tell me. Whatever happened to those sacks, to Nesrin and to Schulz. He wasn't a bad sort, for a German, was he?'

'No, he wasn't and that doctor was right. Basically, he and Nesrin kept you alive, both before and on the drive back to Haifa. We had to stay off the main roads to the border and some of the tracks we followed were pretty rough. But we made it, and there we parted company. Schulz had given us his word that he wouldn't try to escape as long as we took his fellow officer, Haller, back with us. He wanted him to have a decent burial, you see.'

'I don't think I ever saw him.'

'You didn't. He stayed in the Jerries' car when they first caught up with us. It was strange when they caught us the second time. We'd had a flat tyre, remember? Anyway,

Nesrin and this chap Haller were pretty much held at gunpoint by those two others and Schulz was even shot in the arm by one of them when he ordered them to cut out the rough stuff. He told me that they were SD, wholly separate from his military intelligence outfit. He was sure we'd all have been killed, had Frobisher not shown up with his patrol.'

'From what I know of the SD, I'd say that Schulz was absolutely right. They're bastards to a man! What happened to them?'

'Both killed in the shooting and good riddance to the swine. After we got to Haifa, I put in a good word for Schulz and Nesrin. I know he's an Abwehr man and she, in some senses betrayed us. But, hang it all, neither of us would have survived had it not been for them.'

Blake seemed to fight an inner battle, before nodding decisively. 'Yes, you're right, Milton. We'd have been shot by those SD brutes the first time we were caught, had Schulz not intervened. So where is he now?'

'I managed to persuade the Army CO in Haifa that he should be given the choice of imprisonment or, because he had helped us, to return to Istanbul. I understand that, after Haller had been buried with full military honours in Haifa, he and Nesrin returned to Istanbul. I can't imagine that it was a happy return to Switzerland for him. After all, he'd failed in his mission. Maybe the fact that he was wounded will mitigate that. I hope so. He was and remains our enemy, but he's a decent man.'

'Maybe at this point, we should stop talking about Nesrin,' interrupted Pym, 'her real name is Melek Benli and, as you know, she is an officer in the Emniyet.'

'What do you make of her, sir,' asked Milton in genuine confusion. 'Whose side was she really on?'

The Professor sat back and heaved a heavy sigh. 'I suppose in wartime and, especially in undercover work such as she had taken on, it's often a question of shades of grey rather than black or white. I've spoken at length to those who interrogated her in Haifa and I'm as sure as I can be that they have her motivation pretty well nailed.' The younger men exchanged glances before Pym went on, 'She was obviously very pleased, at her age, to have been given such an important assignment. Women are still making progress towards equality in Turkey and, when the chance came to replace the original guide, who, by the way, is safe and well, she leapt at it. Schulz seemed so cultured and civilised and Turkey is, after all, traditionally pro German. Anyway, it does appear that she gradually changed her mind as the mission went on. I think both of you clearly made an impression on her. But with you, Stephen, I think it was a bit more than that.'

'She fell for him, you mean?' asked Blake, without any of the hostility that might previously been on display in such a situation.

'I think that's pretty certain, Bill, yes. Anyway, in the end, she wasn't concerned at all about the documents, only that no harm would befall you. She had that undertaking from Schulz, but of course, when Blake's clever ruse was discovered, he lost control of the German side of the operation.'

'Is she back in Istanbul?'

'Yes, and from what we can gather, her involvement has not been regarded as a failure. Thanks to Schulz speaking for her, Germany is, publicly at least, grateful for Turkish help. At the same time, as things worked out, Britain's interests have also been preserved. All in all, a pretty good outcome for a neutral country.'

'Thanks for telling us this, Professor,' said Milton. 'I'm sure that we're both glad to learn that Nes… sorry, Malek and Schulz are both back where they belong. For myself, I was whisked off by rail to Cairo pretty quickly and a plane was waiting there to ferry me back to London.'

'And what's happened since,' asked Blake sharply. 'I mean, was the whole damn thing worth it?'

Milton again sought permission to speak from Pym, who indicated that he could go on. 'Well, when I returned home, there was the typical utter cock up. They couldn't even agree where the bloody guns should be produced, let alone organise the machine tools and skilled labour to get things moving.'

'Christ,' muttered Blake, 'just what I don't want to hear. The desk jockeys bugger it all up. And after all our work too.'

'Relax, Bill. Shortly after I returned to Britain a chap called Goodfellow was given the job of sorting it all out. And, by God, is he well named! He quickly identified some unused railway sheds at Ruislip, which could easily be converted into factory buildings. From then on, he remorselessly chivvied away at the top brass, until they basically caved in. Architects were rushed in and machine tools began to arrive, initially in insufficient quantities. Even with all Goodfellow's pushing, things looked grim at the end of October. But now, I'm delighted to say that production has just begun at Ruislip and we expect to deliver the first home produced Oerlikons to the Navy by March next year.'

'And does everyone agree that the gun is so much better than the alternatives?' asked Blake hopefully. 'I'd really like to think so.'

'I can say with absolute conviction, Bill, that enabling production of this gun in Britain will make a very significant contribution to the Navy's ability to defend itself from aerial attack. What you did will undoubtedly save the lives of many hundreds, if not thousands of seamen, ordinary blokes like you and me. You should be very proud of yourself.' Blake coughed gently and turned his head away from the other men for a few seconds. Milton glanced anxiously at Pym, who made a gesture of reassurance and swivelled his head to indicate that it was time for Milton to leave.

'Well, Bill, it's been great seeing you again and I'm delighted that you're very much on the mend. But I really have to be getting back to the factory. Can't let production slip back now, can we?'

'Of course not. It's been good to see you again Milton. Keep in touch, won't you?'

Just as Milton was turning to leave the table, Blake raised his hand. 'By the way, what happened to those sacks? Did you ever get them back? After your trick with the bus?'

Milton beamed down at his friend, 'I should bloody well say so. Those jewel centres were nothing less than a lifeline for the RAF, after the losses they incurred during the Battle of Britain. A lot of airmen owe the accurate functioning of their instruments to you, Bill.' As Milton walked purposefully through the dining room, Blake reached into his pocket for a handkerchief and blew his nose. Sensing that it was not just his nose that he was wiping, Pym said gently, 'You should learn to accept praise, Bill. On this occasion, it's richly deserved,'

'Well, that's as maybe, Professor,' Blake muttered in response, 'but I should be pushing off as well. Thanks for the lunch, I've really enjoyed myself.'

Pym raised his right arm to indicate that Blake should remain seated and said, 'Can't you just hang on a minute, Bill. There's someone else I'd like you to meet. In fact, I think he's just arrived.'

A tall, rangy man approached the table. His slightly long, fair hair gave him a somewhat boyish appearance, whereas his eyes suggested a wealth of painful experience. 'Good afternoon, Professor,' he said in a cultured and pleasant voice. 'I hope I'm not late.'

Pym rose to welcome his new guest and, having shaken hands warmly, turned to Blake. 'Let me introduce the two of you. Bill Blake, I'd like you to meet John King.' With an unmistakable twinkle in his eye, he added, 'and please, do sit down both of you. As it happens, I have a very interesting proposition to put to you.'

Author's Note

I first encountered the amazing story of the Oerlikon gun, whilst undertaking research for a planned novel to be based on the invasion that never was; Operation Tannenbaum, or Germany's planned invasion of Switzerland. As a resident and now citizen of Switzerland, quite how the Alpine Republic had managed to avoid occupation by the forces of the surrounding Axis powers had intrigued me for some time. However, as soon as I read about the 'Gun from Switzerland' I was hooked and determined to base a novel on the heroic events of the late summer of 1940.

What follows is a brief outline of what is known about this whole story, I leave it for the reader to judge whether I have done it justice. Several 'real' people feature, including Louis Mountbatten, Claude Dansey, Captain J C Leach, Director of Naval Ordnance, Lieutenant Colonel von Ilsemann, German Miltary Attaché in Bern and Captain Otto von Menges , who was given the task of producing the first plan for Operation Tannenbaum. Stephen Milton is based loosely on Steuart Mitchell, whereas all other characters are the product of the writer's imagination.

In order to appreciate the significance of the Oerlikon weapon, one has to go back to the period after World War One. The attacking potential of aircraft was only just dawning on military leaders when that war ended. However, by the late 1920s, the British Admiralty was so concerned about the risk to its capital ships of attack from the air, that they had commissioned the development of at least two specialised anti-aircraft weapons.

Both of these had noted disadvantages, either being bulky and expensive or firing light, ineffectual bullets. Lord Louis Mountbatten was one of the naval officers most concerned about the dangers from air attack and it was in his capacity as a Commander in the Naval Air Division, that he was first made aware of the Oerlikon 20mm cannon. Not only was this weapon specifically designed to cope with the new threat of dive bombers, it also had a very rapid rate of fire and was comparatively light and easy to move and mount. It was also marketed by an extremely gifted salesman in Antoine Gazda. After arranging for an initial demonstration of the weapon's capability, Mountbatten faced a wall of indifference from the Admiralty and throughout 1937 and 1938 he fought a pretty much isolated campaign in support of the Oerlikon.

It was only when Sir Roger Backhouse, an ex-gunnery officer himself, became C-in-C, Home Fleet, that Mountbatten acquired an ally in high places. When Backhouse became First Sea Lord, the door was open for the Oerlikon and in 1939 an order of 1500 was placed with the Zürich factory. As an indication of their real interest and concern, Steuart Mitchell, a member of the civilian staff of the Chief Inspector of Naval Ordnance, was sent to Switzerland in April 1939. Also an ex-gunnery officer, who had been invalided out of the Royal Navy, Mitchell's role was to prove crucial. Initially, however, things did not go to plan; such were the delays and complications that a mere 109 of the planned 1500 had been delivered by the time that France fell to the German Blitzkrieg.

Having arranged for his wife and two Naval Attachés to return to Britain on June 16th 1940, before France fell, Mitchell himself attempted to escape the almost encircled Switzerland. He took with him vital technical drawings and two sacks full of jewel centres for aircraft instrumentation. The documents were absolutely crucial, because even though an agreement to franchise production of the guns in Britain had just been reached, the British had no specifications, on which to base their production. Without the drawings, therefore, it is inconceivable that production of the 20mm cannon could have begun in Britain. Moreover, the sacks contained sufficient scarce jewel centres to keep a very embattled RAF going for several months.

As might be expected, Mitchell attempted to reach Spain by car, via southern France. However, as described in the book, he found his way across the river Rhône blocked by a detachment of German army motorcyclists and was unable to proceed. Having returned to Switzerland, he then made his way to Egypt, finally flying back to Britain from Cairo. Little detailed information on his precise route is available and in developing my plot, I tried to combine what is known of his journey with what was possible and plausible at the time. The fictional Milton's departure by air from Locarno to Belgrade was, arguably, possible, although there are different views on these flights. Some sources state that the special Swissair flights from Locarno to Belgrade took place only in May and June 1940, whereas other sources are less precise over their timing. What is certain is that they were used to move gold on behalf of the Union Bank of Switzerland and as a route out of Switzerland by British military personnel. I trust that those who believe my use of this escape route for Milton to be anachronistic do not find their enjoyment of the book overly spoiled by my timing one of the last of these flights on August 1st 1940.

The Simplon Orient Express continued to run from Lausanne to Istanbul (via Belgrade) until October 1940. The most plausible way to reach Egypt and Cairo from Istanbul would have been via the Taurus Express, which crossed Turkey, Syria, the Lebanon and Palestine. It was the case that, at that time, the Taurus Express ran with a road section between Tripoli and Haifa.

Yeşilköy was a military airport in 1940 and bizarrely, German engineers were actually working on its improvement. The German paver, so vital to the plot is, however, entirely my creation.

Domestic production of the 20mm Oerlikon cannon began at Ruislip in late 1940 and the first deliveries were made to the Royal Navy in March 1941.

The RAF Regiment, which was that section of the air force responsible for the defence of airfields from enemy attack, also made great use of this weapon's anti-aircraft capability. The Oerlikon was also the main armament used by its Light Anti-Aircraft Squadrons operational in North Africa, the Middle East, Italy, North Western Europe and the Far East.

While there are no specific statistics on the number of guns built in Britain, it is known that by 1945, some 55,000 of them were in active service in the British and

Commonwealth navies. Its small size, easy installation and lightweight quality made it ideal to fit as a defence weapon on submarines and smaller ships. Indeed, some Auxiliary vessels of the Royal Navy still carried the Oerlikon in 2006!

I'd like to thank you for reading the second in the Spymaster Pym series and to express the hope that you enjoyed it. Ratings and reviews are extremely important to all self published authors and I would be very grateful if you could spare the time to post one of these. I also really enjoy direct contact with readers and you can always contact me via my website apmartin.co.uk.

Printed in Great Britain
by Amazon